"Going well beyond Keller's *Miracle Worker* days . . . Sultan convincingly imagines that this much-admired if oversimplified icon wanted nothing more than to be treated like a woman."

—*Booklist*

"Eye-opening and thoroughly involving . . . This well-written novel will appeal to those who enjoy women's fiction as well as readers of historical and biographical fiction. A thoroughly enjoyable read that should entice many to seek out one of the biographies Sultan recommends in an afterword."

—*Library Journal*

"With empathy, imagination, and vivid sensory detail, Rosie Sultan's *Helen in Love* gives voice—and scent and touch—to an iconic American heroine during a little known chapter in her life."

—Jane Mendelsohn, author of *I Was Amelia Earhart*

"In this richly imagined and moving novel, Rosie Sultan brings alive the history of Helen Keller—the brilliant miraculous creature who stole the heart and sympathy of the world—while also exploring how she must have felt as a woman: the loneliness, longing, and great vulnerability. The result is a vivid, sensuous portrait full of sound and vision."

—Jill McCorkle, author of *Going Away Shoes*

"*Helen in Love* is involving, passionate, and deeply felt. It tells this little-known, remarkable story with a loving heart, beautiful language, and great commitment to its heroine. Helen Keller was a woman with blood in her veins—this book makes you feel it."

—Martha Southgate, author of *The Taste of Salt*

Praise for *Helen in Love*

"Captivating . . . A riveting story."　　　　—*Good Housekeeping*

"Rosie Sultan is adventurous—and brave. She has immersed herself in every available piece of information about Keller and, to an amazing degree, puts herself into her heroine's silent, dark world. Sultan looks within, telling Helen's story in the first person. We are taken into the isolation and limitations that Keller lived with her entire life. . . . *Helen in Love* is touching and fun to read. . . . Sultan has given the adult Helen Keller a new voice and reminds us of both her brilliance and her humanity."
　　　　　　　　　　　　　　　　　　—*The Washington Post*

"Ambitious. Sultan's sensibility is consistently contemporary, a wise choice given Keller's distinctly modern views. An advocate for women's rights, an unapologetic socialist and fierce opponent to World War I, Keller exposed and challenged oppression and prejudice in all its myriad forms. Her voice in this novel is evocative of any current celebrity's. She feels imprisoned by her reputation and her fans' expectations of her, weary of being the meal ticket for her family, and harassed by the press. As much as she loves and needs Annie, she also chafes at their interdependence. And above all, she is unashamed of her own sexuality, eager to express it, and resentful of her mother and sister's determination to keep her pure and caged within the confines of propriety. . . . Sultan does a fine job of demonstrating how Keller navigates the world with just three senses."　　　　—*The Boston Globe*

"Imagining your way inside the head of a historical figure is surely hard enough, without that figure being one who lives in a silent, unseen world, 'a marble cell of dark,' and communicates with others through finger spelling. . . . Considerable research girds Sultan's fictional account of Helen Keller's brief, real-life affair with her secretary, Peter Fagan, which gives the tale a solid foundation."　　　　—*The New York Times Book Review*

"Quite an accomplishment . . . Through illustrative language, readers get a believable glimpse into the mind and emotions of Helen Keller."   —*Montgomery Advertiser*

"Rosie Sultan has taken on a major task with a blind-deaf heroine. The prose is elegant, and the author deftly shows us Helen's world through touch and smell."   —*Historical Novel Society*

"Debut novelist Rosie Sultan spins a tale of forbidden love, invoking scents, textures, and tastes on every page to show how Helen 'saw' the world. She grounds the story in well-known incidents from Helen's childhood, but draws on later biographies, speeches, and letters to show Helen as a woman, intelligent and determined but forced by her handicaps to be dependent on her family and employees. . . . Sultan skillfully expresses Helen's main frustrations: at the public for refusing to take her seriously when she speaks on political issues unrelated to blindness, and at her family and friends for refusing to see her as a grown woman, with a woman's desires. *Helen in Love* holds readers' attention with a fresh depiction of a woman famous for overcoming her physical handicaps, forced to fight for her right to love."   —*Shelf Awareness*

"Sultan's story carefully builds Helen and Peter's affair, layering their more intimate scenes into an evolving bond of love and connection. With everything told through Helen's sense of touch, we painstakingly feel Peter's scent: muskrat, hot rain, and tar. Lover and muse wade deep into the sparkling waters of Kings Pond at her home in Wrentham, Massachusetts, and all that is sexually pent-up inside Helen finally comes alive. . . . Thoughtful yet passionate, Sultan treats Helen's battle between filial duty and sensual pleasure evenhandedly and with great sensitivity, steering us through the minefield of betrayal to a hoped-for marriage, to a manipulative family, who in their ignorance, arrogance, and selfishness cruelly sabotage Helen's journey in following her heart's desire."   —*Curled Up with a Good Book*

PENGUIN BOOKS

HELEN IN LOVE

Rosie Sultan won a PEN Discovery Award for fiction and earned her MFA at Goddard College. A former fellow at The Virginia Center for the Creative Arts, she has taught writing at Boston University, the University of Massachusetts, and Suffolk University. She lives with her husband and son in Brookline, Massachusetts.

To access Penguin Readers Guides online,
visit our Web site at www.penguin.com.

Helen
in Love

ROSIE SULTAN

PENGUIN BOOKS

Previously published as *Helen Keller in Love*

PENGUIN BOOKS

Published by the Penguin Group
Penguin Group (USA) LLC
375 Hudson Street
New York, New York 10014

USA | Canada | UK | Ireland | Australia | New Zealand | India | South Africa | China
penguin.com
A Penguin Random House Company

First published in the United States of America as *Helen Keller in Love* by Viking Penguin,
a member of Penguin Group (USA) Inc., 2012
Published in Penguin Books 2013

THE LIBRARY OF CONGRESS HAS CATALOGED THE HARDCOVER EDITION AS FOLLOWS:
Sultan, Rosie.
    Helen Keller in love / Rosie Sultan.
        p. cm.
    ISBN 978-0-670-02349-3 (hc.)
    ISBN 978-0-14-312339-2 (pbk.)
    1. Keller, Helen, 1880–1968—Fiction.   I. Title.
    PS3619.U455H45 2012
    813'.6—dc23   2011039574

Printed in the United States of America
10 9 8 7 6 5 4 3 2 1

Designed by Carla Bolte

This is a work of fiction based on real events.

To my husband, David Rudner, and our son, Gabriel Sultan,
who mean everything to me.

I am so blessed.

Helen
in Love

Chapter One

✦❊✦

I wait under a night sky pocked with stars I cannot see. I lean forward on the porch, the *chrr-chrr-chrr* of crickets thrums the warm air that vibrates against my skin; the wooden railing I hold feels cool after the day's heat. The night around me is a bitter cup of ink, drained into my cells. Those weighty caverns of water under the earth—hungry mouths, waiting to take me in.

I cannot account for my behavior.

I have lied—to my teacher, my mother, the world. I hid from them the second miracle of my life this fall night of 1916. Because I have a secret.

I've never told this story. I don't know if I can tell it now. But it's a story I have kept out of all the speeches I've ever given and every one of the books I've written. Yet it's the truest story I've lived.

Thirty-seven years old. Deaf, blind, mute. I have taken a lover, and I am in love. I can't publicly marry because my teacher and my mother forbid it—it is their only hope of keeping me close.

But I defied them. I lied to Annie. I was tired of being perfect Helen Keller. Helen the pure; Helen the tireless worker, the saint, the good girl. I wanted to break free. And it happened very suddenly. Last summer I met a man who awoke all sorts of demons, mad cravings in me. A man who tasted like night.

Since October we've been secretly engaged. This is the night we will elope. I'm ready. Beside me sits my leather suitcase as I wait all through this steamy Alabama night on the porch of my sister

Mildred's house in Montgomery. I wait in silence—nothing new to me. But this silence, this dark, is not a casket; it is an opening. Life calls from the tangy woods at the edge of my sister's house. Woods from which Peter will creep under cover of night, take my hand, and race me off to Florida, where a minister friend waits to marry us.

The night gets cooler around me, and the silence deeper. One hour, two, then four hours pass. Yet I know he will come. The people who know me best—Annie, my teacher; Mother, asleep on the second floor—could never have imagined I would deceive them, or marry and have someone to care for.

The longer I wait here the more the woods give off a vicious scent as morning breaks. I had crept out of my upstairs bedroom, suitcase in hand, at two a.m. and waited in the rocker by the piney railing for four hours, my listening feet pressed to the porch to feel the *thrum, thrum, thrum* of Peter's footsteps.

I waited even as my sister Mildred heard me rocking, and got up. She woke her husband, who told her not to be afraid—it was only me on the porch: Sister Helen, he called me. They didn't know I kept in communication with Peter Fagan; that I packed my leather bag and came down to wait for him as they slept. This is the story you will never read about in my books: how Helen Keller waited all night on this porch to elope with her lover.

Here's the date I'll never write: November 27, 1916. Did Peter sense trouble, and decide to stay away? Did Mildred's husband pay him off? Or did the men come to blows in the woods? Did Peter fight back, push Mildred's husband away, saying, "I must see Helen. She belongs with me?" Doesn't he know I am waiting, will wait some more—will keep waiting even as this bitter sun rises—hoping to feel his footsteps on the stair? He must come.

Burning, the Alabama sun. People ask me: How can you tell the difference between night and day if you are blind? I tell them that night air is lighter; day feels heavier, more sodden with life. And as I stand up, pick up my suitcase, admit to myself that maybe my lover will not come, this air of daylight weighs more heavily on my skin than any blindness ever did.

My throat is a red knot, unraveling. I can't go back in the house to Mother and Mildred. The sun rises like a plume of smoke, trailing until daybreak comes and the silence deepens more than any I have ever known.

I am alone. Still, he still may come . . . Because we had an extraordinary, passionate affair. When I think about it now, it makes my breath move fast, fast, like a train . . .

Chapter Two

Peter Fagan was a miracle I was not prepared for. On a hot Wisconsin night, midway through my lecture tour across the Midwest, the warm scent of corn, pond water, and dirt filled the tent where a crowd of farmers waited for Annie to lead me up the steps and call out the story of my life. As I stood at the base of the three wooden steps leading to the stage, I gripped the stair railing—its cool metal vibrated with the shuffle, then stomp of heavy boots, an angry tint to the air. The crowd had been waiting for a half hour.

"I can't do it," Annie spelled into my palm. "I just can't." A cough rattled her chest, and she doubled over beside me.

The steady vibration of impatient feet shuddered the ground, and I stood holding the railing.

I felt desperate, hollowed out inside. This cough kept Annie awake nights, made her skin damp as constant rain, and exhausted her so badly that for the first time since I was a child, she couldn't climb the wooden steps to the stage; she couldn't translate for me day and night as she always had for thirty years.

"Write to John," I spelled into her hand as she struggled to lead me up the stairs toward the rickety stage. "After the show. Please. He'll help. I know."

"John wouldn't help me if I were the last woman on earth," she spelled into my palm.

"He's still married to you."

"Married? He's a husband in name only. He lives in his own

4

apartment in Boston with that deaf hussy. At least she won't have to listen to him blabber on, like I did for fourteen years."

"Annie," I spelled into her damp palm. I felt a whoosh of air as she pushed back the stage curtain and led me out toward the waiting crowd. "He *must* help. He's all we've got."

On the stage Annie cut short her introduction of me. Her hand shook in mine as she called out to the crowd, "I bring you Helen Keller, the miracle."

One thing no one tells you about being blind and deaf is this: You say what people need to hear. You leave out the rest. After our lecture, Annie walked me across the dusty road from the tent to our motel and sat me down at my Remington typewriter. "Maybe a flunky from John's newsroom can help. But God knows he won't respond to me. You'll have to do the writing." From the warped desk in our Appleton motel I pressed my fingers onto the typewriter keys. I didn't write the whole truth. I wrote what John needed to hear:

Appleton, Wisconsin
August 1916

John Macy
Boston Herald
Boston, Mass.

Tour a great success. Several towns in Kansas, Nebraska, and now Wisconsin. I had my picture taken with the mayor of Wichita back in Kansas. Crowds everywhere. Enough profits for Annie and me to go on a vacation to Cape Cod when we get back in September.

Please, John. I know you don't care for us as you once did; perhaps you still care enough to help us. Annie has developed a hacking cough. But the tour must continue. You above all others know how I depend on her. We still have dates to finish in Wisconsin. Can you send me a private secretary?

Helen

I didn't write that the mayor of Wichita, Kansas, had refused to shake my hand when I told him I was a Socialist, or that we slept in drafty motel rooms to save money, Annie so ill she coughed into the morning.

A week later, over a breakfast by the train station on the way to our next town, Annie spelled John's telegram into my palm:

Helen: Boston, Mass., 1916
Peter Fagan arrives Wisconsin Monday August 25. Work Experience: laid off *Boston Herald* reporter. Special Qualifications: long on time, short on cash.

Wants the job.

The cost is yours.

John

The thought of being alone with a stranger, a man, was illicit, and thrilling. All night during the long train ride through Wisconsin, I imagined my fingers tracing his cheekbone as he moved his face close to mine. The train rocked beneath me, and as I slept I dreamed Peter's scent clung to my skin: a scent of woods and heat that made me feel deep in my being that he would change my life.

The night Peter arrived, Appleton, Wisconsin, smelled of rain. Annie and I sat despondent over the failure of that night's audience to listen to our Chautauqua lecture when Peter slid into the billowing, creaking tent—in the night his scent came easily to me: I inhaled typewriter ink, cigarette smoke, and the strange muskrat smell I always associated with men. I held the edge of my chair and felt his footsteps as he swung closer to the stage where Annie and I sat. Annie shifted beside me, saw him, and spelled her impression into my hand: "he flips open a brown reporter's notebook, waves a cigarette with thin, long fingers." I lifted my head, sensing electricity in the air.

"Is he handsome?" I asked, nervously smoothing my hair.

"All I can say is thank God you're blind." We both laughed.

"Is he that bad?" I spelled back into her hand—familiar as my own. I cocked my head. Peter felt closer. Annie said, shifting in her chair, "He's looking left, now right." Annie went on, her fingers flying in my palm: "Jesus, Mary, and Joseph, his *shirt* is unbuttoned. And he's got that shifty look of a person ready to flee."

"Flee?" I leaned closer to Annie.

"His family fled Ireland," Annie went on. "The famine. He's a Socialist now," she told me. "Another supporter of lost causes—like *you*."

We both laughed again, but I felt a slight mocking in Annie's palm. "Do I look all right?" Always I've liked men better than women; even at age seven I'd ask Annie to make me pretty. Now, dress tugged down just a bit, I sat up straighter.

"He doesn't see you," Annie rapped. "But he *is* looking. He's turning this way. Dark hair, he's shaking his jacket off his shoulders, and oh, brown eyes." Relief washed through me as Peter rounded the table. Through the soles of my shoes I felt the *sssaah, ssaah* of his boots until he swung up to the table and grasped my hand.

"Miss *Kel*-ler, a *pleasure* to see you." I touched his throat to hear his words and felt a twinge, very slight, that moved to the center of my heart. His voice, rough as twine, thrummed through my fingertips. I felt incapable of taking my hand away. Warm air pressed down inside the tent; the thump of footsteps told me that the crowd was filing out. Still, Peter waited for my response. With my ring finger on his vibrating larynx and my forefinger on the rough stubble of his cheek, I felt his parted lips with my thumb. A pent-up energy moved through me. Annie always told me, "For God's sake, Helen, when you're touching a man's face, move fast: Read his words, then drop your hand. People gawk at you enough without seeing you lingering over some man's drawl."

But Peter drew me *in*.

"The pleasure is *mine*," I spelled into his rough palm.

"The famous Helen Keller," he repeated. "Engaged in making the world a better place." With a quick flick of his fingers in my palm he spelled, "I've been following the press on you: a sold-out lecture tour across Canada in 1914, and now this current tour—two lectures a day, twenty-five cities, three different states since you left Wrentham last spring. All in the service of raising money for the blind. Am I right?" That night, under the hot dome of the tent on Wisconsin's lakeshore, I grasped Peter's hand in mine and felt the delicacy of his fingers.

But Peter didn't know the whole story. The truth was harsher. Our tours—including this one—were to raise money for the blind and deaf, yes. But how could Peter have known that my father had stopped paying Annie's salary when I was ten years old, and since my graduation from Radcliffe College, Annie and I had done our show in too many cities to count to pay the bills. We had to keep ourselves afloat.

"I'm so glad," I blurted out. "That you're here to help us."

He just threw his head back and laughed, his throat a lush drink of creamy milk. "Yes, I'm engaged in the important mission of taking over for Miss Sullivan and getting you two safely home," he said. And I believed him.

Peter turned to Annie. "I'll take her to dinner if you'd like." As always when I'm with two people, I held Annie's hand with my left hand and listened as she spelled. At the same time I held my other hand to Peter's lips and lip-read his response. His mouth moved quickly, excitedly under my fingers; Annie's spelling—usually up to eighty words per minute poured into my palm—was weary.

Peter looped his arm through mine; he led me through the tent robust with the odors of farmers, dirt tracked in on their shoes, and the scent of machinery still in their clothes. And when Peter said, "Watch your step," I knew we were about to cross from the inside of the tent to the rough, patchy grass outside.

Just as we stood at the tent's edge the cool night air hit me: it was filled with the vibrations of the dinner bell—pulsing and fading on Lake Bally's shores.

"Let's eat," Peter said beside me. "Are you hungry?"

"Starving," I said right back.

The steady thrum of the dinner bell chimed in the night air. As I felt its vibrations in my hands I hesitated, then stopped on the threshold of the tent.

Before walking out into the night the bell stopped tolling, leaving a fist of empty air—and I can tell you now what I did not know then: that bell was just like Peter. Booming with joy. But soon empty. Gone. I held his hand more fiercely in mine.

I live in a tangible white dark. My blind world is not shot through with blue, sultry green, or shouting red. But neither is my world black. It is not a casket; it does not close over me like death. No, my world is more a deep fog, rough to the fingers, the color of flesh.

That's what I spelled into Peter's smooth palm when we stood together at the threshold of the tent that Wisconsin night. He'd just asked me what everyone wanted to know but was usually too polite to ask: "What's it like to be blind?" he'd said. "To live in the dark?" We waited for Annie to catch up; she had gone backstage to get our paycheck from the Chautauqua tour manager. My stomach rumbled with hunger; beneath my feet I felt the resounding smack of hundreds of people striding out into the night from the tent: the rapid, sharp *thonk* of their feet across the grass telling me they wanted to get away; our talk was not what they had wanted to hear.

"It's not dark," I said again. "It's more like something I can touch." I didn't tell him my whole body is a vibroscope: I remember conversations with my fingertips. Instead I leaned back against a metal tent pole as he said, "Stay here. I'll go find us a table for dinner. They're setting up outside the hotel across the street." And when I leaned back, alone, I felt the air splinter, crack open a bit, as Annie, far inside the tent, was racked by a fit of coughing.

The tent pole shuddered under my hands: I couldn't go to dinner until Annie, or Peter, came for me. In new places I couldn't walk alone; I needed a guide. Through the soles of my shoes came the vibrations—first soft, then more insistent—of Peter's footsteps as he came toward me across the grass. I reached out for him; he took my hand with great happiness and he spelled, "How did you know it was me?"

"I can tell people by their scents," I said.

"All right, nature girl," he spelled to me. "Let's eat."

All the way across the lawn to our hotel, where tables were clustered in a patio facing the lake, I felt like I could touch our shadows—Peter's tall and lanky, rough to my fingers, yet blending into mine, into one.

Chapter Three

They say that love is blind. But fame can blind a person, too. That night Peter led me across the grass outside the Chautauqua tent to where rows of metal tables behind the hotel were stacked high with food: country hams with salt, yeasty breads, the sharp, green scent of peas, even the iron scent of radish floated past as he sat me down under the cool of a trailing willow tree. I moved my fingers over the slim knife, rounded spoon, plate, and thick-rimmed tumbler atop a rough place mat. Immediately "seeing" them in my mind's eye, I picked up chicken, beets, grilled corn from heaping platters. Peter, his dark hair curling down his neck, eagerly took his place beside me when I touched him in the heat of the night— he was a slender, regal animal. "I'll feed you," he laughed.

"I'm blind and deaf," I spelled back. "Not dumb. Do you think I can't feed myself?"

I knew I wasn't the woman he expected—and I liked it. Chicken in hand, I offered Peter a taste and he opened his mouth to bite.

"Stop." Annie had crossed the grass from the tent and put her hand on my arm. Peter lowered his chicken leg to the plate. "Before you eat, you work," she said to Peter, all the while rapidly spelling her words into my palm. "First, you translate the daily newspapers, then the correspondence. Got it? If a newspaper comes, you spell it to her. A letter: the same thing. You translate everything—and I mean everything—conversation, radio news reports, bits of speech on the streets as you pass by—into Helen's hand. You can start with all this mail."

For eighteen hours a day, seven days a week, for over twenty years Annie had spelled into my hand. She got migraines now. Her trachoma made her eyes burn so that she picked at her eyelids till her eyelashes fell out. At that moment a cough racked her again; at times that cough seemed a relief, if only because it would give her the smallest time away from her endless duties with me.

I felt Annie push the heavy mailbag across the table, closer to Peter, its *ssshhuh* making the table vibrate just slightly beneath my hands. A slight shift of air followed by the scent of ink told me Annie had pulled out a newspaper. "The *Boston Globe*," Annie said, handing the paper to Peter. "Read to her."

"Ah," spelled Peter to me. "I'm your voice." His stomach rumbled. "My appetite will have to wait."

"You're her link to the world," Annie said. He reluctantly slid the newspaper open and turned to his job as secretary.

I felt lit and burning as a fuse.

Peter licked bits of cherry-apple crumble from his lips, rearranged his tie, his mouth moving fast under my listening fingers when he read of the Red Sox in the lead for the pennant—maybe they'd finally win the World Series, the bums!—then suddenly his lips turned to pools of sorrow, as he flipped to the world news:

SPECIAL TO THE BOSTON GLOBE BY NOAH SANDER

SOMME, FRANCE, JULY 5, 1916 – Yesterday, 57,000 British soldiers were killed in one day at the Battle of the Somme. Tens of thousands were wounded. The battle rages on.

"What a stupid war!" I burst out. Peter's fingernails pressed into my palm as he read, more furious, then softer in sorrow. No one

wanted to hear my opinions about politics, world events, or Socialism. And certainly not that I was against this war, and urged all
Americans to stop President Wilson from entering this foolish waste
of human life in the name of capitalism. The *Brooklyn Eagle* said
that as a blind woman I had no right to speak about politics, but
Peter's hand warmed mine and I heated up in rage. "President Wilson," I said, "is as blind as I am. Fifty-seven thousand soldiers killed
in one day in France? For what?" The battle in Europe raged. And
even though the United States remained neutral, daily President
Wilson called for our entry into the war. Weekly my desk was piled
high with desperate letters from German, French, and English soldiers blinded in battle, letters pleading for help.

Peter laughed at my comment about President Wilson.

"Why, Miss Keller," he spelled, "you're calling the president blind?"

"Why not? He promised peace, but now there's talk that he'll
raise the U.S. military from one hundred thousand to eight hundred
thousand in the next year. Is he blind to the consequences of that?"

"I'm a radical, too, but he is the president."

"And I'm Helen Keller. I've met with every sitting president since
Grover Cleveland," I spelled into his palm.

"I know, I know. You were the darling of kings and queens by
the time you were ten. They kept abreast of your activities in newspapers worldwide: how you could read Homer, and they all saw that
photo of you posed so quaintly with your little white dog. Your
Radcliffe graduation was front-page news in 1904, and Dr. Edward
Everett Hale wrote that your future upon graduation was unlimited."

"You . . ."

"I'm not a crack reporter for nothing. I've done my research."

We sat together, the mailbag giving off its musty canvas scent. I
didn't want to tell Peter there was one thing that was very limited
in my life.

Men.

———

Foolish, I know. But I believed love would be like the romance novels I secretly read. As I traced my fingers over the Braille print of those books, I knew my lover would be torrid. A darkness at his core. I would struggle against him, try to keep him away, but he would win my love by his kindness: he would know without my telling him just how to take care of me. I had dreamed of it. I can tell you now that in romance novels women have little power. I had too much. I didn't know that a man doesn't want to compete with a woman. They want to shine, to be the real star.

Peter rattled the mailbag so its inky scent rose to me. "Helen, can we get back to work here?" he spelled. "You rant against President Wilson. But it's a wonder the U.S. government hasn't thrown a net over you yet. Don't you know that people are being tarred and feathered out in these parts for speaking up against the war?" His hand felt jittery, excited in mine.

"Apparently, Mr. Fagan, you haven't kept up with the news. Wisconsin's Senator La Follette is against U.S. involvement in the war against Germany. When he spoke out last week Teddy Roosevelt called *him* a skunk."

"Teddy Roosevelt is rich, and famous. And you are . . ."

"Famous."

"Well, one out of two isn't bad."

I can't remember a time when I was not famous. After Annie taught me my first words when I was seven, she wrote to Michael Anagnos, the head of the Perkins School, of my success: the Fifty-Sixth Annual Report of the Perkins School, published worldwide, called me "a phenomenon" and "most remarkable." The news of my "miracle" spread. Religious leaders said I was proof of the purity of the human soul. Alexander Graham Bell called my progress "without parallel." The *Nation* profiled me. Half of Tuscumbia visited my house. Reporters swarmed at my door, even while we slept.

I was ten years old.

Stories of me were carried around the world: soon President Cleveland had invited me to the White House, I was enrolled at Perkins for free, and overflowing crowds met me wherever I went. By the time I was sixteen Andrew Carnegie had invited me for dinner. I wrote my autobiography as a sophomore at Radcliffe College, and when it was published Mark Twain called me "a wonderful creature, the most wonderful in the world."

The truth is, I was never unknown, but often lonely.

I reached for Peter's hand.

Then I felt him reach into the bag and pull out a letter. It gave off a dampness. He tapped the contents of the letter, from the sister of John Beutler of Cologne, Germany, into my hand:

> Miss Keller,
> My brother John, he quit the typewriter factory at sixteen to fight in the war. Sent straight to the trenches and into the French line of fire. But Miss Keller, he didn't die.
>> Only woke up in a hospital blind.
>> Help him.
>> > Sincerely,
>> > Hannah Beutler

Peter pulled away—but I edged closer to him. I felt my long nights of blindness invade the life of this boy, this soldier, and I burst out impulsively that the Germans loved my autobiography, *The Story of My Life*. What if I give the profits of the German edition to soldiers blinded in the war?

Peter dropped the letter, leaned forward, and put two fingers on my cheek.

"If you give money to blinded Germans, you'll be marked," he said. "I told you, Socialists are being arrested left and right for protesting the war."

"I'm doing it. And when you next come back," I said, "mark the rest of me." At that moment I was doubly blind: I didn't realize how my fame would protect me, but in the months to come Peter would have no such protection.

I took out a Braille pen from my bag sitting on the chair beside me and scrambled through it to find a piece of notepaper to write my letter right away. "What are you doing?" Peter asked. "It's too dark to write." Then I felt his hand pause, until I laughed.

"Watch me," I said. While I pressed the pen to mark the page, Annie walked up to the table and leaned in, tracing her hand over the Braille letters to my publisher, telling them to give money to the German soldiers.

Peter pressed toward me until I felt his approval of me glow like grass. I knew then that I would cling to him. I was not foolish—I was terrified that Annie would sicken and die, that my mother would be the only person left, that I would be sent to live in the cold, dark cell of Alabama.

But I wanted to be loved, and this was my chance. *I am yours* I wanted to say as Peter traced his thumb in my palm. My two-dimensional world ballooned out: rounder it felt, smoother, larger.

I breathed in fully for the first time.

After we devoured our dessert, Peter led me past the hotel's grape arbor and into the grassy expanse by the lake's edge, where, he said, a wooden windmill creaked and groaned. We stood there together, unsure of what to do next until I said, "Annie needs me. I have to go inside." When Peter led me past the windmill it turned at a full surge as he and I puffed and panted up the hill toward the hotel.

Chapter Four

⊰⧉⊱

"Helen, don't be foolish," Annie spelled to me moments later when Peter and I reached the hotel's front porch. She was waiting there for me, and the floorboards gave off that queer midwestern scent of whiskey, prairie dirt, and corn. Annie shook my arm and said again, "Foolish girl. You can't afford to give money to *anybody*." I stood between Annie and Peter, the willows that circled the hotel cooling my arms, and regretted that I'd just told Annie I would donate money from my autobiography to German soldiers blinded by the war.

"We barely have enough for ourselves," she said, her hand heavy in mine.

"You're tired," I spelled, my fingers erratic in her palm. "Are you all right?"

"Don't change the subject."

But I interrupted again. "Where's Peter?" I turned toward the street, where the rumble of cars shook the porch. "Has he left?" Annie's palm tightened under my fingertips, telling me her temper was about to flare. From the first day that Peter and I met—even though she hired him to help—his very existence rattled her. It was partly that I might be taken in, but it was more that she might be replaced.

"Hold on," she said. Her footsteps receded to the end of the porch, then I felt the sluicing of the porch swing. The swing, Annie showed me that morning, hung from the wooden ceiling from two metal hooks. The clink of the swing's metal chains against them now grated the night air and suddenly mixed with the scent of sulfur and cigarette smoke.

I tilted my head toward the swing. Peter was in it, surely, slouched into the swing's cotton cushions, his fingers on the cigarette as he inhaled the smoke.

"Now," Annie said when she came back across the porch and took my arm. She led me inside the hotel's heavy front door. "He's far enough away so we can talk." She sped me across the lobby, and as we rounded the corner by the coffee shop I stiffened. Through an open window Peter's scent of smoke drifted toward me as we passed. I wanted to stop there, but Annie hurried me toward her room, all the while talking as we walked rapidly down the hall: "If you give money to Germans—*Germans*, Helen, even blind ones—the press will have a field day. I can see the headlines now: 'Helen Keller, Traitor.' Then who will come to hear our talks? We get paid to do them, remember? We get paid by the number of tickets collected at the door. Helen, come on. We barely have enough money to make it back to Massachusetts at this rate. If you give money to Germans, believe me, it will be much worse."

I turned to move farther down the hall to my own room, but Annie squeezed my hand harder. "What's going on?" she demanded, leaning against the doorjamb of her room. "What gave you this idea?" When I said, "Peter," she leaned forward. "Why did you talk about this with him first, and not me?" Her voice under my fingertips slightly oily, the color of dark.

I felt the whoosh of air as she pushed open the door to her room. The scent of the coffee cup she'd left on her bureau mixed with the tang of her leather suitcase just inside the door. "Watch your step." I knew Annie was sloppy and she warned me about her clothes on the slippery bare floor, and with her hand looped in mine, she kicked the clothes aside, led me in, and rapidly closed the door. "Stay here." She crossed the room to the small desk sitting by the far window, came back, and said, "Look at this. I'll show you how crazy your idea is."

She had scooped up a loose sheaf of papers from her desk and now handed them to me. "Helen, listen." She read them quickly. The top letter said, "American Investment Warning: Stocks at a Loss, Balance Zero."

Then Annie said, "Listen up, Helen. If people stay away from our talks and our stocks keep falling . . ." She paused. "We won't be able to keep our house more than another few months."

"Don't worry, I'll fix it," I said.

But Annie pulled my hand as if to shake me. "Face facts, Helen. Your father stopped paying me my salary twenty years ago, when you were ten years old. He was supposed to pay me until you were eighteen, but you know his will made no provisions for my salary. And you didn't get your share after he died, even though your sister and brothers did. We've paid our own way since you were twenty-three, by God knows how many lectures, your books, that yearly money from Carnegie and Sterling. But it's different now. I have this damned cough day and night. You may have the strength to cross the country still, six months of the year. But Helen, I just don't."

At that moment her cough seemed like a retreat. Some place safe where she could stop living our life, ignore our troubles, and just be alone. From the open window by her bed came a breeze so cold it tightened my chest, but I kept Annie's hand in my own.

"Keep this in mind. Peter will cost us plenty. But we need him here if I'm too sick to work."

At the mention of Peter's name I wanted to run from Annie's side, just to be near him.

But Annie's scent of defeat called me back.

She led me across the room to the bed by the windows and sat down.

I turned toward her. "Stay with me," Annie told me. "It'll be all right. It's probably just a scare." But I pulled my hand away and moved to the window facing the porch. Its glass cool under my fingertips. The glass trembled with the vibrations of a train hurtling across the countryside just past the hotel. I imagined I was on the train with Peter, moving into the night with him. Instead I walked back to the bed where Annie sat and took her hand. She needed me so much. Was it wrong for me to want Peter—any man, really—to help me find a life apart?

The train in the distant woods left a taste like iron in my mouth.

One thing I never said was how tired I was at times. What people respected most about me was my stamina. Especially that summer of 1916 when we fell into debt. Annie and I never liked paying bills, never liked to feel their envelopes, and now that our lecture tour was a failure because I kept talking against the war, we needed our investment returns; without them we couldn't pay the maintenance on our house that August, or for the rest of that fall. Still, we never missed the chance to buy a new fur on Newbury Street instead of paying the water bill or the mortgage.

Why didn't we have enough money? Andrew Carnegie gave me a pension every year. The Sugar King of Boston, John Spaulding, gave me stocks to protect my welfare. Even Mark Twain, whom I met on a warm Sunday in New York, at a lunch in the home of Mr. and Mrs. Lawrence Hutton when I was fourteen, got his friend the "robber baron" Henry Rodgers, of Standard Oil, to help pay for my college education. I had no debt from those years.

But as I sat in the upholstered chair next to Annie's bed, I knew the truth was that Annie was dependent on me for a living, and all the money we made from lecturing, from my books, went to protect her and pay for my secretaries. Annie and I both needed food, clothes, a new roof on our house, and all the people we required to keep me looking "normal" in other people's eyes.

———

"The Star of Happiness." That's what Annie called me during the four years we performed as the "serious part" of a vaudeville show. From Boston to Los Angeles, in theaters ripe with the scent of workers' boots and whiskey, we went on stage twice daily. I was thrilled; Annie, despondent. For our act she parted the velvet curtains to walk alone onto a stage arranged to look like a residential parlor. Silk dress rustling, the theater's cigar smoke stinging her eyes, Annie stood beneath the hot lights to call out that no matter what trials I faced, I always met them with optimism and love.

Then I came onstage.

Guided to Annie by the tart scent of her rose perfume, I was exuberant. Backstage I had put on my own makeup, and as I walked out to my audience I smiled as I inhaled their warmth. Then Annie spoke my words. I was the Star of Happiness, because I knew the most important thing in life: love. Love and connection to others. That is what brought true happiness, I said. And I meant it. Music came up as our act ended. As the curtain fell, I felt the audience's wild applause through my shoes.

But we didn't do vaudeville just for love.

We also did it so that Annie would have money as she grew old.

No matter that our fellow performers included a man who ate tadpoles. I was proud of myself. In our hotel, Annie, however, spelled into my hand just before sleep, "We have been miscast in life."

So we fell into debt that summer of 1916. Nothing new. We'd been in and out of debt for years and had tried everything: we had tried not reading the investment reports, we had tried tying them in bundles and putting them in sacks, we had tried making money by lecturing, vaudeville, but by age fifty Annie was worn out. This cough seemed a good reason to do what she had always fought so hard against. To lie down.

And if she wanted to escape, it would be my duty to provide for the one person who gave up her life so I could have my own.

Then just as the bedsprings shuddered and Annie's heavy body leaned into the bed she said the magic words: "Helen, we've got to have Peter full time as your secretary when we get back home. I just can't do it anymore. I'm going to make some arrangements. He needs to live nearby."

I'd never felt so alive—or afraid.

Chapter Five

⊰⊱

A marble cell of dark. Without sight or sound, sometimes my
life felt like a prison. But in our Wisconsin hotel room, where
the smell of cornfields and night rain filled the air and I knew Peter
would be by my side, that cell of dark broke open.

I sat head up in Annie's room, shoulders back, feet planted solidly
on the wooden floor. I was going to be left alone with a man for
the first time in my life. "Are you sure?" I asked Annie, my hands
searching for her mouth. I lip-read her response by pressing one
finger on her throat, one on her lips, and another on her nose, so I
could "listen" to her words. I didn't want to mistake her answer.

"For God's sake, what choice do we have?" I felt the dry, wry
tone of her voice through my hands. "Stuck in this godforsaken
town with another talk to give tomorrow, and no way to get home
by train if I'm this sick—he's our savior, Helen. A flawed one, that's
for sure. If you saw the way he eats—crumbs all over his fingers—
and I'd rather break stones on the King's Highway than hear him
spout off about politics. If I hear one more thing about those young
girls who jumped to their deaths from the Triangle Shirtwaist Factory fire, landing on the streets of New York, I'll scream."

I didn't move.

"Perfect he isn't, not even close." Annie's fingers rapped my palm.
"But he's all we've got."

I said nothing, as if my breathing would give me away. The clock

23

on the wall above my chair made a ratcheting vibration as one minute, then two went by.

"But he's still a man." Annie's palm gave off the tautness she
always had when she felt an enemy was near. "You're not to let him
touch you. From here up," she gestured from my waist to my
mouth, "nothing. And from here down." She passed her hand over
my waist, hips, and upper legs. "Absolutely nothing." I was so taken
aback that I wanted to jump up and leave the room.

The upholstered chair beneath me scratched. "Yes," I joked back,
to get her mind off how much I wanted Peter to touch me with
those fingers of smoke, whiskey, and twine. Instead of answering
me Annie leaned forward. The door to her room shuddered as if
someone was outside.

"Who is it?" I asked Annie.

"A crowd of latecomers tromping into the lobby, no doubt. They
shouldn't come in this late. I saw them clambering out of their car
this morning after a hiking trip to George's Falls."

Hoping to keep her attention on them—on anything, instead of
Peter—I said, "A whole family and they didn't bother to come to
our talk?"

"Barely anyone comes to our talks as it is. Don't you see?" She
tried to lie against her pillows in bed, but her cough forced her up,
and I held her as she bent almost double, her back under my hand
a long tense coil. Then she got her breath and went on.

"We used to talk about your 'miracle': how you came to read,
write, go to Radcliffe—succeed. That's what audiences want to
hear. They don't want to hear you now, going on about President
Wilson and your ideas that this war is a capitalist disaster. For God's
sake, Helen, you can't encourage people to form a general strike
and refuse to go to war."

"Why shouldn't I?" I said. "The capitalists don't care—"

"I already heard that speech," Annie said, "when you gave it in
Carnegie Hall. Helen," she shook my arm, "come out of the clouds.

I just counted the receipts from tonight's lecture: it's *half* of what we got this time last year." She dropped my hand and exhaled so hard I felt it in my bones.

"In your talk tomorrow, no talk about war. Not a *word*. And drop that letter to the Germans in the trash. Do you hear me?"

"Do I hear you?" I almost started a joke, but then remembered that Peter might laugh, but not Annie, not now. "I don't want to argue." I shifted toward the door to the porch. "Peter's going to take me on stage tomorrow?" I asked again. "Where is he now? Is he still out there?" I felt her stiffen. I moved toward the door and swung it open.

"Close that door." She walked up behind me and put her hand on the doorknob. "Were you raised in a barn?"

A warm wind mixed with the scent of brandy as she swung the door shut. "But Peter?" I said. My palm still held some of the warmth of his thumb.

"He's still out there." Annie turned to the windows that faced the front porch. "You should see him. Pacing the floorboards like a loyal dog." She paused. "What on earth is he waiting for? Why doesn't he go to his room for the night?"

"He's waiting for me," I said. Annie's palm turned hard, almost metallic. Her suspicions rose between us, tightening the night air. "Why would he be waiting for you?"

I kept my fingers still in Annie's hand.

"He works for us." I was afraid to breathe. "Maybe he's waiting for us to tell him to go." Just like that she threw her blanket off, crossed the room in a *sslap-sslap-sslap* of her bare feet, and swung open the door. Peter's footsteps moved quickly across the porch floor, until he plonked up the hotel's stairway to his room, where he would stay until the next day.

"No funny business tomorrow, Helen. I mean it."

"Trust me." I lied so easily. I took her hand and squeezed it good night.

When I felt my way to the door, then down the hall, the pine paneling rough under my hands, it was all I could do to stand at the bottom of the stairwell and then go on to my room beside Annie's instead of climbing those stairs to Peter.

Chapter Six

❦

"Do you dream in color?" people ask me. "In your dreams can you see?" I wrote a book about how the world comes to me through scents, taste, and that divine medium: touch. In that book I wrote of a dream I had about Annie. I was ashamed to admit that dream, but now it's time to say it once and for all.

The night Annie told me we were almost out of money and that she was sick, I fumbled my way into my room but avoided the bed. I could not sleep. Instead I sat heavily in the desk chair by the door and read in the dark. My fingers traced the Braille pages so easily. But even that wouldn't calm me.

Because Peter would be my private secretary for the rest of the summer.

As morning's faint sunlight fell on my arms I pitched into an uneasy sleep.

And I dreamed that Annie was perched high above Niagara Falls as I pushed her straight to the waters below.

When I woke up, that image—heavy, murky in its shape— hovered at the dark edge of my memory. The Wisconsin air was heavy with rain, a sodden scent, and I couldn't wait to see Peter, tell him I needed him by my side that day. If I didn't go to him then, I might not go. So as the heavy thud of farm trucks labored up the road outside, I felt my way to my closet, picked a fresh dress from the first hanger, then crossed to my door and slowly made my way up the stairway. In my own house I have memorized everything—

tables, chairs, rooms—and walk quite fast. But in new places I am lost; I can't find my way even from one room to another without a hand on my shoulder to guide me.

In my well of dark, I held the railing, climbed one stair, two, until my foot reached a pocket of air. I was at the top of the stairs. One door, two, three, I worked my way past the first three rooms and stopped nervously outside the fourth door.

Two quick raps woke Peter. He opened the door and led me into his room, around the coffee table to sit on the settee by his windows. He leaned back easily against the cushions, the scent of night, whiskey, and tobacco on his skin.

"Come on. Spill the beans. What is it?" he said, as if it were a normal occurrence for a woman to bang on his bedroom door at seven a.m. I shifted beside him, aware of his palm on my arm. "Okay," he said after I told him Annie was too sick to take me on stage that morning, and that I needed him with me, well, all day. "We'll trot over to the café, have a bite to eat, then do your show."

I paused, but he didn't seem to notice. I felt him flip his wrist to the side, and guessed he was checking his watch. "Right, we have enough time," he said. "I'll get ready, then we'll shoot over there."

Still I didn't move.

"Or, maybe you've had breakfast?" I stood stock still, and he paused.

"How would I get breakfast without Annie, or you?" I finally said. "The waiters don't know fingerspelling, and I can hardly read the menu or tell them my order, you know." I smiled, but I could feel in his fingers the realization that I really couldn't go out and do the simplest things on my own.

"Well, let's get on it," he said, and strode off toward the stairs. The *carumph* of his footsteps receded from me in a rapid *tap, tap, tap*, and then, as I leaned against the doorjamb, they came right back.

"Another blunder." He gave me his arm. "I lead you, right?" And when he stepped off quickly down the hall and led me out into the day, the weak rays of early sun fell on my bare arms. We crossed the bumpy grass toward the restaurant and the scent of waffles and hot coffee, the mist of the distant lake rising in the air. When I tripped over a thick root sticking out of the grass, Peter clumsily grabbed my arm, lifted me back to my feet, and said, "Don't even think of saying it."

"That cliché?" I said back, eager to feel the sinewy warmth of his arm as I hung on.

He sped me across the grass. We got to the restaurant and he pulled out a chair for me, its metal frame sending a tingling up the backs of my legs as he dragged it across the floor. He said, "Yes, don't say that cliché."

"About the blind leading the blind?" I tucked my napkin into my lap, hungrier than I'd ever been.

"That would be the one."

He slid a menu across the table to me. I felt a sudden vibration as he pushed his chair away from the table. "Nature calls. Pick out whatever you want. I'll order when I get back." I felt his footsteps receding, and I picked up the menu, its creased edge pin sharp in my grip.

Waiting. The curse of the deaf-blind. Not only couldn't I read the menu myself, I also couldn't ask one of the waiters to read it for me, either. Menus weren't in Braille, and the waiters—like most every-one—didn't know the manual fingerspelling language I used. So I tapped my feet, sat up straight, and pressed my hands into the cool tabletop, waiting for Peter's footsteps to thud across the floor so he could translate the menu.

I sat taller, to suppress my impatience. It was infuriating, this waiting. I was thirty-seven years old. And like a child, an infant, really, I was at the mercy of others. Hour after hour of my life was spent waiting. Waiters brushed past my chair, the scent of raspber-ries and sugar trailing from their trays as they passed.

———

"Onward, missy." Peter returned, scented of pine soap, and when he pulled out his chair he sat close to me, his leg brushing mine. He picked up the menu.

"Read it?" I spelled cautiously into his hand.

"Yes, ma'am. Even the descriptions."

I leaned forward.

"If being your private secretary is this much work, you're going to have to pay me extra." His voice hummed through my hand.

"I'll pay whatever you want." I pressed my fingers closer to his lips. I couldn't wait to taste the pancakes with wild blueberries, pockets of flavor in my mouth.

Over breakfast we practiced my talk, until the bell clanged its metallic *thong* into the air at ten and Peter led me across the grass to the Chautauqua tent, all the while saying he didn't know why the American flag hung so easily over the tent when we were approaching war.

That morning he and I bounded up the three wooden steps to the makeshift stage, the rustling of the crowd a welcome wave of warmth. After flattening his tie against his shirt with one hand, and then faltering a bit—I felt his weight press heavily into the wooden floorboards—his voice rang out into the air. For ten minutes he told the crowd of how at age seven I was a child with no language who fought Annie at every turn, but after weeks of spelling words into my hand Annie finally took me to the water pump in our yard. In the heat of the day Annie splashed that water over my hand, her fingers flying in mine: w-a-t-e-r. W-a-t-e-r. I leaped up, awakened. Everything had a name. Life penetrated my muffled world.

Beside Peter, I held his arm, and the way he pulled me close told me that the story thrilled him.

The crowd applauded my "miracle" for so long, the stage reverberated under my feet.

The truth is, I don't remember the moment at the water pump. For two decades I've heard it hundreds of times. I know it like my name. I've stood by Annie as she told crowds in Boston, New York, Chicago, Los Angeles, and tiny towns like Albion, and Rock Creek, Michigan, about my awakening. I've even written about it in my books. But I have no memory of it at all.

What I do remember is this: It was June 1888. Annie took me to be examined by Alexander Graham Bell, then a prominent doctor for the deaf in Washington, D.C. Was there any way my hearing might be improved? I was eight years old. Dr. Bell said no, I would never hear. But he told Annie that he had an exciting new invention. It allowed anyone who didn't know manual fingerspelling to "talk" with the deaf.

"This could work for Helen," Dr. Bell said to Annie. She spelled his words to me, and then he slid a large, bulky "glove" over my small hand. Printed on it were letters of the "normal" alphabet. Raised, they could be felt by the wearer. I felt them on my palm. Dr. Bell tapped first the *h*, then the *e*. Then, he pressed down harder, on the *l* two times. Last came the *o*.

"Hello," I answered back. A feeling of intense pleasure flooded through me.

With my free hand, I took his. I had "spoken" to someone without Annie interpreting. Dr. Bell said that with practice, hearing people could easily learn how to use his invention to talk to me. "Helen will have freedom," he said to Annie, who spelled his words to me.

I couldn't wait.

All the way back to Tuscumbia on the train I spelled to Annie that soon I would be able to speak with Father, who never was good at the manual fingerspelling, and my Auntie Ev, or anyone else.

"No," Anne spelled back. "It's not a good idea." She said I wouldn't need to communicate with others because while she was with me, she would tell me everything I needed to know. I wouldn't need to talk to anyone else.

She wanted to keep me close because of her own loneliness. People say together we were miraculous. We were. But we were also isolated; loneliness engulfed me in those years. I'm older now. I realize I want more than a story frayed from its telling.

As the Wisconsin crowd's applause receded, the stage became still. I held Peter's hand more tightly in mine as, fingers tense, he introduced me to the crowd: "For twenty-five years Helen Keller has called for the rights of the deaf and blind around the world. But she has more to say than that," Peter said, spelling his words into my hand, then giving me a nudge so hard I almost bolted forward.

So as Peter called out my words to the audience, while I spelled them into his palm, I said everything Annie warned me against: the floorboards of the stage jutted out and warped beneath my shoes as I stepped forward, my hand in Peter's, aware that he would boom my words out to the waiting crowd. "Let no capitalists send our innocent boys to slaughter. We've suffered long enough at the hands of a government that sends boys to war for its own profit. This must *stop*. Strike, strike, strike against the war."

I believed then that Peter would set me free.

When the crowd filed out, the show's manager came up on stage to give us our night's wages. Right after he left Peter said, "Helen, is this really all you get for all this work?" He told me he'd taken out the manager's 20 percent, and then the thirty dollars for his own salary. "The ticket sales were lower than ever, and twenty people asked the manager for their money back," he added.

I wasn't the Helen Keller they expected, or wanted. But I didn't care.

"It was worth it," I said.

———

"Jesus, Mary, and Joseph," Peter said later that afternoon after the show. I'd wolfed down two hamburgers with him at a burger shack by the hotel—Annie would never let me eat burgers in public: too vulgar, she said. But I couldn't help it. With Peter I wanted to eat hot dogs, wear high heels, drink gin. "Here's the problem as I see it," he said. He'd just paid the lunch bill and was scribbling down the costs for the hotel and the food for our trip back to Boston the next day.

"You don't mind how much you take in, and I don't know enough about your situation to give you advice." We started across the lawn for the hotel. The sharp scent of pine trees filled the air, and the pine needles underfoot made the ground yield to my shoes. Into the bed of needles the day's happiness slipped away. "If this keeps up, we'll be lucky to get back to Wrentham with a few cents."

"We'll work it out," I said, my face suddenly cool as we walked under the hotel's covered front porch. That afternoon I napped on my hotel room bed. I slept a deep, dreamless sleep. Night would come, and with it, Peter.

I had no fear.

Chapter Seven

The blind are idolized for the wrong things. It's strange. The praise I got for being "Helen Keller the miracle." Everyone loved that. Some people even praised me for becoming a Socialist—a Wobbly, even—supporting the Lawrence strikers, working to wipe out slums in New York City, and rallying against wars around the world. I believed that plutocrat President Taft when, at a speech for the New York Association for the Blind, he asked, "What must the blind think about the Declaration of Independence, since they are not granted the same rights as others in our society?" In my blindness and deafness I proved I was equal—more than equal—in my intellect. But no one, from the time I was a young woman, would accept my having a lover. It was unseemly, somehow, a blind girl in a love affair. Torrid, almost. So I didn't speak my desire, I hid it. While I marched for birth control, stood up for Margaret Sanger when she gave out leaflets in Brooklyn saying women could limit the number of children they would have, I wasn't allowed to even marry, or consider having children of my own.

I couldn't accept that fate. That wasn't enough for me.

In my hotel room after my nap, the air was heavy with rain, and a wind blew in the ripe scent of the nearby town. Down the bare hall outside my room I detected the rapid, determined footsteps of waiters entering the dining room for the dinner shift, sorry to have left their girlfriends or wives. And me? At that moment I wasn't idolized by anyone. I was a woman alone in a room, with nothing to do, and no one to guide me outside.

The audience's applause seemed very far away.

All afternoon I waited. I read a German Socialist magazine in Braille, restlessly moving my fingers over the raised print, then walked to my window. The slanting, metallic vibrations meant workers were dismantling the Chautauqua tent. A rapid succession of blows followed. The high metal poles that held up the dome of the tent were being knocked down, reminding me of endings.

The thumps and plunks of the dinner crowd faded; the granite rocks outside my window turned from baking hot to cool. Evening had come, the tour was over. Peter and I would leave the next day for Boston. Surely he would realize that he should come downstairs, read to me, take me to dinner. I felt my way from window to closet, then, with an armful of clothes, tossed them into the open suitcase at the foot of my bed. Still, no Peter.

The blind are excellent guides. A telltale rap on the ceiling of my room told me Peter was awake; he had swung out of bed and was pacing the bare floors.

I decided to make a racket to guide him downstairs.

I sat on my suitcase so I could fasten it tight, then pulled it over to the door and dragged my desk chair, with great banging, away from my desk and sat down heavily. At the oak desk I swept up my hair to show off my bare neck, the way women in romance novels always did, and unbuttoned the top two buttons of my blue dress and sat at my desk just in time. Within minutes Peter came into my room and took my hand.

"Sorry, boss, I slept through my afternoon shift. Wait a minute." He leaned over me and saw the Braille letter I had been reading at my desk. "Come to think of it, I'm not sorry at all. Look at you!"

He took the letter and read to me that a farmer in Indiana, a

German American, refused to pay his war bonds, and a mob attacked his house. Hang him! they cried. Traitor! Until his wife convinced them to let him live.

"You work so much it makes mere humans look bad," Peter said. I put my hand on his cheek and felt his voice dip.

"That German farmer needs help." I was suddenly defensive. I'd thought I could bring Peter closer to me by showing him my intensity. But as I spelled to him he opened and closed his palm, as if he were drawn to me but also pushed away.

"What's going on out there?" I jerked my head toward the window to get his attention away from me. The floor beneath my feet vibrated with the arrival of cars and trucks; even the arms of my chair rattled under my hands. "What are all those people coming for?"

"There's a carnival outside. Can't you tell?"

"How would I know?"

"I thought you were the scent expert. What, can't you smell the popcorn? The fireworks, at least?" He was right. There was a singed, burnt scent in the night air. "Let's go." He pulled my chair back from the desk. "The carnival awaits. I get the inside seat on the Tilt-A-Whirl. Otherwise I get dizzy as hell. You in?"

"No." I held tight to the edge of my desk.

"Why not?"

"Do I have to explain?"

"Explain what?"

"I can't just go outside. Look out the window. I'll bet you dinner at least two photographers are out there, with press tags from the *Wisconsin Tribune* dangling from their shirt pockets. One man is right outside the hotel, his camera trained on the door." I felt Peter jolt a bit with surprise. "Most likely the mayor of Appleton is smiling for one of the photographers, and the minute I walk outside, he'll demand a picture with me."

"Great. You're psychic," he laughed. "I really am doomed."

"Lesson one on the life of Helen Keller." I tapped his chest with one finger. "Always be prepared. Every public event I go to with Annie, the local newspaper sends a photographer to snap a picture of us with the mayor, or any other dignitary who is there. I guarantee if I go to the fair there will be front-page photos of me in the papers tomorrow." I felt Peter stand perfectly still, listening to me. "So I have to get ready. Annie insists I always look normal, better than normal if I can pull it off."

"I like you the way you are." He touched my face.

"Yes, but you're not the public that pays to hear me speak. I'd go to the fair with you if I could—I'd take the outside seat on the Tilt-A-Whirl and go in the dunking booth, too."

"Seriously, Helen. Do you always live for everyone else but yourself? Your public always sees you poised, perfectly smiling, the happy deaf-blind girl. Don't you ever get tired of the charade?"

"That's enough." I suddenly felt self-conscious, and missed Annie. She would understand.

Peter acted as if he didn't hear me. "Come on." He pulled my chair out and gave my shoulders a shake. "Let's get outside. Be part of the crowd." The rumble of the Ferris wheel shook the room, making the air press against me. I still refused to move, and he said, "I get it. Maybe you go only where you're invited to speak? Be up in the front, where everyone can see you?"

"That's a bit harsh." I stood up straight. He *was* my employee, after all.

He took my hand. "Come back here."

It was my turn to pull away. No matter how much I argued against being idolized, I was ashamed to hear from him how much my public image meant to me.

I had learned early to live for others. To say, often, what they wanted me to say. When I was ten and already well known, my Mastiff dog, Lioness, ran into Tuscumbia's town square, and a policeman accidentally shot him. I wept. When I wrote about my loss to Mr. William Wade, one of the wealthy men who provided money for my education, he published my letter in *Forest and Stream*. Thousands of letters arrived in my Tuscumbia mailbox: people around the world wanted to buy me a new dog.

I was elated. But Annie told me to write back to them and say, "I don't want another dog. I would like to use your kind offer of money to send a poor little blind and deaf boy named Tommy Stringer to school." I wrote down Annie's words in my square handwriting.

My letter was carried by newspapers across the country.

My words raised enough money for Tommy to attend Perkins for two full years.

I was always helpful. Careful. I had learned to show only part of myself to others. Then people would never leave me. I would not be alone in my darkness.

Ten years later, when I was at Radcliffe College, my composition teacher was one of the first people to tell me to write what I knew—that I had original thoughts. I responded that all my life I had written what I was told, or, at times, what I thought people wanted to hear, but in his class, as a young woman of nineteen, I wanted to express my real thoughts. Because it wasn't just in my writing that I had lived for others. In newspapers published around the world there were pictures of me meticulously dressed, dancing the fox trot with a young man, but I had never been allowed to date. The world saw me riding a horse on my own, when outside the photo someone always held the reins. The photos were fun, yes. But they were untrue. They did not show my real life.

Peter leaned over the hotel room desk. The moment of my annoyance with him passed. I suspect it was my bare neck that called to him.

"I've written to my publisher," I said, "telling them to give the royalties to blinded German soldiers and sailors. We've done it!—you and I. Annie would have my head if she knew, but not you. You're a radical, like me. Together we can even help the Austrian soldiers."

He put my hand to his mouth, and ran my fingers gently over his lips. "Don't you want more than that for yourself? Why *shouldn't* you?"

The pounding of the carnival rides shook the windows of my room as Peter recounted the way I spoke out to audiences in Kansas, in tents in Nebraska, by lakes in rainy Wisconsin over the summer. How the audiences waited to hear about the "miracle" of this deaf-blind woman who speaks her mind.

I felt as if a light fell over me. His voice flowed through my fingertips.

"Don't you ever want other things?" he said.

I leaned into him.

"Do you want to hear this?"

"Yes."

"Helen, kiss me."

I felt his warm breath on my mouth. "Wait. Not yet." I fumbled with the little glass figurines on my desktop, suddenly unsure. "Will you—" I moved suddenly toward the door and opened it for him to leave. "Give me some time?" I said, and stumbled over my opened suitcase. When I slipped, Peter steadied me.

"I'm getting pretty good at this."

"Catching me?" I picked up the hem of my floor-length calico dress and swept it free of dust.

"Keeping you on your own two feet is more like it." He followed me back into my room.

"Kiss me." He pulled me back to him.

His mouth salt, willow trees, pear.

I held his face with my hands, his button-down shirt scratchy as he pulled me close. His hands warmed my back.

"Annie is sick. I have to check on her upstairs."

"Right. Another person who needs you." He stroked my cheek.

I leaned forward. "We'll be home soon. When we get there, walk down the hill behind my house to King's Pond. Meet me there for a swim. I promise you'll like what you see."

He paused, his palm tentative. "Listen. I can barely do the crawl. But if you want me in the water with you, I'm there."

I was so relieved that I joked, "If you start drowning I'll let you sink like a stone."

"You're not my lifeguard?" He felt the smile on my face, and pulled me closer. "Helen, if I start slipping under, I'll take you down with me."

We both laughed.

Chapter Eight

Why was I so brazen—so forward with Peter? I was thirty-seven years old and had never before been alone with a man, never mind with a man with a mouth like night. And yet I'd always preferred men's company to women's. When I was at Radcliffe, Annie wanted to hire a smart young man to help me with my studies. But Mother immediately stopped her. She'd met with the young man. With his deep brown eyes and lovely Italian hands he was far too handsome to work with me, Mother said. I might be taken with him, and forget about my studies. She ordered him replaced. Now, with Peter near, all that was pent up inside me came alive. I was a rushing train.

He saw so much—maybe too much—of me.

I waited, fidgeting, on the hotel's sweltering front porch the next day. The morning air crackled around me, the *ting-ting-ting* of the flagpole's metal reverberated in the breeze, and the scent of motor oil and rubber tires rose from the hotel driveway. I inhaled Peter's scent of pine soap and coffee as he ran up and down the steps. I knew he was packing the waiting taxi cab with our six trunks.

Just then the slap of footsteps on the porch made me stand up straight. "Where are our suitcases?" Annie had come out of her room and stood beside me, brushing her fingers against my hand. I inhaled her menthol cough.

"Peter put them in the cab."

"Well, at least he's learning how to treat women. Not like most men we know." Her hand was tense in mine, and my heart sank at how sick I felt she was. Then Peter returned for us. He installed Annie in the front seat of the cab. The closing door made a reassuring thump.

He took my arm.

"I'm sure you're a crack navigator." Peter guided me into the backseat. As he slid in beside me, I was oddly relieved that Annie was in the front.

I felt the car roar to life.

"Boston, here we come," Peter yelled. The cab swerved through town. I rolled down the window. The scent of the bakery, the gas station, and then the camphor scent of the Baptist Church I knew stood at the far edge of town told me we were leaving Wisconsin for good, but then the cab came to a stop. The rumble and bustle of Appleton's train station moved through my arms and legs.

"Train station. Time to get out."

"Wait a minute. Aren't we taking the bus?"

"I checked the schedules. The bus takes seventeen days. Nothing personal, but you'd die of boredom. I can't spell into your hand for that long and she"—he jerked his head toward Annie—"looks to me like she needs to see a doctor pretty quick."

"But you read the paper to me this morning. The local railroad workers are striking for an eight-hour workday. I won't cross a picket line. We'll hire a car."

"Quiet, lady." Peter went on, "Annie's too sick to share the driving. And as far as I can tell you're not exactly an ace behind the wheel."

"You've got a point there." I felt the cold air as he steadied me by the open cab door. Annie slept fitfully in the front seat. I hoped she wouldn't wake up just yet. I didn't want her to detect what I was feeling. I wasn't his idol. I was just Helen. I would follow wherever he led.

——

All my life I've wanted to fit in. I was the first blind deaf-mute to go to Radcliffe College. I thought I'd make friends with the other girls, but they avoided me in the hallways. They didn't know the manual fingerspelling language, and I couldn't speak to them. They gave me a puppy I named Phizz, and nights when the girls were sledding in Boston's cold with their boyfriends, I sated my hunger for company with Annie, both of us unsure if we'd ever fit in.

Only one of my professors bothered to learn fingerspelling, and since most of my books weren't available in Braille, Annie had to spell their contents into my hand for hours each day. During classes she sat by my side and spelled the lectures word by word to me.

On those hot summer nights, when the other girls were out past curfew, Annie slept in her room in our apartment on Boston's Newbury Street. And I pushed away my copies of Cicero in Latin, and Molière in French, and pulled out the romance novel *The Last Days of Pompeii*. I ran my fingers over the Braille pages about the blind slave girl, hips undulating in the garden, while men picked flowers from her basket. As I read, branches scraped my window. In the night's heat I felt strangely excited.

But Annie came into my room and pounced on me: "Caught, discovered, trapped!" She pulled the novel away. If I read books like that, she said, she would not utter one word to me for an entire twenty-four hours. Without Annie spelling into my hand in the Radcliffe classroom, isolation would surround me. I slid the book away.

Annie needed me to stay childlike.

But Peter treated me like a woman.

"Right this way, madam." He led me deeper into Appleton's station. Annie followed, her scent like sour rain. As we moved toward our waiting train, he said the walls above the ticket counter were peppered with posters supporting the war in Europe.

"Don't get carried away," Annie spelled as she walked by my side. "Most of the loafers in here are just reading their newspapers, checking their watches, waiting for trains. They don't care about the war at all. You two can talk antiwar propaganda when we get on the train. As for me, I'm going straight to bed."

The trees outside the train station sent sparks of pine scent into the air as Peter led me and Annie up the metal steps, while he repeated the conductor's shout: "Last caa*aaall* for Pullman train one seventy-five to Boston." I felt the metal door slam shut. Peter installed Annie in a sleeper car in front of us, and led me to the club car.

The train whistle shirred the air as our car moved down the track.

As I slid into a leather seat by the window, Peter passed a packet of letters to me. I felt his hand as he plied open a bulging envelope. "Your latest bills, I think."

"Let's get through these as quick as we can." I drummed my fingers on the table. "And then it's time for lunch and a drink."

"Yes, boss." He covered my fingers with his. "The sooner we finish these the better."

Roof repair:	$1,750.00	Payment thirty days overdue
Painting:	$900.00	Payment due immediately
Taxes:	$1,400.00	Unpaid. Penalty due

"Helen." He took my hand. "You and Annie run a bit of an unsteady ship."

The train rocked so unevenly that I held the table's edge. "You've been with us one full week already, and you're just realizing that?"

"Well, I am a quick study." He steadied me with his hand.

I breathed easier. "I'm suddenly thirsty." The passageway thudded with the tread of other passengers lining up at the far end of the car for lunch. "Will you get us some drinks?" I could smell the coffee, the tang of whiskey sours in the club car. "And some lunch?" I pushed him toward the edge of our seat. "Let's put these away for now." I slid the envelope of bills back toward him.

"Your wish is my command. If you want to deny you have problems, I'm with you. When I come back with lunch we'll talk about what will happen during our Wrentham swim, instead." He moved away, leaving behind a pocket of air. He would soon realize the extent of the trouble Annie and I were in. But I pushed that thought out of my mind and thought about his return instead.

I learned denial early. At age seventeen, I first felt sexual desire; it was while I was reading a romance novel. Then one morning I asked Annie about sex and she said, "Forget it. That's not for you. Channel it into your work." And I did. Fifteen cities in two months and I earned enough money for our house, clothes, and food. My very life depended on my never seeming different from those in the sighted world. My motto, according to Annie, was simple: never complain. So as the train shook furiously over the cross-country tracks, and I felt Peter approaching, I did what anyone good at denial would do. I picked up my paper napkin, and spread it over my lap.

I was ready for a hearty lunch. Peter handed me a lunch bag. I pulled it open, plucked out a ham sandwich, with its scent of salt and the smokehouse, and bit in. I was famished. "Read me the news?" I pushed the newspaper toward him.

While munching on his grilled cheese sandwich, Peter rattled the *New York Times* from where it had fallen to the floor. He shook it open to an article on the war wounded and read. "Listen to this. There's this medical officer—Charles Meyers—who's coined a new diagnosis. It's called shell shock. It happens when soldiers—kids, really—see and hear too much death and they lose their minds. Some even become blind and mute. One seventeen-year-old in the trenches in the Battle of the Somme saw a shell explode fifty feet away; he was unconscious for days. When he woke up his hands and feet shook uncontrollably. The doctors found nothing physically wrong. Still, he was blind and mute."

"Like me."

"Not exactly." Peter's voice moved faster as he read. I kept my fingers close to his mouth to keep up. "This kind of blindness, or muteness, is all in the mind. According to the paper, two thousand seventeen men were sent to one British hospital for shell shock."

"Peter." I turned and ran my fingers over the taut skin of his cheekbones. "Why don't *you* write an article about that? I can just see it in the *New York Times*. 'Special Report from Peter Fagan, Correspondent.'" I picked up my napkin, wiped my mouth, and hoped there were no crumbs.

Peter leaned toward me. "You're a mess, missy." He deftly brushed the rest of the crumbs from my blouse. I wished I had made more of a mess.

"Sure, I can write a piece on shell shock, but the *Times* will never take it. I'm just a former stringer for the *Boston Herald,* remember? Now let me clean off the rest of your pretty dress."

"Stop that. Eat your lunch. Keep your hands off me." I laughed. "They'll take it if *I* ask them. I wrote for them. They'll take it if I say so. We'll be a team. We'll make the money we need."

"What do you mean, 'we'? I'm just your secretary while Annie's too sick to work. If you don't mind my being so bold, it looks like the burden is on you. You're the one who's world famous."

He ran his fingers over my cheek. "I love that you're an independent woman." He lit a cigarette, the tobacco ripe and tart.

I nodded, my jaw tensed.

"Isn't it something?" What I didn't tell him is that I'm more dependent than he thinks. There are some things about which I keep mute. Because I have no intention of losing this man.

"Wait." I stopped Peter from reading more. "I think I've heard enough for one day."

Peter let the paper slide from his hands.

For the first time, we sat together without anything to say.

I leaned back in my seat and breathed in the hot air, the singed ash from the train, the acres of barley, wheat, and corn fields as we passed. And I daydreamed that Peter peeled back my dress. I arched up to him and we tossed and rolled together in a world without end. Through the night, the train-fast night.

Chapter Nine

In that way Peter brought alive cravings in me, like an empty mouth. To be with someone who didn't idolize me. Who saw me as a grown woman who wanted a life of her own, instead. But I didn't know about the cravings I brought alive in him. Some were for fame. Others for some kind of power. All were contradictions. None of them really were clear. I told Peter none of this.

Instead I betrayed my loyalty to Annie—I should have been by her side in her sleeping car; she was so sick. But no. I followed Peter, eagerly, into the club car just to sit by him that first day on the train, and the next day, and the next. I stayed by his side all the way home to Boston, then out to Wrentham, where we installed Annie in her second-floor bedroom, then we went outside, to be alone in the night air. The hot-tar scent of the street and the smoky traces of a nearby barbecue wafted toward me on the breeze. I slid my fingers into Peter's open palm when he said, "Massachusetts has a hurricane season?"

"We never have hurricanes here." I paused, smiling at what I knew would come next.

"Not by the looks of this place." I felt him move his head back and forth, taking in the disheveled state of my house. "What on earth happened here?"

Through the windows opening onto the porch, I knew he saw the living room lit by a lamp. There, two ragged chairs that felt like oats, rough to the touch, faced each other in front of the enormous

fireplace, a rickety table between, a Braille Monopoly game, newspapers, old books scattered across other tables and the floor, and
wisps of dog hair from my Great Dane, Thora, clung to the ragged
braided rug. "John used to help us keep things up. But it's hard now
that he's gone."

Peter said nothing at first, at the mention of John. Annie's husband, a ne'er-do-well who walked out on her two years ago, was
Peter's boss at the *Boston Herald*. An odd tension made him close
his hand into a fist. "I know he's your boss," I said. "I'm not criticizing. But when he and Annie were married and he lived here, he
did the odd jobs—built bookcases, put in the screens for summer.
He even stretched a wire a half-mile long across the stone wall in
the woods so I could walk alone. But now that he's gone, well . . ."
I faltered.

"I hardly know the man." Peter stretched his fingers and traced
my palm. "Besides, he *was* my boss. You're the boss now. In fact
I'm taking the train into Boston tonight to pack up my apartment.
Annie rented me a house nearby so I can be at your beck and call
from now on."

"And don't you forget it." I was so relieved and excited that he
would be near that I didn't even mind if he noticed the living room
ceiling: after a storm, while Annie and I were away on a lecture
tour last year, great patches of water leaked over two-thirds of the
ceiling, leaving it a sodden, dark, tea-colored brown. She had fin-
gerspelled the disaster into my hand.

"Here's what I don't understand," Peter said. "It's you and Annie,
traveling the country to paltry audiences this year, as far as I can
see, yet you've got this house, and me, and if I'm not mistaken there's
a servant inside lighting the lamps and priming himself, eager to
see you the minute we walk in."

"And?" I was ready to be more honest than I should have been.
"You want to know how I manage this? How a deaf, blind woman
in 1916 can afford her own house?"

"Something like that, yes." He smelled of clover and fresh-cut grass. I would have said anything.

"This house cost me my life," I said.

"What?"

"You know." I waited. "The book . . ."

"Oh, *The Story of My Life.*"

"Paid for it," I exhaled. My autobiography had been published to critical acclaim when I was only in my twenties.

"Looks like you bought this place in the halcyon days." I felt his fingers peeling the decayed paint from the windowsill. "Spent money you couldn't afford. But that's not the strangest part. Let me get this straight. You wrote the story of your life when you were what, twenty-five?"

"Don't age me." I gave him a poke. "I was twenty-two."

"Tell us all about yourself," people urged. So I wrote *The Story of My Life* when I was a college student. The tale I told in my autobiography was one of utter triumph: of how Annie, then the Perkins School for the Blind, then Radcliffe, all carried me closer to the shores of the normal, sighted and hearing world. Books were my dearest friends, I wrote, making up for the lack of human company. But for all the success of that book, underneath there were so many things I never said. A dark jealousy burned. I tried so hard, in my writing and my books, to seem exactly like a normal, hearing and sighted person that I never showed how discouraged or disappointed I was at times. I wanted to show perfection.

Later in life I wrote, "What I have printed gives no knowledge of my actual life." Strangers, the people closest to me, no one liked hearing that.

I felt Peter pivot so my hands moved from his chest to his back. "Okay," he said. "You've got twenty-four acres, some outbuildings that seem to be sinking into the earth—"

"They're not that bad," I interrupted.

"Well, the roof needs repair, even the lawn needs mowing. But this place really is something," he tapped into my palm. I felt his fingers spell *I'll see you tomorrow.* "No offense," he added, "but I hope Annie needs a long mending period before she takes over again. I'm beginning to like this job."

"I'm beginning to like being the boss."

"Have I told you how much I like a woman in charge?" He pinched my lower back hard, sending a jolt to my skin. "Do that again," I said. "And you're employee of the month."

Pain is a dark star in my life. It's always been with me. Even now, thirty-five years after I lost my hearing and sight, I still remember the burning, like a fireplace poker turned around behind my eyes, at nineteen months old when my fever broke, and I was going blind. Day by day, the sunlight pierced my eyes like fire. Slowly my sight burned to ash. Nothing left. My fingers still ache with the felt memory of how fiercely I rubbed my infant eyes of pain.

And my blue eyes? The ones you see in my photographs? So bright and clear that reporters say they are mesmerized by my gaze? They're glass. I had them put in during an operation when I was a young woman so that I could look more normal, less blind.

But no pain is like the one I had when I went to Annie's room our first night back in Wrentham and realized she knew I wanted Peter near me, and that she had made plans to send him away.

The truth is that it was Annie alone who really knew me. She read my moods instantly. With a touch or by a look I was exposed to her, like a child. After Peter left for the night I walked carefully inside the house and, touching the hall table, then the velvet love-seat by the far wall of the entryway, found my way to her room. Slowly, I went in.

The queer aluminum scent told me that Annie sat up, alert in bed, and the shrill pock of her fingers in mine once I crossed the thick-rugged floor to greet her was like an electric shock. With great force Annie threw back her quilt and told me to sit down. She must have run her eyes over me—the top buttons open on my dress, the heat in my face from being with Peter—because she said, "Sit down, now. You look like a chicken about to be plucked."

"Don't you mean a flower?" I idly picked up the bristle brush on her bedside table and started brushing her hair. "Your hair's so tangled it's like a pelt." She bowed her head. I tugged the brush through the knots.

"Animals have pelts, Helen. Not humans." She kept wanting to teach me, even though I was no longer a child.

"You're curled up like an animal, a hurt one, in bed," I spelled. Her bathrobe was matted beneath my fingers when I touched her sleeve; the breakfast tray on her bedside table gave off the odor of untouched eggs and cold coffee.

"Careful or I'll bite." Annie made a snapping motion with her mouth, and I was so thankful she forgot about Peter that I laughed.

"Do that again." I held her to me.

She leaned back so I could brush more. Her shoulders, thick with muscle, weight, and worry, sank beneath the even strokes of the brush. Gradually, her breathing slowed.

The familiar scent of just we two together made the thought of Peter fade away.

Vaguely, then more strongly, a childhood memory came to me. I am seven years old, sitting at Annie's knee in my bedroom in Tuscumbia, Alabama. Annie is filled with nervous energy: it is my first Christmas since she arrived. Annie, in order to tame me, had taken me from the house where I lived with my mother and father, and moved us into a two-room house, where just she and I lived. Every day she taught me words; every night I slept, a child, by her side. She was nineteen, an orphan. And that Christmas day she wrote a letter to her former teacher—a Braille letter I later read. In it Annie crowed to her friend, "With Helen, I have found someone who will love me completely—and can never leave." And I never wanted to leave her, until Peter.

Annie sat up, took the brush from my hand, and said in the eerie way she had of reading my mind: "You were to be with me on the train. Instead you were alone with him—Helen, after everything I said, you've disobeyed?"

Before I could protest she said, "It's done. I've sent for your mother. She's already left Alabama by train; she'll be here in a week. She'll stay with you, every minute of the day, mother hawk that she is, until I'm better."

"You sent for Mother? From Alabama? Without talking to me first?" I turned my head toward the window; a steady shake-shake of the floorboards told me the Boston-bound train thudded through the far woods. Peter was on that train, due to return the next day to Wrentham and the house Annie had rented for him, to be close to me. Every cell of me filled with anticipation, hummed with it until the train rushed over the slight hill behind our house.

"I thought you rented a house so he could be near." I steadied myself by holding her bedpost.

Annie's hand was sweating and silent in mine.

"I changed my mind." She turned to lie back again, exhausted. "Too many things are changing around here, Helen. When your mother gets here everything will go back to normal." Annie struggled to sit up. "When Peter gets here tomorrow I'm telling him I'm back in charge. He has to stay away."

But even as I touched her soft hair, my fingers filled with love for her, I wanted to tell her the truth: Before Mother arrives, I will make my move. Nothing will stay as it is.

Chapter Ten

⊰❦⊱

In the books I've written about my life I never told the whole truth. Once Peter and I came back to my rattletrap farmhouse outside of Boston everything changed for me. I know I wrote about how Peter and I had a "little isle of joy" in our love together, but I don't think—no, I *know*—I never wrote that I did it this way: I betrayed, cut off, lied to, people I loved.

Here's another thing I never wrote in all those books: I would do it again.

It was the second day we were back. The heat was sweltering. King's Pond gave off the scent of wet acorns and oak leaves as Peter pulled me toward the wooden cabin set in a grove of pines by the shore. "Come with me. For a minute." The ground gave way in soft pockets under my shoes as he led me toward the cabin. I stumbled over the rocky path, the damp air of the woods around us. Peter pulled open the cabin door and the musty odor of bathing suits and picnic baskets reminded me of summers on King's Pond.

"We'll tell Annie—and your mother when she gets here. Just not yet," Peter said.

"But when? We can't hide out here all day. The second Annie sees you she'll have you driven to the train."

"More like she'll have me shot." Peter laughed. "I saw her myself at breakfast. If looks could kill, you'd be digging my grave right now."

"And get this dress dirty?" I picked up the hem of my favorite sassy blue dress. "Sorry, but you'd have to call the undertaker your-self."

"Your concern is touching. Still, we have to tell her."

"Tell her what, exactly?" I cocked my head. That morning over a hurried breakfast of oatmeal and blueberries in our kitchen, Peter dabbed at bits of blueberry staining my mouth as I told him Annie wanted to replace him.

"We'll tell Annie that I'm staying put. The rental house is mine, I'm your private secretary, and that's that."

"And that's because . . . ?"

"That's because we're . . ." Peter stopped.

"We what?" I was still a post-Victorian woman. No matter how much the people Annie and I knew preached free love, I still couldn't claim a man as my own.

"We're . . ." Still he waited.

"Comrades? I do have a Bolshevik flag hanging in my bedroom."

"Then you must be armed. May I frisk you?"

"Only if I can frisk you back."

"But we're not comrades, we're not a couple."

"No."

"Not in love."

"Definitely not that."

"We're . . . interested parties."

"What are we, lawyers?" I laughed again.

"Lawyers?" Peter's voice turned rough under my fingers. "They commit about as much high crime as bankers, in my book. We're definitely not lawyers. But we are adults. Two consenting adults."

I bit my lip so I wouldn't say more. I'd gone too far. What was I consenting to? I understood Peter didn't see the complexities of my personal life. He could never really take on the responsibility of caring for me.

"Maybe there are no words for it," I lied, smoothing Peter's hair. "But whatever we tell them, at least we're in this together."

"Right." He pulled me toward the cabin. "Come inside."

"Lead on."

Something was wrong inside that cabin. I can tell people's moods by their hands: a shy hand gives off a tentative feel; a bold, brash person's hand vibrates with fervor. And the liar? The liar's hand shifts and trembles while the liar's words say yes, but the hand says, "Don't listen to me." I trust what people say with their hands. People control their faces, they don't want to show their emotions to the world. But their hands? I'll say this. They give a person away.

I trusted Peter's hands. I trusted them on me.

But I also trusted how they shook, ever so slightly, that day.

He leaned me against the warm wooden wall and said he wasn't afraid: with his hands on me he said we would tell Annie and Mother that we were a couple, that he'd stay on as my private secretary, their wishes be damned. But his hands had the soft, marshy feel of someone wanting to flee.

It was his hands that told me what to do next.

"Can you be quiet?" Peter backed me up against the cabin's wooden wall where every summer I'd hung my bathing suit on the third peg. Far off, I could feel the thrum of a motorboat crossing the pond.

"Can *I* be *quiet?*" I laughed back. I wanted Peter to undo the seedlike buttons of my silk dress. But he reached behind me to grab my bathing suit.

"Why don't you take off this pretty dress, and put this on? It's about time I got that swim you promised me."

"I never break a promise." *My flirtation was working.*

"I can only swim in circles," I said, as we headed out into the warm air and across the sand to the pond. "Mostly I just hold on to the raft."

"So hang on to the raft. It'll save me from having to watch you. I've got to work on my tan."

"To look good for me?"

"If I have to look after you, I might as well look good for you."
The pond waters sent waves of cool air toward us.

"Keep an eye on me," I said.

The waters of King's Pond shivered up my bare legs. Peter's
scent—muskrat, hot rain, and tar—stayed with me when I waded
deeper into the pond water. The sun on my arms was weaker; noon
had passed. My skin adjusted to the shock of cold water. I sensed
Peter's strong strokes behind me and said, "I thought you couldn't
swim."

"You really thought I would sink like a stone? When I'm built
like this?" he made a muscle with one arm and placed my hand there.

"You lied."

"I keep some things to myself." He splashed water on me, and I
laughed.

I squished the pond's swampy silt beneath my feet.

"Let's move," he said. "Race you to the raft."

"It's ten feet out."

"So? Hold tight to my shoulders." He kicked water up furiously.
"I won't let you go."

Peter's wit, scent of water, smoke, and fury took me in. He dissolved
me. We immersed ourselves in the water, and my flickering awareness that he had lied washed away. The realization that he said he
couldn't swim so he wouldn't have to carry me faded in the pleasure
of being surrounded by him. His hands reached for me as the water
swirled. "If you think I get lost on land . . ." I gripped his hands
tightly.

"Don't talk."

I felt him guide me to the raft several feet out from shore. "Come
on." He moved my hands till they gripped the ladder. "Up you go."
I willed myself up onto the warm wooden dock and Peter, sopping
wet beside me, said, "Hear the birds?"

"We have loons around here. They're eerie." I was relieved to have climbed out of the water.

"They're crazy birds." He unbuttoned the top button on my suit.

"Yes, crazy, crazy birds."

Call me desperate, afraid that Annie and Mother would stop me from having him close by. But I not only let him unbutton the top button, I undid the next two myself. I had to be courageous—to take advantage of this moment before Annie came down to the water. I led Peter closer to me. I quickly took off the shoulder straps of my suit before he could guess my next move. That was my way to keep one step ahead of him, to keep him following me.

"Let me help you with that." Peter eases my black, knee-length bathing suit away from my shoulders. He tugs the damp, rubbery straps. The sun turns me warm, breadlike.

I feel the sharp intake of his breath.

"You are a miracle." He traces his fingers across my bare collarbone.

The water ripples under the rolling dock. I feel Peter staring at one thing only. Me.

That moment on the dock Peter did the strangest thing. He put my hands behind my back and held my wrists tight so I couldn't resist. "Kiss me, Helen."

I leaned into him.

I felt him touch my mouth with his fingers. Then he took my hands from behind my back and led my fingers to the warm center of his chest. I felt his heart beat beneath my fingertips.

"Kiss me there." He dipped my head.

And I did.

The skin of his bare chest deliciously cold, his scent of scotch and night risky, outside the law.

"How was that?" I asked.

"A-plus." He raised me up slowly, his hands on my bare shoulders. "I love a girl who takes direction."

"I'm nothing if not compliant," I lied again. I wasn't compliant at all. I had wanted him near me. He had been afraid. But now I knew by the steadiness in his hands that his resistance had slowly faded. His fear was gone.

Suddenly Peter untangled his arms from mine. "Come on, lady, let's swim. Act like nothing's up." He slid me off the dock. "Annie's coming through the woods."

The sand felt suddenly slippery beneath my feet. I struggled to stay steady but Peter grabbed me, guided me to shore. This time his hands told me he was mine.

Chapter Eleven

Blindisms—the rocking, the hair twirling, the things that iden-tify us as blind, I tried to keep those things from Peter. Years ago, Annie trained them out of me. When I was seven years old and had just learned language, I wanted so much to talk that when Annie wasn't around I spelled to myself. All day and night, my fingers moving so I could talk, talk. Annie said it looked strange, and to stop me she tied my hands behind my back to "cure" me, to spare me the humiliation of being different. But she didn't want me to be totally normal. I could look like other women, I just couldn't have the pleasure women had with men.

So the moment Peter guided me to shore, the sand gritty under my feet, I suppressed my shame when Annie marched up to me and said, "Helen, stop twirling your hair!" Her scent was heavy with camphor and cough drops. I stopped the twirling, but I did take Peter's hand. I was about to betray her.

"We've got news," Peter said as we both dripped water, standing before Annie.

"Like hell you do." Annie stepped between us. "I'm the one with news. And it's for Helen's ears only, if you don't mind, Mr. Fagan. Now if you'll excuse us?"

"Anything you say to me you can also say to Peter." To my sur-prise, I blurted this out before thinking.

"Foolish girl. This is critical. Get rid of him, now."

I did not move. For years Annie had claimed emergencies: When

John fled the house after their marriage broke up she kept me up nights, weeping on my shoulder in a way that was heartbreaking, and then stopping only to lean heavily on me and saying, "Well, Helen, at least we have *your* story to tell." Then, in the months after he left she became so hopeless that some nights she ran off and couldn't be found. Early mornings she'd return, the emergency passed. Only later would I learn that she'd spent the night curled up like a child under our rowboat. She would return distant, unmoved.

How could I turn her away?

"Give me a minute," I said to Peter.

"Take your time. I'll be in the house. I'm not going far."

I stood in place as the sand gave off the *whuff, whuff* of Peter's footsteps fading away.

Annie approached me at the shore. "Years of practice, Helen, and you're alone for two minutes and you do this? Pull these straps up—damn you!"

When I struggled into my bathing suit—the suit weighted by water—I felt her cool shadow over me. But when I came out from behind Annie into the warm sunlight she said, "Don't tell me you were working down here at the beach?"

"Working, chatting . . ." I betrayed Annie again.

"This is no time for socializing." She led me over to a wooden bench. "Sit down." Her palm shook. "Listen." The coolness of shade made me lift my head as I sat on the rickety bench.

"What?"

Annie snapped back, "Not now, Helen. Don't act up with me right now. It appears you're too busy with Peter. You've ignored me twice already, so why should you listen now?"

But just before Annie stalked off she said, "Sorry to have interrupted. It's nothing, really. Just urgent news."

My nostrils quivered with the scent—pond water, salt, brine—that told me Annie was gone.

———

I sensed Annie's footsteps over the pine needles. She did not tell me her news. Instead, she walked off as she often did. I tried to follow her—clumsily, rapidly, I tried to make my way into the woods.

Ahead of me her footsteps, *ca-runch, ca-scratch,* on the gravel path, in her finely heeled shoes—because even outside she was well dressed. *Wait, what is it?* I wanted to say, but could not. The chill scent of moss and decay rose from the forest floor but I could not find the path. I stood, lost and unable to catch up with Annie.

But the desire to be with me won out; even from the wood's edge I sensed her return, her resentment rising like steam. As she came closer I sensed her twin desires: to be free of me, and to be even closer, forever.

"Come on." Annie led me to a small clearing where the sun fell directly on my skin. She lay down on the blunted grass and pulled me down, but when I reached across the grass, Annie was too far away to touch.

My breath came shallowly; Annie stiffened further. In desperation I reached out to touch her rough linen dress, and my finger found one ragged hole at the waist.

"What is it? What's wrong?"

But Annie ignored me. Finally she said, "It's Peter. It drives me crazy to have him in the house. He doesn't clean up after himself, he leaves the dirty dishes in the sink, making more work for me."

"Then I'll do the dishes."

"That would make things even worse." Annie stood to go back to the house.

I reached for her hand. "Peter will be watching out for me from the back porch."

"My nemesis," Annie said.

"Your nemesis? You hardly know him."

"How right you are. I haven't spent every minute of the day with him, mooning over him. I haven't disobeyed my teacher, the one who raised me, in order to be with him. You are so right, Helen. I don't know him, and I am sorry to say at this moment I don't even know you. But I do know one thing. I know men."

"You knew John." The minute I said it I knew it was a mistake. Since he'd left we rarely said his name.

"You're right. I knew John. I knew him so well that even though I married him, and he befriended you, he walked out after draining us of as much money as he could get."

"Is that what's wrong? Has John contacted you? Does he want to give the marriage another chance?"

"No," Annie said, tracing her hand in mine. "You forget. He's not a giver. He's a taker. That's all."

"That's not true. He typed my manuscripts all night when I couldn't. He taught me about Socialism, when everyone else thought I had no right to think or write about anything but blindness. He opened up the world to me."

"He opened up our bank account. He drank our profits, took *your* money, Helen, to go to Europe for four months while you and I dragged our sorry selves across the country giving yet more talks. And he left us. He's gone. Staying in a rattletrap room in Boston that he set on fire that last time we visited—too drunk to put out his lighted cigarette. And we're still paying his expenses, my dear girl. Wake up. John was no good. This one"—she gestured toward the house where Peter stood—"won't be any good either. Helen, wake up."

Who was it that woke me up to desire? John Albert Macy, Annie's husband. It started the day of my Radcliffe graduation in 1904 at the Tremont Temple in Boston. The old century creaked behind us. I heard it. I was a woman now. "Stay still," Annie tapped into my palm. She sat dressed in black beside me. All ninety-seven girls waiting for our new lives to begin. I stood on stage inhaling dust, chalk, and theater grease. And just before I walked out to get my diploma I felt the strange, haunting echo of new things to come.

John Albert Macy sat in the front row, watching. He had married Annie the year before, and become part of our lives. Lived with us in our seventeen-room farmhouse. Built me a stone wall so I could walk freely in the woods. Strung a wire across the trees so I could daily walk free—free! As far as I'd ever gone on my own.

Nights he stayed in his study writing his new book. I stayed up late, too, typing fresh pages of my autobiography, then tearing pages out of the typewriter to show him. When we were finished for the night, exhausted, I would go upstairs, put on my nightgown, and get into bed. Under the covers I felt his tread move past my room, a man-tread, heavy, thick, so it ran up the floorboards to my bed where I lay awake. The floorboards suddenly still between our two bedrooms.

I pictured him taking off his shirt, his arms smooth as blended butter. He'd reach for Annie. Under the sheets I stretched my hands over my breasts, my thighs, the darkness suddenly brilliant around my body.

Did I love him? I loved his sexual awakening of me. He was Annie's husband, he never touched me in any inappropriate way, but in the morning he smelled of fir trees, brine, and green apples after making love with Annie at night.

"Helen." Annie shook my shoulder once more as we came out of the woods. "Let's get a move on. We've got to get dinner, then there's laundry, and letters to do, too." The stack of chores was so high that in my imagination it reached the roof of my house.

"All right," I said. "But just tell me. Is Peter still there, in the doorway?"

"Helen." For once Annie felt kind, tender, almost. "Sweetheart. Let's face it. The last time I looked that old saying still stood."

If I had been able to hear, I would have covered my ears. As it was, I tried to withdraw my hand, but Annie grabbed it right back.

"John's the one who found Peter. And you know that old saying, 'The apple doesn't fall far from the tree.'"

For one of the few times in our years together, I formed a fist so that she couldn't tell me more.

"Helen." She opened my hand. "Don't make this harder on me than it already is. I didn't come down here to fight about Peter. I came to tell you my own news."

Then she began to cough so roughly it seemed to break open the air. Her muscles contracted under my hand as I rubbed her back, trying to make the cough stop. She bent over, almost double, and when she finally stood up I said, "It's not just a cough."

"Worst case, tuberculosis. You know. The White Death."

The White Death. Annie had lost a lot of weight, and in my fever over Peter I hadn't noticed. I knew only that tubercular patients were kept, often, in isolation from their families to avoid the spread of infection, their eyes burning, their faces flushed, then pallid, so pallid, as they wasted away. Their bodies empty caves where the skin faded to the whitest of white, as if they were angels, rather than the pale face of death.

Her hand in mine was a hollowed-out shell. I traced her face with my fingers until she shook me off.

"It could be just a bad cough. But we have to prepare for the worst. Now zip your lip. Not a word of this to Peter—or anyone else."

"Yes, ma'am." As Annie and I stood next to the house, her hand in mine, it must have been hard to tell which one of us was blind. Annie was so afraid that her sleeve caught the wire John had strung up for me: she stumbled and I caught her, led her through the twilight as if my care alone would bring her home.

We walked up to the porch. Peter took Annie's arm and helped us up the steps, took Annie to her room, then came back to me.

"Don't take this wrong," Peter said. "But who's handicapped? You? Or her?"

Both, I thought. Much more than you know.

Chapter Twelve

֍

Tuberculosis, the White Death, I thought as I made my way from my second floor bedroom to Annie's at the far end of the hall the next day. The morning sun fell on me. A series of rounded thumps told me the wash was banging against the house from the clothesline where I'd hung it that morning, my fingers fumbling in the basket Annie had set out full of damp dresses, thick wooden clothespins, and instructions to be a little more careful than usual: we wouldn't want Peter seeing our underthings. Those were to drip dry inside the bathroom off the kitchen, away from his prying eyes. But I was not thinking about daily chores. As I pushed open the door to Annie's room I was thinking about tuberculosis.

Trucks rumbled past outside as I walked to her room. Inside, the scent of sulfur, quinine, and bitters led me to Annie's bed. *H-e-l-e-n*, Annie nervously spelled into my palm as I stood by her bed. A metallic scent rose from her sweating skin; a migraine pierced her temples.

Outside, wind drove past the pine trees to the road, flowed down East Main Street, and rattled into town.

"You're going to be all right, aren't you?"

"Do I look all right?" Annie's voice under my fingers was dry sand.

Her cough filled the room with its vibrations. Suddenly a rush of cool air. Annie spelled into my hand, "It's Dr. Webb. It's about time he showed up; I called him hours ago." Dr. Webb strode into the room and leaned over Annie's bed. I put my fingers, gingerly, to his mouth and throat and read his words: his voice felt reedy when, after a few moments, he told Annie, "You'll go to St. Joseph's today for a test."

I felt the *ca-rip* of paper as he handed his orders to Annie.

Is Annie going to die? I thought.

"This is very dangerous," Dr. Webb said. "You may not under any circumstances expose others. And if you have it, you'll go to a sanatorium—"

"No. I know about these 'rest cures.' If you're lucky you come back in a year."

"If you're lucky you come back. Today. Get the test. It takes weeks to process, so don't delay."

"All right, just to show you that you're wrong."

Even in sickness Annie was defiant. I loved her for that.

After Dr. Webb left, Annie and I sat together. Time slid by. Finally she said, "This is perfect. I'm sick, my eyesight is going, and now I have to drive to Boston for a TB test. The luck of the Irish, all right."

I followed her as she opened her closet door and started to dress.

"I'll come with you."

"Helen, no." She patted her hair, and picked up her purse. When I leaned in to kiss her good-bye the onion scent of her breath made me draw back in fear.

"Who will take care of me while you're gone?"

Annie ignored me. She picked up the phone on her bureau and began to dial. I felt the *chut-chut-chut* of the metal disk turning beneath her fingers. "If tuberculosis doesn't kill me this will."

"What will?"

"Isn't it obvious? I'm calling Peter. I can't leave you here alone, but having him here is no picnic either."

Annie taught me the words for colors I could not see. Pink, Annie said when I was a seven-year-old on a rampage for new words, is like "a soft Southern breeze." Yellow is "like the sun. It means life is rich in promise." But I can find no color to describe the day I realized Annie might be sent away from me. Her hand in mine as she prepared to leave the room didn't feel pink or white or even green, as she'd once told me green was "warm and friendly as a new leaf." No. Her hands gave off the white of death. A husky, graspable thing.

"Don't go," I had said. "Stay."

I felt like a cut-down forest tree, rootless.

Annie was slipping away. I began to feel panic. I write this to explain the contradiction in my thoughts. I wanted to stay by Annie and I wanted to bind Peter to me more closely. Maybe because I was desperate. Yes, I was desperate for Peter.

"Cheer up," Annie had said. "The worst is yet to come." Then she kissed me on both cheeks. The thrum of a cab's engine moved through me. Annie closed the front door, then Peter opened it.

He came in.

Chapter Thirteen

At times when I trace the pieces of my patchwork quilt I feel their lightness rather than the weight, as if something new is about to reveal itself. The moment Peter stepped over the threshold I knew things would change in ways I could not have predicted.

"Tell me you don't need me around here." Peter draped his tobacco-scented leather bag over a broken wicker chair in my study, pulled out my desk chair with a scrape, and sat down. The farmhouse filled with cool fall air.

"She looks like she saw a ghost." Peter laughed about seeing Annie rush down the steps to the car and race off.

"Maybe she has." The possibility that Annie had TB filled me with panic. "The doctor was just here. She's very sick. She's gone to Boston today for a test . . ."

"Hallelujah," he said. "Not about Annie being sick, but about having a full day alone with you. Looks like we've been given a reprieve."

"A reprieve? Annie may have TB." I steadied myself.

"TB? Big article about it in today's *Globe*. Apparently it runs in families," Peter spelled into my palm. "Ralph Waldo Emerson had it, his wife died of it. Henry David Thoreau died of it at forty-four. Did you know it's an epidemic in twenty-two states?"

"Peter, if Annie has it, she'll . . ."

"What? Leave you? Helen, you and Annie exaggerate. Make

things worse, or bigger, than they really are." His hand in mine felt heavy, and we sat without saying a word.

Had I exaggerated? Suddenly a strange thought seemed to float in the air. Was I exaggerating who Peter was? His shirt cuffs were frayed in my fingers. He was a bohemian. Did he want a steady job? How long would he be my private secretary? He traveled from place to place not really landing anywhere. I got the sense that he loved ideas more than people. Was he attracted to the idea of me? I had the strange sensation the answer was yes. But I pushed the thought away. If Annie was sick, I'd need Peter to take care of me.

"You two get carried away by things," Peter repeated. "Annie's gone to get a test, she'll be back tonight. I guarantee she'll be bossing you around again by tomorrow morning. And when the results show up in the mail in what, two weeks? I can't tell you what's going to happen. But I can tell you what should happen."

"What?" I breathed clean air.

"You should let me take care of you. Well, as much as any mere human can." He lightly pinched my waist.

"You're right. Maybe it's nothing."

"I didn't say it's nothing. TB is serious—I'm not denying that. But you and Annie do jump to conclusions. Then you work yourselves into a frenzy based on what? Speculation, not facts."

"Are you chastising me?"

"I'm saying you need a good journalist. We follow facts, keep things straight."

Suddenly I felt very tired.

"I'll take care of you."

"Are you proposing?" I said.

"I'm proposing that I'll take care of you."

"Then I accept."

———

To Peter I always said what he needed to hear. I didn't tell him that fear sliced me like a knife, thinking he'd leave, and with Annie sick I'd have no one near. To myself I told the truth. I didn't set out to attract his desire. But once it was within my reach I knew I would not let go.

Peter pulled out my desk chair and led me to it. "Have a seat, lady. Let's get to work. Isn't that why you pay me the big bucks?"

"You're a tyrant." I sat at my oak desk, my fingers tracing the familiar white mantel just above it.

"Yes, but I'm your tyrant," Peter laughed. "And don't you forget it."

"How could I, with you reminding me every minute of the day?"

"Quiet, missy." He put a silver tray with a stack of letters beside me. *Ca-riiiip.* He opened the first envelope, and a limpid scent of onion, musty tenement rooms rose from the page.

"London, England," Peter read: "September 1916."

Dear Miss Helen Keller,
I don't know where to turn, except to you. They say you're a saint, pretty as a statue, and kind.

I blame myself for it. My boy was four. I was afraid. The German blockade of England. No food, we had no food. I held my boy in my arms in the bathroom, dousing his face with water, the acrid smell of garbage filling the alley outside our building. No heat. The air so cold—we couldn't get warm all winter. But that night he was on fire with it, the fever. It's my fault. I didn't call the doctor. By morning it was too late. No money, just my cracked hands, this war, and my boy's cries. My husband bleak. By morning the fever was gone. But he was blind. I still rocked him. Rubbed the white film from his bright blue eyes. He let out a cry—no, a howl like a lost dog—when he tried to stand up and couldn't see the floor.

Mrs. John Murray

I felt a slight movement of air as Peter dropped the letter. Then he said: "Germany fights England, blockades it for months, keeps out even medicines, and this boy goes blind. For what?"

His anger rose.

"I know I'm missing something. But remind me, Helen. What is this war for?"

We sat together not speaking.

Finally I said, "We'll send the mother a check. Annie and I send money to people like this every day."

"For what? To help this one woman, yes. But that won't stop the problem."

"Then we'll send money to the British League for Blind Children." I handed Peter the letter; a slight shudder told me he opened the file drawer to drop the letter in.

"Damn these selfish capitalists. They just want to wage war. Don't you get it, Helen? Don't you see how one donation won't really help this boy?"

It took Peter a minute to realize I wasn't going to say anything.

I kept silent about the hundreds of checks Annie and I sent out every month, every year, to people who pulled us aside on trains, in the streets, in hotel lobbies after our talks, saying they needed money for someone they loved who'd lost their sight, the truth was we sent money all over the place. Even when we didn't have enough for ourselves.

"Poor kid," he said finally. "What he's going to suffer."

"Poor mother," I said right back.

Mother, mother. The image of my own mother—even then on a train heading north—came to mind. But I tried to banish it. I can't think about her because when I do it is like thinking of a long night. A cool night, at times. At times light with a breeze. But underneath, thunder clouds and the threat, always, of a storm.

I can't remember losing my eyesight, or my hearing. That was my good fortune—to forget those days and nights of fever, of pain. But Mother? She remembered it all. It was seared into her, made one with her flesh: the minute she passed her hand over my eyes and I did not blink she said to herself, "It is finished." A kind of dusk fell around her, too. Sometimes, with the birth of her two other children—my sister, Mildred; my brother, Phillips Brooks— or on her travels with Annie and me across the country, that dusk would lift. But most of her life was lived in a shadow of grief that she couldn't save me. The intolerable, blurred image of what I could have been.

"Hold your horses." Peter's hand in mine brought me back. "This just may be the ticket." Peter placed another letter in my hands.

"What is this?"

"A way to help. You're invited to address an antiwar rally in downtown Boston. A few weeks from today. They say they want the world-renowned Helen Keller to inspire the crowds, help keep the U.S. out of this damned war."

"I'll do it."

"Not so fast. If you're so world renowned, why do they want you to speak for free?"

"I'm sure it's not for free. They must be offering an honorarium?"

I felt a slight vibration as Peter shook the letter and read on: "Twenty dollars! That's not even horse feed."

"They don't need to pay me. They need to raise money to stop the war."

"At last count, Helen, you have six outbuildings that need roofing, a lawn that's going to seed, and Annie's treatment, if she needs it, won't be free. Now where will you get the money for that?"

"I . . ."

"By the way," Peter went on. "Your mother gets here tomorrow. Who paid for her train ticket?"

"Annie and I . . ."

"And when she gets here, who pays for her food?" Peter fingered the silky dress I wore. "If she's anything like you and Annie Sullivan—two women who appear to have a severe allergy to anything on sale—who will pay for her trips to Newbury Street for the perfect new shawl?"

"She's my mother. She needs me."

"That sounds strangely familiar." He traced my jaw so softly. "Tell me, Helen, who doesn't?"

"I'm sorry." His criticism of me seemed like a small betrayal. Did he think I forgot that I needed money coming in? The cost of Annie's test and treatment suddenly flooded through me.

"Seems like you're always apologizing." He traced my upper lip with his fingers. "But then you go ahead and do whatever you want, anyway."

I can't remember a time when Mother didn't need my help. She needed me to ease her guilt, her sorrow. When I was almost twelve years old, Annie and I traveled to Tuscumbia in June to find my father very low on money—almost bankrupt. Everything he owned was mortgaged. My baby brother, Phillips, had whooping cough, and my half-brother, James, had what seemed to be typhoid fever. Exhausted, Mother cared for them. She had no nurse, no cook. Annie loaned my father thirty-five dollars of her own, and thirty-five of mine, too, so heavily was he in debt.

My father threatened to have me become part of a freak show, to be an exhibit: people would flock to see the blind, deaf, mute girl talk with her hands.

"They'll pay me five hundred dollars a week," he yelled. The air in our Tuscumbia house so thick it felt like wool around me, so heavy I could not remove it from my eyes, my mouth. My great-great-grandfather had a claim to thousands of acres of Alabama land, Robert E. Lee was a second cousin to my grandmother; my father was a Confederate Army captain—but after the Civil War his title was about all he had left. Finally, Mother snapped at my father, "You'll never use her to support us." But the message was clear: She would fight for me, yes. But the need to make my own life was up to me.

So I told Peter I had to go to Boston Common, I had to be on the podium, in front of the crowd, but I didn't tell him why. That since an early age I've needed a crowd to let me know I have a reason for being. The warmth of their applause slowing, for a moment, the sorrow I, too, carry inside me.

So I turned to him and said, "I have to go. And I'll need you with me."

He hesitated.

"Look. I'll split the twenty-dollar honorarium."

"You're too generous," Peter said.

"It will pay for our train ride—round-trip."

"And two martinis," he laughed. "Okay. Boston Common, here we come." Peter pushed the pile of letters away. "Now, missy, Annie will be back in a few hours and your mother gets here tomorrow, so let's attend to some more important business right now."

We had the whole morning together. And I got hungry. A wild growling in my stomach. Together we walked the hall to the kitchen and had toast slathered with jelly, huge glasses of milk, and a bowl of porridge that I made myself.

Then by the kitchen table, the whole kitchen filled with the scent of ripe peaches, he pulled me close to him until I was breathless, and he said, "Can I see the ripe, bawdy Helen?" With one hand he reached behind me to close the kitchen curtains, then slid a date into my mouth; I bit it, then slid it between his teeth.

His mouth tasted like the earth's deep dark.

Then he lifted up my blouse.

"I'll put up with your mother. I'll help you take care of Annie. I'll even go to the rally with you and take my fee in cold hard cash because it's my job. But pleasure?" He put his fingers on my blouse, and unbuttoned the top button.

"That's free."

Chapter Fourteen

I've written twelve books about my blindness, and in them I said I was an optimist, fully alive since the day in college when I'd read Descartes's "I think, therefore, I am," and decided I could use my intellect to overcome any obstacles in my way. I wanted for nothing. I was as capable as any sighted or hearing person. Yet I never said how much I yearned for that which came so easily to others: the ability to love a man, to have a child. Those things would never come freely to me. So a fury raged in me. I became a burnt fuse inside, nothing but ash. I had to learn to act as though parts of myself simply did not exist.

But Peter made those cravings burn again.

So as heat rose inside the kitchen and the windows let in the bitter scent of dried grass, I let Peter reach for me. In the scorching heat of the day he touched me. It was heart-stopping. Peter's hands held firmly to my waist, and as if we had all the time in the world, I leaned into him again, while the kitchen's air grew warmer around us. Outside in the early afternoon the mail truck rounded the bend in the road, and was gone, leaving us alone, with no one around for miles.

Peter eased my blouse from my shoulders.

"You need some tutoring." He led me across the rough kitchen floor to the divan in the front hall.

"And you're my teacher, I suppose?" I slid back onto the divan. "May I take your advanced class?"

"You're in. And thank God Annie's gone till at least five."

"I won't thank God she's sick," I said. "But the way your hands feel on me are a blessing indeed."

"Don't get all serious on me." He guided my hands under his shirt.

I inhaled sharply as he lowered himself to my ribs.

"Your body is like a temple." He traced my skin with his mouth.

Suddenly he pulled away. "Damn, she has good timing."

"Who?"

"Your real teacher."

"What do you mean?"

"She's here."

"Are you sure?" I buttoned my blouse, fingers flying. The air grew heavy in the front hallway. Only then, with Peter's body away from mine, did I sense Annie's car shuddering into the driveway beyond the maple trees. It seems strange to me even now how calm I felt, as if nothing could go wrong.

"Come on. Her car's in the driveway. Now up you go, missy."

I felt a rat-a-tat-tat vibration as Peter opened the shutters over the hall window and then shut them again. "Damn. It's Annie, all right." We both willed ourselves to sit apart, to straighten our clothes. There was a pause and then Peter said, "When's the last time she repaired that car? It's dinged up on the fender." Then he stopped. "Oh, that would be—"

"John's parting gift. He went on a bender one night before he left and came home so late he didn't see—or couldn't see—the front porch. Banged the car up good, and left Annie to repair it."

"Well, she never did. That car looks like it belongs in a used car lot."

"Annie says she'll never fix it. That it's a good reminder to stay away from men."

Peter laughed. "Well, that's a warning you're clearly not going to heed."

"You said it."

———

Annie and I never spoke of the most pressing reason she stayed away from men. But the truth is Annie damaged the car. I can never forget that night last summer, ten years into Annie's marriage to John, when she finally realized that she and John would never have a child. Annie was too old, or too sick. Who knows? But she couldn't conceive, wouldn't. Year by year her face a blank, disappearing thing.

So John started an affair. He took a lover. The radiant, stimulating Myla, a deaf-mute sculptress, mouth like a lotus, Annie told me. It was the night Annie drove into Boston and, finding John and Myla together in bed, then drove home to Wrentham so blind with rage that she took the turn around the drive too fast, and I found her in the wrecked car. All night she spelled her sorrows into my hand.

"Never trust a man," she said over and over.

The air smelled of mint, fading rose impatiens, and the damp soil Annie kept in pots on our front porch. I felt her step out of the car, her footsteps harsh on the asphalt. But even then, Peter didn't rush. Instead, he lit a cigarette. He inhaled slowly, breezily, and then, as if reading my mind, he said, "I know about the affair, Helen. John parades this woman Myla around the newsroom six days a week." He paused, his hands queerly tense. I felt the *ting-ting-ting* of the cigarette being tapped into the ashtray by the divan. "I want you to know that—"

"That what?"

"That I know Myla's pregnant. With John's child."

"That's none of your business."

"You are my business, Helen. And what concerns you concerns me. Do you think I don't know that you and Annie still send John money, even when you know another woman is having his child?"

"He's still Annie's husband." I suddenly couldn't wait for her to walk up the steps, to be by my side.

"Helen, I want you to know that if you ever—"

"Ever?" His hand touched my belly.

"If you?" he said.

He pulled his hand away. So I said the words he was afraid to say.

"Are you asking me what I'd do if I got pregnant? Why, Mr. Fagan, we haven't even—how do you say it?—fully consummated our affair." I laughed, smiling so broadly I felt the room around me widen, grow softer.

"Helen, do you *want* to have a child? In your life, I mean?"

"Do you?" I said right back.

The room smelled of forest trees, damp rain.

I wish I had let him answer. But I felt an odd, watery feeling in my veins. As if whatever he was about to say would be too much to bear. So I rushed ahead. Covered his fear with my words. I couldn't help it. I was in love. "I already have a child. Aren't you ten years younger than me?" We laughed at the same time, and the watery feeling disappeared.

I knew what I wanted then: I wanted to marry him, to have a child. There were so many obstacles to overcome: Annie, my mother, and, if I had listened, Peter himself. The truth is he tried to tell me. I just wouldn't hear.

"It looks like our day just got even better. Annie's getting out of the driver's side. But she must have . . . Helen, is your mother by any chance a tall, slightly stooped woman with enough luggage for a year?"

"My mother?"

"Yup. That must be her. She's got broad shoulders, like you. And by the set of her jaw she's got that Keller fighting spirit. Now I'm really doomed."

"She's not due here till tomorrow." I laughed. "Stop joking with me."

"Joke's on you, blondie."

Sunlight from the open window fell on my arms, my face. I moved even farther away from Peter. "Do you think she saw us?"

Peter still exuded warmth, cloves. "If I'm not mistaken, Mrs. Kate Keller is straightening up, stretching after a three-day train ride. But if she finds me in the house with you, that's a disaster."

He quickly led me down the cool hallway to my study and straight to my desk. He guided my hand to the Bolshevik flag on the wall. "Shall we take this down? Before she comes in?" he said with a laugh.

"She doesn't exactly share my Socialist views."

"You mean she's not a firebrand? Not a hothead, like you?"

"She's a southerner, born and bred. When I donated money to the NAACP she hardly left the house: it scandalized her southern neighbors so much I had to apologize in print." But never once, in all my years, had she let me be close to a man.

Through my feet I felt Annie and Mother move onto the front porch. "Any minute they'll call me." I stood up, ready to go downstairs. But first I had to tell Peter the truth. Not the large truth—that I sensed that day his fear of having children—but a smaller one.

"I guess I mixed up the days," I said. "I thought Mother was getting here tomorrow. I guess you now know the truth."

"What have I missed?"

"That I'm deaf, blind, and—"

"Helen. Don't say you're dumb. You're the smartest woman I've ever met. You're the woman I'd marry, if I could."

People fool themselves all the time. I fooled myself then, as his footsteps moved across the wooden floor. Foolish, foolish me. So thrilled, dizzied, really, that he said he wanted to marry me that I ignored the last three words: *if I could.*

I didn't ask.

He didn't say.

Chapter Fifteen

⧦

One thing I never told anyone was that I had learned to put other people's lives before my own as a survival skill. One thing I never knew about myself was how quickly I would turn against Annie and my mother once Peter offered me a way out, a life of my own.

I was haunted by my own status. That was my problem. I learned language at the age of seven but that wasn't enough to help others when they were in despair. So I took enormous care, starting when I was still only nine, never to stay still, rarely to save things just for myself. When I went to the Perkins School for the Blind as a child I had a double handicap, but I bought presents for all the little blind girls. I made myself indispensable, because without sight or hearing I needed a way to bind others to me. But there was a price.

So by the age of thirty-seven I was giving my royalties to blinded German soldiers, as well as supporting John. I was writing letters to newspapers against the war. Yet I wanted to escape from the existence I'd created, to merge myself with Peter. I turned my back on Annie and my mother. How eagerly, how recklessly, I let go of my obligations to them, and to myself.

So as Annie fumbled to open the front door downstairs, I resisted the impulse to run to her. I stayed by Peter, instead.

"May as well look as if we're working. That will impress your mother and Annie." Peter tore open a letter from a Mr. Lyon in France.

"You know the way to their hearts."

"I know the way to yours." He fingered the buttons on my blouse. I laughed and pushed him away.

"Listen," he said, reading. "*Le Monde* has published an article lambasting your gift of royalties to blinded German soldiers. A Mr. Lyon protests that you took pity on them. He writes, 'Don't the blinded French deserve Miss Keller's help more?'"

"If any of my books were published in France, I would immediately give the royalties to the French blinded," I dictated to Peter, and he tapped out my response on my Remington typewriter.

The steady thrum of the typewriter was punctuated by a rounded thump. Annie had dropped her bag on the hall floor just inside the front door to rustle through the mail. A second thump told me Mother had dropped her luggage by the door, too, and in the rush of incoming air I smelled the brisk, almost acrid scent of a storm.

"I've got to go down." I turned to leave the room.

"Stay here." Peter, cigarette in hand, leaned closer to the window. His voice under my fingers was joking, but it was also tight, as if he expected me to prove my loyalty to him.

"I haven't seen my mother in two years."

"But once she and the feisty Miss Sullivan come inside you won't see much of me, I'm sure."

I felt weary, and could not answer.

I have always been forced to choose sides. First, when I was seven and groped from place to place, without an *I am*, Annie forced my mother to let Annie and me live alone together in the small house next door. We drove for blocks in my father's wagon, then returned to the house next door so I would not know my mother was near. All night I cried, stormed. I wanted to go home. But Annie demanded allegiance. And in two days I was hers.

At age sixteen at the Cambridge School for Young Ladies I was forced to choose between my mother and Annie. I chose Annie.

And I blossomed. I believed Mother would always be there when I needed her, and I also knew that I had to move forward, had to make my own way. But in my dreams at night the image of my mother grew smaller and smaller as I grew larger, riper in the world.

So I waited for Peter. I waited for him to let me go to my mother, to Annie downstairs. I waited for him to let me go so I wouldn't have to choose again, take sides, leave someone desperate, helpless, alone.

As if sensing my weariness Peter said, "Helen? Why not just come in here?"

He led me behind the screen in the corner of my study and patted an old chair. "Sit, rest. They'll think we went out for a walk."

"And we'll get a little more time alone."

"You're a mind reader. Let those two hens settle down."

"They're not hens," I said.

"Well they're going to peck at you for being alone with me."

"I'll peck on you." I stood close to him behind the screen.

"Promises, promises." He opened my blouse. "When we're done here you can saunter downstairs all fresh and perky, and I'll come down later. Like we've been apart all day."

"You're a master planner."

"I could be a spy."

"Maybe you are."

"Maybe I am."

It was a perfect escape, if only for a while. We stood glued together behind the Chinese screen propped in the corner of my study. I couldn't have been happier. I felt the tread of Annie's footsteps on the stairs. Peter and I stood stock still. Finally the door opened, I smelled the scent of Annie's hair, then the door closed and her footsteps faded away. Within moments I inhaled the scent of car exhaust and asked Peter, "Is Annie leaving?" He spelled back that

Annie was furious: she had yelled that there were no groceries, she was going shopping, and Mother was going to nap in her room. I noticed that Peter tried to seem easygoing, relaxed, but there was something tentative in his hands. I wanted to keep him by my side, so I did the only thing I knew how to do when situations got tense.

I took a deep breath and said, "I'm itching to get out of this house. We've been here for days since our Chautauqua trip. I like to keep moving. How soon till that speech in Boston?"

"It's in . . ." He slid his fingers over my back, then down to the desk to grab the letter. "Five days."

"Wait a minute," I said. "That's when Annie's test results come in."

"She'll be fine. And then we'll have three things to celebrate."

"Three?"

"Annie's health, your rousing speech, and . . ."

"And?"

"And the fact that you've agreed to marry me."

"Marry you? You haven't asked me properly."

"I've seen you with your top off, missy. Don't talk to me about proper."

I smiled, waiting for him to go on.

"Am I to get down on one knee? To beg?"

"Yes."

"Yes, what?"

"I want you to beg."

"Beast. You want me to prostrate myself before you?"

"Absolutely."

"Your wish is my command." He lowered himself to the floor and said, "Thank God I have this."

"A ring?"

"Better. One exquisitely sharp fingernail." He scratched the back of my bare calf and then pressed hard on the inside of my bare thigh.

"Do you say yes?"

I couldn't answer.

"Helen, let's marry. Let's run away."

I couldn't move.

"I'm begging," he said, his breath warm on my thigh, his hand inside my skirt.

I called his name. My voice, which I hardly ever used in front of him, was ragged, but I couldn't help myself. *Yes.*

As I pulled him toward me his curly hair, rough in my hands, smelled of teak, a kind of far-off tree. My senses told me that even as he proposed, fear pitched through him. He knew I was not like other women. Every day, in recurring, relentless ways, he would have to care for me. Strangely, I was not afraid. We would marry, run away. So when I felt him pull away from me I reached for him.

His skin was slightly slippery. He pulled hard at my hands and said, "You'll marry me?"

"Yes."

"You'll let me deal with your mother and Annie?"

"Yes."

Why didn't I realize that Peter acted strong but was really frightened? It wasn't clear to me then, when I put aside my loyalty to Annie, to my mother, even to myself, that Peter was what Annie called a paper fighter. A person who fought in print, through words, but when real people were involved, he would dissolve. I couldn't see it at that moment. I didn't want to see it.

There are so many ways to be blind.

We celebrated our engagement that afternoon. "Shhhh," Peter said as he led me down the back stairs, past my mother, who napped in the first-floor bedroom, her rose perfume filling the air. "Let's go outside." With a shudder of the back door we were free: out and running across the bumpy grass to the edge of the yard.

"What do you want to do?" he said.

"How about you teach me to drive?" I laughed. "If I'm to be your wife, I'll need to be at least your equal, maybe more."

"For now let's try a bike." Peter laughed. "Let's ride the tandem bike." Peter yanked my hair loose from its pins. "Come *on*." We dragged the heavy bicycle out of the garden shed, pulled on gloves, and off we flew over the bumpy New England roads, my hair flying as we pedaled up hills and down dales.

What seemed like an hour later we reached a field, where he dropped the bicycle on the grass with a chunky *thonk* that I felt in my legs. We were sweating.

"I'm no athlete," he said. "That's probably the last time we do that."

"I'll drive next time," I laughed. "Put me up front. I can steer like a madwoman."

"I'll bet you're a menace behind the wheel." He trapped my wrists above my head so I couldn't move.

Then he put some wildflowers in my hands.

"Your favorites, missy."

The buttercups' rounded flower heads were dense with something that burst straight from the earth's center.

Then he opened my mouth and slid in a yellow bit of flower.

"Are you hungry?" he said.

I remembered how, when I was young, I pounded the table, craving meats, sweets, anything to put in my speechless mouth. I had the same feeling with Peter. Some new hunger flooded me.

"Starving," I said.

Chapter Sixteen

By a slight quiver in my nostrils I could sense a storm's approach. A flood of earth odors washes through me when a storm closes in. So I was not surprised when rain started to fall later that afternoon as Peter and I paused on the back lawn, crickets shirring open the hot air. Peter lit a cigarette and blew the smoke into the air. "Time to face the music." He nodded toward the house.

"You know I can't hear music." I laughed.

"Excuse me for forgetting your handicap. But you're lucky you can't hear Annie stomping around inside."

We both paused on the back steps.

"Do you think I can't tell how angry she is?" The staccato of Annie's footsteps crisscrossing the kitchen sent splinters through the floorboards of the porch.

"You want to face her alone? I'll come with you." Peter came up the steps.

"No. She'd tear you apart. I'd better go first."

"Helen," he said. "You act so strong. It's not a sign of weakness to ask for my help. I'm here when you need me."

The smoke from his cigarette smelled bitter.

It's strange to me now, how as I walked through the downpour of warm rain and into the house my acute senses felt nothing to fear at all. The truth is that when I moved into the house to meet Mother and Annie I felt stronger, more alive, than either of them had ever been. The sweet scent of corn, the bitter tang of radishes, the warm scent of bread told me Annie was back with the groceries. She thumped and banged cabinet doors open in the kitchen as she unpacked the bags, and when I felt my way into the room Annie was so annoyed at seeing me that she slammed the French doors.

She herded me into the stuffy kitchen, where she drew the curtains against the rain. "Don't make me ask, Helen. Just spit it out. Where have you been?"

"I'll help with the groceries." I tried to pry a bulky bag from her arms.

"Stop." She dropped the bag to the counter. "Stop trying to distract me. Just tell me the truth."

"The truth is I'm worried about you. How was your test?"

"It was nothing. A poke in the arm and I was done. A whole day wasted."

"Today wasn't wasted . . ."

"You're right, Helen. Today wasn't wasted. I left the house at six a.m. with my chest feeling like it was on fire, and I came home five hours later with my ears about to burst: your mother talked nonstop from the time I picked her up at South Station until the minute we came up the driveway, and where were you? Were you here to listen to her torrent of words about Mildred, and the new baby Katherine—"

"Is Mother okay?"

"And Mildred's most excellent mincemeat pies, how Mildred is the best housekeeper in Montgomery, and the Junior League just can't *function* without her. I swear, Helen, you *know* I love her, but then we come in here, practically kicking our way through the books and parcels scattered in the front hall, there's no food for dinner, I have to turn around and go back out to grocery shop and you—the reason she came here—you are nowhere to be found."

Too delirious to answer, I just laughed.

"It's not funny." Annie whacked me with a rolled-up newspaper. "You couldn't have cleaned up?"

"I should have, you're right." I smiled—it was so absurd.

"So? Where were you?"

"Oh, out walking." I smoothed my dress, one button still open.

"It's pouring, Helen." I felt Annie step away from me, examining me from head to foot. She patted my dress.

"You're soaking wet." She came closer and sniffed my collar, my neck, my hair. "And you reek of cigarette smoke."

I was determined to keep my secret about Peter to myself. I couldn't give Annie the chance to stop me, to end this happiness.

A great silence fell over the room.

"Peter loves his vices, doesn't he? Have you become the newest of them?"

I wanted to say, "I am engaged. I am to be married—Peter and I, we're going to run away." But again I lied.

"I was in the barn."

"In the barn?"

"Ian, the boy who cuts the lawn, he was smoking out there."

"And you? What were you doing? Reading those trashy romance novels you hide in that rusted metal bin?"

"Guilty." I smiled. "What's my punishment?"

Annie laughed and poked me on the arm. Then she unpacked the rest of the groceries while I followed her around the kitchen as if nothing at all had happened.

The blanketed air in the room told me Annie was still angry, so I pulled her toward the kitchen table and spelled, "You're tired. Please, sit down. Read, have some tea, *relax*." I gave her the newspaper. To my relief she took it and settled into a chair beside me.

"Oh, this is classic," Annie said moments later. "Another big shot idealizing the blind."

"What?" A car rushed by outside. I felt it through the floor as I held her hand.

"Here, in the paper." She shook out the newspaper, its wet scent rising to me. "They're quoting this Indian swami. A temple in his name is being built in Boston. According to this article, a blind person asked the swami if there's anything worse than losing one's eyesight. The swami replied: 'Yes, losing your vision!'"

"Who said that?"

"Swami Vivekananda. Born in India in 1863, died in 1902, believed we are all one. Traveled the world saying so. He's one of your type: he's met with everyone—Harvard professors, the common man, heads of universities from here to Kingdom Come."

"Well, he's right. Peter has a vision," I spelled to Annie. "He thinks everyone—even people left out of the system—should take their place in the world."

"Peter sees what he wants to see." Annie's hand turned harder in mine. "Helen, have you even noticed that we're using only half the kitchen table this morning? Do you have any idea why? It's because your Mr. Vision, as you call him, is too busy idling about to help keep this house going—and don't tell me he's too good for that work. We *all* pitch in here. Here, feel this." She laid my hand on a stack of books that were spread out over the table's entire right side. "Recognize these?"

"My Braille books," I said.

"Right. I asked Peter to take them down and clear out the bookcase. It's dusty, and we always clean it this time of year. So what did he do? He pulled down all your books—and you know together they weigh tons—and left them piled here for two days. He's too busy dreaming up schemes to improve conditions for the women of the Lawrence Mills than to help the ones right here in this home."

"You could have asked me."

"When you do housework it's like a tornado has gone through the room. And Peter doesn't have a practical bone in his body,"

Annie spelled, her fingers staccato in mine. "You need someone to buy sugar and milk every week, to set up your next speaking engagements, to get you there and back, and to make sure there's food to eat when you get home again. Not to mention holding reporters at bay, and tracking the finances to keep this whole ship steady."

At that moment, I was so elated about Peter wanting to marry me that I refused to see anything else. I didn't think about how we'd secretly marry or, once married, how we would work out the details of our life together. All I could do was run my hands over my Braille books, sure that we would find a solution.

"Peter possibly may have a vision." Annie shoved the books to the corner, and the floor vibrated beneath my feet as she dragged a stepladder to the bookshelf. A shudder told me she climbed up, repositioned the heavy volumes, and came back down. "But God knows both of you can't be blind."

Annie was not finished, not by a long shot. She was strangely attracted to what she suspected was happening between me and Peter. Even as I got up and walked to the dining room to set the table for dinner, feeling my way around it, one hand on the edge as a guide, the other placing napkins to the left of three plates—for Annie, Mother, and myself—Annie followed me, eager to talk. With a strange unease to her fingers she tapped, "I asked around about your Mr. Fagan today."

"What?" I stopped and fiddled with the edge of a plate.

"In Boston. I stopped by the *Herald*—"

"Was John there?"

"Yes, well, no. Not for long, but I—"

"You saw him? Annie?"

"I . . ." Annie held up her hands. I imagined tuberculosis floating like bits of ash in her lungs. She was afraid. She wanted John back.

But by the limp feeling in her hand I knew he had no intention of coming to Wrentham again. "Mr. Fagan's a new hire, not much experience. Helen, are you listening?"

"Yes." I'd finished setting the table and collapsed on a chair by the fireplace, unsure what Annie would say next.

"He's engaged."

"Oh, he's engaged, all right."

"He's engaged to a Miss Dorothy Eagan."

"No, he's not."

"I have John's word on this."

"That couldn't be true."

"At least I know this: he'll stay away from you."

I knew John would say anything to hurt Annie and me. I never doubted that he had lied about Peter. But how fine, how really liberating, that Annie now thought she didn't have to worry. As we waited for my mother to come to dinner I thought I was almost free.

Chapter Seventeen

Some people smell of fire. My mother swept into the dining room and the afternoon stood still. I inhaled her and remembered when I was four: the smell of floor wax, lard from the huge iron pots hanging over the kitchen fireplace, and the churned butter as my mother worked alongside the Negro servants, all the while me clinging to her skirts.

"You two need a little time alone," Annie spelled into my palm. "I'm going to put dinner on." Then she spelled only to me, "For God's sake, Helen. Behave yourself while I'm gone."

She started to cough, that ratcheting mixing with the vibration of her shoes as she left the room.

Mother never liked talking about difficulties. Even with the scent of Annie's menthol cough drops permeating the room, Mother didn't mention tuberculosis, or the fact that if Annie died, the only person left to take care of me would be Mother herself. So, as the curtains billowed, filling the room with hot, damp air, Mother moved her fingers in mine as if counting. Her hand was not rough and sinewy, like Peter's, nor increasingly wan, like Annie's, but softer, more yielding, scented of the ferns, yellow roses, and ivy that surrounded her Alabama house.

Still, her wedding ring parted my right thumb from my fingers, as if she specialized in taking things apart.

"How long has it been, Helen?"

"How long has what been? Annie's test? Two, three days."

"No. How many years has it been since Annie came to us?"

"I was seven, so thirty years."

"And she's still as . . . tempestuous as ever?"

"You mean moody? Yes."

"That's amazing."

"What?"

"Not that she came—she needed work; we needed a teacher. It's only amazing that she stayed."

I was so anxious to keep Mother's mind off of Peter and me that I brought up one of her favorite stories.

"You said Annie looked like a ragamuffin when she got off the Boston-Tuscumbia train. The cinders had made her eyes swell, and she lost a shoe in Baltimore so she came limping off the train, one eye squinted shut, and you thought, '*This* is the teacher Perkins sent us? *This* is the valedictorian of the 1886 graduating class?'"

"That whole first year she fought every night with your father over dinner about how the Yankees won the Civil War, and she was so furious at your father's insistence that the South deserved to win that I can't tell you how many times she packed her bags to leave." Mother laughed.

"And I was terrorizing the dining room."

"Helen. You were never that bad."

"You're right. I was worse."

My mother never wanted me to tell the truth. But at the age of seven when Annie arrived in Tuscumbia my shoelaces were strings, my hair a knotted mass, my voice a bitter rage when anyone tried to rule me. When I wrote these things in my autobiography, my mother said it made her look unfit.

How could I know the dark hallways my mother paced, alone, searching for a way to help me? How at night, unmasked, she felt helpless, terrified, at having to raise me, wondering what would happen to me if she died. How both jealous and proud she felt when Annie civilized me.

The savory smell of pot roast and potatoes from the kitchen told me Annie was hard at work. "Still," Mother continued, "I've never gotten used to you and Annie talking to each other and my not knowing what you're saying."

"You mean what Annie just said to me?" I stalled.

She waited.

"We said you never looked better." How easily I lied.

"And you look quite . . . robust." I felt her move back to inspect me. "You've been outdoors quite a bit?"

"Swimming, biking." I bit my lip.

"You've taken up exercise."

"I've taken up some new habits, yes."

"They suit you. You've never looked more radiant. But Annie looks pale."

"Oh, you know, we're busy."

"Perhaps Annie has been too busy." She paused.

"Too busy for what?" I fiddled with my teacup.

"To stay home, to take care of herself."

"Mother. You know we have to work." I stopped.

There was a long pause.

"Yes, the Keller trust fund didn't exactly work out, did it?"

I felt the narrow wedding band on her finger. Mother never spoke of the sweltering Alabama summers when she took Annie and me with her and Father to our retreat house high in the mountains. That house surrounded by pine forests, the tinny scent of red fox, and the dark-cave scent of bear. Annie, Mother, and I sat on the veranda, hungry because there was so little to eat in the house, while my father stalked the woods hunting with his friends. One day he plunked up the veranda steps to pack his bag and return to Tuscumbia, leaving us three in the woods with no money and no way home.

When I wrote about this in one of my books Mother said I brought the family shame.

Now I spoke up and told the truth. I wanted a changed life. I was not afraid. The dining room air shook ever so slightly with Annie's cough as she rattled the plates in the kitchen.

"All the work's taken a toll on Annie."

"Mother, you can't think that our travels made her sick."

"I have never been able to tell you what to do." Mother laughed. "But if Annie had stayed home more . . ." She was too well bred to mention John's abandonment of Annie. I felt her turn slightly toward the head of the table where John always sat.

"Mother, that's over."

"Well, from what Annie tells me there's another man in the house."

I said nothing.

"A single man. Am I right, Helen? Or formally single. Annie tells me he's engaged."

"Right."

"But you're not." Mother waited for an answer. "Helen? But you're not."

"I'm—"

"You're a single woman," Mother went on. "So I trust while Annie's been ill you have not spent time alone with Mr. Fagan."

"Mother, he's my secretary."

"As long as Annie was with you that's fine. But from now on I'll be in the room with you two whenever you do your . . . letters."

A headache began to throb behind my temples. To be fair, my mother never imagined the grief she would have after I became deaf and blind before my second birthday. How could she have known what to do? She was the spoiled daughter of a wealthy Memphis family, and when I couldn't see or hear, some of her relatives demanded that she send me to the Alabama Asylum for the Insane and Infirm. She refused. She found me Annie, fought with my father to send me to school, and for all that I loved her, loved her beyond myself. And for the second time in my life I would bring her unbearable grief.

"I trust you behaved yourself."

"You have my word." I withdrew my hand and picked up my teacup, its porcelain so thin.

Chapter Eighteen

Unlike Annie, who was partially blind from the age of seven until she was sixteen, my mother never learned the shape of the earth by touching an orange, as Annie taught me to do, never walked past a factory so filled with heat that she thought, as I did at age seven, that the sun had fallen to the earth; she never felt her way down an alley, fearful of getting lost.

No, blindness was foreign to my mother—for that I am grateful.

But I never said this: I traveled the world, I rallied crowds of thousands outside factories on behalf of workers' rights in New York, Boston, and Chicago, found my way down streets in Berlin, Paris, and Rome, places where my mother never ventured.

Imagine my pride—and my sorrow: I had vast stretches of loneliness and fear, but still I was freer than my mother, who lived mostly alone.

I had to lie to her about my engagement to Peter. I didn't have the will to confide in her when I had a new life to live—my own.

Annie came in, and the slight shaking of the table told me she was tapping her shoe against the floor. Mother and I sat side by side, and after Annie passed us platters of pot roast, scented with rosemary, and biscuits, she sat down and handed me a letter.

"Helen, did you write this letter lambasting the French?" Annie spelled to me.

"Where did you find that?" I said.

"In your study. Now did you write it or not?"

"Yes." I kept my hand in Annie's. I felt her lean toward Mother to tell her what I'd done. I held my breath, waiting for Mother's response.

"Perfect, Helen," Annie spelled to me. "Your mother wants to know if *I* put you up to this."

I said nothing.

"It was that Fagan, Kate," Annie spelled to Mother, and to me. She then passed a bowl of peas. "I left Helen alone with him for one day and she goes and acts like a traitor."

"Mr. Fagan put you up to this?" Mother took the bowl from me, her fingers smooth in mine. "When exactly did this happen?"

"Yesterday. When Annie was at the doctor's. Peter whipped out my response on the typewriter. That's his job, Mother." I tried to ease the tension in her touch.

Mother turned from me to face Annie.

"You left Helen alone with this man?"

"He's not important," Annie said. "We have more important things to worry about."

"Helen." Mother took my arm. "How did this happen? With this Mr. Fagan? Wasn't Annie supposed to *watch* you?"

Annie, never one to avoid a fight, sprang up to defend herself. Almost choking on her cough, she said, "*Watch* Helen? Kate, in case you haven't noticed, this is the same Helen who punched out my front tooth when she was seven years old. You want me to *watch* her twenty-four hours a day?"

"Annie, if I'm not mistaken, it is your job to keep Helen away from this—or any—man."

"How am I to do that," Annie snapped, "when I may have to move six hundred miles away?"

With a final bang of the door she was gone.

Mother pushed back her chair and rose to her full height. "Bring Mr. Fagan downstairs."

I rapped three times hard on the floor for Peter, in our signal.

"But first I have one more objection."

"Yes?" I stood.

"*F-a-g-a-n.* What kind of name is that?"

"Mother, please."

"Where is his *family* from?"

"Ireland. They're Catholics."

"Helen, you keep up with the news. Surely you've read about the trouble Irish Catholics are causing these days. They don't hold down jobs. They've rioted in New York. Think of your family, Helen. First you defended the Negroes in that letter to the newspaper—"

"That was fifteen years ago."

"And they still haven't forgotten about it in Montgomery. Every time your sister, Mildred, has her card club over, someone says you disgraced the Keller family. Now these people."

I said nothing.

"They're immigrants first, American second."

"He's a U.S. citizen."

"And whose side will he be on when the United States enters this war?"

"He'll be on *my* side."

I have never told my mother I know the sorrow I brought her. I have never let go of the burden of causing her grief. "We had a few brief months of happiness," she often said to me about the times before I became blind and deaf. But I want more happiness. My life is not shrouded in grief. I want to live with Peter, have a family of my own.

She would never allow it.

But I was reckless. I did not care. I felt Peter's footsteps as he strode into the dining room, kicked a tasseled ottoman in the corner, and then stood by my side.

"Have you met my private secretary?" I asked Mother.

"I haven't met you but I've heard about you."

It was suddenly hard to swallow in the warm room.

"I enjoy working for Helen."

"As long as it's only work."

"I do what Helen asks me to do, ma'am."

"You work for the Keller family." My mother stood straighter. I felt the rustle of her floor-length silk dress. "With Annie sick you'll report to me."

I forced myself to stay still. I imagined my mother disappearing, fastening her cloak, climbing up the steps to the train headed for Alabama.

"You coming, Helen?" Peter's hand gripped mine.

I let him begin to lead me out of the room; his fingers were so tense.

Why couldn't I have Mother, Annie, Peter, *and* my own life? Because my responsibility was to be loyal to those who helped me—without them I had no world. I stopped before we reached the door.

"Helen. Your mother wants me to leave. But I'll be back tomorrow afternoon to help you write your speech for the rally. Meet me in your study at twelve thirty. Will you?"

Peter's footsteps moved away. First they gave off a birdlike scratch. Then they grew stronger, heavier with a *crack-snap-crack*. He walked out like a newly determined man.

Chapter Nineteen

I've always longed to fit in. In my autobiography I wrote that being deaf and blind was like being trapped on a gray, silent island. Far off there was a distant land where people talked, laughed. But I was alone, only able to reach them by tossing out a long lifeline, so desperate to be among the living. I dressed up, learned to read and write, rode horses, learned Latin, French, and Greek, and was the first deaf-blind person ever to graduate from Radcliffe College, cum laude, at that.

But the more I tried to be like everyone else, the more a frightening space opened up between me and the people I loved. It was always there, that chasm. So I followed Peter onto the porch, and when he slipped his warm hand into mine I was not alone—I was with a man who drew me into the world instead of keeping it at bay. I eagerly let Peter lead me away from the house, where Mother paced the dining room floor and Annie tossed in bed.

"You didn't tell me the Kellers celebrated Fourth of July late." He leaned against a maple tree at the yard's edge.

"The fireworks?" I had to laugh, thinking about Mother's outburst.

"You got it, missy. But the show's over."

Suddenly I wanted one thing only, to run away with him.

"Please pardon my rudeness last night," Mother said. "I had a long trip." The noon sun warmed the living room the next day. Mother and I faced Peter as he came into the house.

I felt Peter shuffle his feet.

"So if you'll oblige, I'd like to take you both to the Devon House for lunch." Mother took my arm and swept me alongside her out the front door. Peter followed, just as the heavy maple panels shuddered behind us with a *whap*.

"Peter can drive. I assume he is your chauffeur, too?"

Peter snatched the keys from her hand, and as soon as we climbed into the car he gunned the engine to life. We whizzed up the road, past the murky, mossy water of the lake. Finally Peter pulled the car into the Devon House parking lot.

"Annie usually takes us here the day after I arrive," Mother said to Peter, who spelled it into my hand. "But with Annie sick, well, traditions must be kept up, isn't that right, Helen?"

"I'm for new traditions."

"Fine. As long as I'm in the room when they take place." Mother walked ahead.

I followed her, with one hand on the railing, up to the restaurant's front door. Peter grabbed my elbow, and as he guided me over the step to the lobby I wobbled a bit.

"Thank God I'm steady on my feet," Peter said.

"You?" I said right back. "Between the two of us, mister, I'm the stable one." I laughed, but I had no idea how right I would be.

Peter led me into the dining room. I smelled the bleached linen tablecloths, felt the dragging of chairs. With my feet I sensed the vibration of musical instruments, a trumpet and drums. "Is there a band?" I asked.

"Yup. Can't wait to do the fox trot with you." Peter swung my hand and followed Mother right past the dance floor to a cool section of the dining room, and we sat at a table for three.

"Looks like the bandleader's going to make an announcement," Mother said. "He's dedicating the first song to the men, women, and children in Britain suffering under the German blockade as starvation sets in."

Peter grabbed my hands under the table.

"I'm hungry, too. For you."

"Where are your antiwar sentiments? Shame on you."

"Oh, I have sentiments, all right." Just then Peter scraped back his chair and stood up.

"Where are you going?" I asked him.

"The bandleader wants people to donate money to the war effort. I'm going to donate my words: I'll ask the guy if I can speak. Tell people they should resist this immoral war, this war of useless death and destruction."

His hand slipped from mine, and as he leaned toward the stage, he gave off the eager scent—I know this comparison is wrong—of Father's prize hunting dogs, their bodies taut, ready to charge deep into the woods after something tantalizing, exciting, and they were born to go after it.

Cold ran through my veins. What Peter craved was an audience, a voice. That was his instinct, what drove him.

I tasted copper in my mouth.

I was almost certain then that he wanted fame—no, not fame. He wanted to be in the center of things. And I would be the casualty.

Only then did Mother speak up.

"Mr. Fagan. Sit *down*."

I wish I had accepted then how much Peter longed to be in front of a crowd, how the more sought after I was, the more diminished he felt. All I wanted to believe was that he craved me, so I sat back, sipped my cherry cola, and did not interfere with Mother as she spoke rapidly to Peter, all the while spelling everything into my hand.

"Don't be foolish," Mother said to him. "It's not you they want to hear. It's *her*. *You* haven't met presidents, you weren't beloved by Mark Twain, as Helen was since the day he met her. *You* never

vacationed in Nova Scotia with Alexander Graham Bell." Mother's
hand shook slightly.

In the summer of 1901, Annie and I had stayed with Dr. Bell at his
summer cottage perched high above the Nova Scotia cliffs. His
house—thrumming with the activities of his two daughters and his
deaf wife, Mabel—was a haven for me: everyone knew manual
fingerspelling, so I could talk freely. The guesthouse was filled with
aviators; Dr. Bell was flying kites, trying to discover the path to
human flight. But he put his work aside one evening and spelled to
me that he was concerned about my being so alone. None of the
joys of womanhood should be denied me, he said, his hand warm
on mine. I had no hereditary handicaps to impede a marriage.
Someday Annie would marry, and leave me. I would need a husband of my own.

"I shall never marry," I said. "It wouldn't be fair; any man who
took me for a wife would be marrying a statue." But Peter had
changed all that.

"Mr. Fagan, sit *down*," Mother said again.

"It's a free country, Mrs. Keller," Peter said to Mother and spelled
to me. "Anyone can speak."

"If anyone is to speak here, Mr. Fagan, it's Helen."

"I may not be famous, but I'm—"

"You're an employee."

"I'm not just an employee. I'm—"

"Peter." For one moment I thought he was going to announce
our engagement. Mother couldn't know, not yet. So I changed the
subject.

"The band is starting up."

"I'm not in the mood to dance."

"What are they playing?" Through my feet I felt the solid, round
thump of the drums.

"'Keep the Home Fires Burning,'" Mother said.

Restlessly, Peter tapped his feet.

My fame drew Peter to me, yet at the same time it pushed him away. He wanted to be up on the stage, bringing the crowd to its feet when he denounced the war, its debauchery, the way France had become a bloodied war zone that nothing could cure. Within moments a strange murmuring moved across the restaurant until it ran up my back.

"They know you're here," Mother said to me. "Sit up straight. People are watching. And don't order the soup. It's too hard to eat in public."

"Mother, I know." I felt Peter push a menu across the table to me. "Peter, did you forget I can't read regular print?" His hand cool to my touch told me he was bored translating the menu.

"Say good afternoon to the bandleader," Mother said as she drew my hand into his.

"Miss Keller, we're so honored to have you here."

"Congratulations are in order for Peter." I changed the subject to get the attention off me.

"For what?" Mother sat straighter.

"Peter's going to write an article on shell shock for the *New York Times*."

"Does the *Times* know that?" Mother said.

"Not yet. But they will." I sipped my cola.

"You don't say?" Mother slid a napkin under my drink and I felt the bandleader move away. "You're having a fall full of successes, Mr. Fagan. Annie tells me you're engaged," Mother said.

"That's true."

"Who is she? Would I know her?"

"Actually, you know the name . . ."

"Peter, stop," I said.

"Do tell." Mother leaned against me.

"It's a prominent name."

I nervously pulled my hair.

"That's all I've got to say," Peter said.

"About the article," Mother said. "I thought you were a cub re-porter?"

"I'm more experienced than that, Mrs. Keller. I've published articles about the labor movement, the war in France . . ."

"How nice that you've put your work aside to help Helen."

"I'm an excellent helper, ma'am."

During the return trip Mother sat without comment in the back-seat while Peter sped the car toward home.

Chapter Twenty

All my life I've feared things falling. Now, with Mother upset, it felt as though things were falling apart, but the more unstable I felt, the more closely I bound Peter to me. With Mother napping in the farmhouse, no one knew I was alone with Peter. How easily I let him persuade me to drive up the road to his little house in the woods. Once inside the kitchen, a tiny, sweltering-hot room, I felt the *chunk* of the front-door lock.

"All's secure." He dropped his head to my neck.

"Wait. I wish it had been easier with Mother."

"Judging by that reception, I think it's safe to say we won't need an in-law suite in our house."

"Once we're married?" I leaned against the cool icebox.

"Yup."

"Probably not."

"Though your mother's chill tells me if she did live with us, our house would be cool on the hottest damned days of summer—"

"Peter. That's enough. She is my mother."

"And she loves you."

"Yes."

"Even if she can't stand the sight of me."

"I've never disobeyed before."

"First time for everything." He slid one finger inside my blouse.

"You don't say?" I leaned farther back.

"I do say." He smoothed my hair. "The forces are closing in on us here, Helen. Tell me you'll go with me to Boston soon."

"For what?"

"A marriage license. Even a radical like you can't marry without a license from the state."

"Tell me when."

"How about now?"

"The day of the Boston rally is better. But let's practice now. Now is good."

He pulled open my blouse. "I say, is this office open?"

I felt a rush of warm air on my bare skin.

"Yes," I laughed. "The office is open."

"Is it open all day?" He slid his hands under my shirt.

"All day."

"Nights, too?" I felt his teeth on my neck. The heat of his breath was beautiful.

"Nights, yes." I had never known the pleasure of this.

Peter slid his hands further inside my blouse. He lowered himself so I felt his breath near my breastbone. Then he lowered his hands so they gripped my waist. He unzipped my skirt.

"You need to relax."

"I do." I could barely move.

"I can help with that. Let's go to my bedroom." He tried to pull me down the hallway.

"Give me a minute." I traced the small of his back.

He slowly unbuttoned the long row of buttons on the back of my skirt. He leaned in and kissed me on the mouth.

"Time for a quiz, smart girl."

"Test me," I said.

"Give me an hour."

"For what?"

He raised my skirt, laid his teeth on my skin. "To show you the world."

When I was younger I suspected I had a strong sexual drive. But that was nothing like Peter's rough, tearing hands on my waist. I believed in free love; so did he. I believed in a woman's right to physical pleasure; Peter did, too. And Annie had talked to me about sexual desire: You must use it, she told me, in other ways: your work, your writing. In that you may be a force in the world. But she never told me what this would be like, to be alone with a man who kissed me without end.

"Wait."

"All right." His hands traced my skin.

"I've got to get back. Mother and Annie will never forgive me for running off."

"Those two firecrackers are burned out." Peter's wrist turned as he examined his watch. "Three fifteen. It's hot; maybe they're still napping." He led me to his bedroom, and we stood by his bed. He traced the outline of my breasts and said, "Recite the names of the trees we passed in the woods."

"Is this a party game?"

"Yes. An excellent one."

He lowered me onto my stomach, and placed one knee between my thighs.

"Okay, nature girl. What trees?"

"Apple."

He pressed harder.

"Spruce."

He ran his hands up the backs of my legs.

"It's hard to concentrate. Did I say elm?"

"Not yet."

"Elm." He pressed open my knees.

"Say pine." But I couldn't say it: he slid his hands over mine so my hands were above my head, his whole weight over my body, and as he raised his hips I inhaled the scent of the woods, aromatic and sharp.

"Helen, what do you want?"

I flipped over, took his hand.

We were interrupted by the shirring of the telephone's ring. Peter grabbed his shirt from the side of the bed, tossed me my skirt and blouse, and then answered the phone, listened for a second, then hung up. "Damned Annie tries to protect your chastity from five miles away. We've got to get back to your house."

"I can't move," I said.

Approaching the house, Peter slowed the car. "Helen, I . . ." Through the open window I inhaled fresh-cut wheat from the farms that rolled up and down the hill from East Main Street, the musky scent of leaves starting to fall.

"Helen, I forgot to tell you." He rounded the last curve just before my house and then pulled over.

"I got a tip this morning."

"A tip? What are you, a waiter?"

"No, a reporter from the *Boston Globe* tipped me off that they're onto something. They're coming out here today to chase down the story."

"To my house? What story?"

"What you said about the war . . ." We drove up the bumpy drive, but just outside the house Peter left the car running. "Is this place ever quiet? Damned O'Rourke and Danson from the *Globe* are on the front porch."

"It will kill Annie—and Mother—to find reporters here."

"Your mother's too cranky to die. She'll be around to haunt you for another thirty years. She's as stubborn as you are. I'll put money on it: she's made of more steel than the Manhattan Bridge."

"So kind."

"By your side, madam, I have a chance to live forever. You put me in one of your books and boom—I'm a household name."

He revved the engine so that the car seemed to leap forward, and I held on to the dashboard.

"Don't have an accident," I joked.

"Accidents happen."

Chapter Twenty-one

I t started that night, the crack in our relationship. Peter eased the car slowly up the drive, where pine needles under the tires gave off a metallic scent. "Jesus, they're here en masse." Peter slowed the car to a stop. He reached over and locked my door so I wouldn't jump out.

"Who's here?" I felt him frantic, reaching for the key in the ignition.

"The reporters."

"Let me at them."

"Helen, stop. There are one, two—damn—three out there on the steps. Frank O'Rourke, that bastard from the *Globe*, itching to scoop me on any story he can get, he's on the bottom step, ready to jump as soon as you get out of the car. That's one." Peter held me back with his arm. "Danson, too, he's worthless. The other one I don't know, but I do know this: they'll pepper you with questions the minute they see us."

"Welcome to my life." I opened the door with an easy click. "You translate their questions and my answers. We'll be done with them lickety-split."

"Lickety-split. Where did you learn words like that?" A rush of air told me he'd opened his door.

What I never learned was this: how a man like Peter did not want to be upstaged by me, and how easily I would do it. I knew about fame. I just didn't know—or I refused to see—that Peter wanted to be cheered, toasted, revered, yet by my side he would become smaller. I wish now I had paid attention to the distant touch of his fingers as we left the car, the reporters clamoring for me, their notebooks scented with whiskey, tobacco, air.

The reporters clustered by the front door: "Miss Keller." They peppered me with questions when Peter and I moved up to the porch. Peter spelled their words into my palm, but pulled away slightly.

"Miss Keller, sorry to bother you at home."

"You're bothering me, all right," I said to Peter, who told them.

"Is it true," they demanded, "that you gave royalties from your autobiography to blinded German soldiers? Isn't that treason?"

"Yes. I did do it," I transmitted through Peter.

Peter gripped the front porch railing facing the reporters. I felt him grow more resolute as he spelled to me and said to them that I was right to denounce President Wilson and to call for aid to *all* shell-shocked and wounded soldiers, not just Germans. He turned to walk me indoors, but then, as if he wanted to linger with the reporters, he turned back.

"Are there any more questions?" He edged so close to the reporters that he moved away, dropping my hand.

I stood alone by the front door. Isolation surrounded me. Where was Peter? Confused, I stepped forward, toward the scent of his tobacco. I reached out, but touched only air. The shudder of porch floorboards told me to keep moving forward until my hand grazed Peter's arm. I took his hand and relief flooded me. He was my door to the world.

"Tell me what they—"

"Helen, they're talking to *me*," Peter spelled.

"But I need to know . . ."

"All *right*. O'Rourke from the *Globe* wants to know if I . . ."

"If you . . . ?"

"If I want to be Mr. Helen Keller."

The reporters laughed; I felt Peter's hand flinch in mine. I wanted to pull him away, but he refused to leave.

"We just heard that Henry Ford's leased a ship for influential Americans to sail to Britain to negotiate a peace." Peter spelled Danson's next question to me. "Will you accompany Helen if she goes?"

Peter stepped back, closer to the house.

"Isn't this house partly paid for by Andrew Carnegie? The same Carnegie whose money supports the war?" Peter's spelling grew faint in my palm.

"No, the house has nothing to do with Carnegie."

"Don't the Kellers—even you—get their support from Carnegie, after all?"

I felt the porch light, so hot on my head.

"Peter, let's go."

He tightened his hold on my wrist, and pulled me inside the house.

I was startled by his forcefulness.

You're deaf. Can you hear music? People ask me this when I go to concerts, or laugh along at musicals and Broadway shows. How? Because as a band plays I "hear" soundwaves along the floor. I sit in a theater or concert hall with both feet flat under my chair and I listen with my feet: I thought of that as Peter and I stood alone in the front hall as the reporters crunched their way down the drive to their cars, but not with the same gait. One of them walked gracefully, with a light step, while the other rushed past to the beat of some inner discord.

That's how Peter is, I thought, as I slowly walked by his side into the living room. Not the reporter who walked smoothly, in sync with the world, but the other, more agitated one. Did Peter think I wouldn't notice how upset and confused he was?

We sat uneasily by the fireplace.

"I don't care about the Germans." Annie paced the living room, her bathrobe warm to my fingers. She had waited in her bedroom until the reporters drove off, then walked in to confront me, determined to make me tell her where I'd been. I told her what happened on the front porch. She paused beside me and I felt her face. Worry lines, yes, but something new was there, too. There was a parchment-paper thinness to her skin, as if tuberculosis had already drained her. I kept my hand by her mouth to hear her speak, and even her voice was thin as string.

"I was worried they would say you two were marrying. *That* is a headline I don't ever plan to read."

"What would be so bad about that?" Peter said.

"Everything. Especially since you're fired."

"What?"

"You're leaving at the end of this month. Kate is here, and we don't have enough money to pay you, anyway."

"I'll fix that." I stood perilously close to Peter, even with Annie nearby.

"Helen, for God's sake, no miracle is going to appear this time. We're nearly broke. He's got to go."

"I'm going to pray about it," I said.

"You're not religious?" Peter acted as though he'd touched a snake.

"Yes."

"Bibles as big as a dining-room table," Annie said. "You haven't seen them? Whole passages she's read so many times the Braille is rubbed away."

"Good grief," Peter said.

"She's a Swedenborgian."

"A what?"

When I was young, people thought that I couldn't be influenced by false ideas, sorrow, or death. So no one ever spoke to me of those things. One day Annie and I walked through a cemetery, and without knowing where we were I sensed the stillness and asked, "Who died here?" People wanted to think of me as some kind of angel. At a young age I asked Annie if I could study the Bible. "Who made me?" I asked Annie, and even though she had no belief in religion she said, "God." I asked, "Who made God?"

I learned in the Bible that people who are blind and deaf are just in a narrow passage in this life, that in the next one their sight and hearing will be restored. Later, in my adulthood, I learned there was a name for this kind of belief: Swedenborgianism.

Yet even as I was comforted by this religion and the Bible, no one knew the dullness of my nights, the chill of winter days when I sat alone, no sound, no motion, no life around me.

I stood between Annie and Peter as if to cause a slight thaw between them.

"You wouldn't catch me in a church if it had a door straight to heaven," Annie said.

"Maybe Helen needs something else to believe in," Peter said.

"Like a soon-to-be-unemployed man?"

"I prefer the term 'income-free.'"

"I'm not blind," Annie said. "I've been married to a loafer."

"He was a drinker. I'm not."

"John was a drainer. When he arrived we had a house fully paid for, and Carnegie money; ten years later the house is mortgaged to the hilt, we're about to lose it, and our income's so small a cricket couldn't make a bed with it."

"I have news. John's volunteered to drive an ambulance on the Western Front. Seems as if he wants to change things," Peter said.

"He wants to help people in foreign lands," Annie said. "Just not those close by."

Peter turned serious. "And he left you with nothing but bitterness and debt."

"He left me, Helen, and . . ." Annie stopped.

"Maybe Helen wants something different," Peter said.

"Over my dead body," Annie said.

At the mention of dying, a single ash seemed to float in the room, and Annie choked, deeply, as if she were drowning.

When she stopped she said, "If death comes to me and Helen marries you, I'll come back and kill you myself."

"The second coming at last," Peter said.

All night I sat by Annie. Coughs had racked her body so insistently in the living room that she needed my help to make her way down the hall to her bedroom. Once in bed, furiously kicking off a quilt I put over her, she held my hand.

"Get any ideas you're having right now out of your head."

"What ideas?"

"Running-off-with-lover-boy ideas."

She held my hand like a vise.

Chapter Twenty-two

⊰⊱

Here are the things I regret in my life: lying to Annie, lying to my mother. What I regret most is that I fell asleep in the chair beside Annie's bed, and when morning came I did not notice that she had slipped out of the room. If I could go back and change that moment, I would.

Because minutes later she hurried back in and shook me awake. "Come quickly," she said. "I have news. Helen—*now*."

"What?" I yawned. The slow rumbling of a passing car made me turn to the window. Had Peter and Annie argued? Maybe that was his car, leaving.

"Is it Peter?" I felt for Annie's hand.

"It's a letter."

"Your tests? You have the results?" The floor felt chilly under my feet.

Annie brushed my hair back and urged me up from the chair.

"Annie, tell me. Are you very sick?"

"For God's sake, Helen. I've been sick all my life." She shook my arm. "I don't know anything yet about the TB. Those slowpokes are keeping me on tenterhooks. They'll tell me at the last minute, after I've not slept for two weeks."

"They'll tell you you're fine," I said.

"They'll tell me I'm doomed." She tapped her foot, waiting for me to get up.

———

Here's what I imagine when I stand by Annie in her room, terrified that she might die: I am seven years old. Annie has not yet come into my life. I pat the damp ground of Tuscumbia, Alabama, next to our cook's daughter, Martha Washington. Her skin dusky-dark, Martha grunts beside me, making a house of twigs and sticks with pasty mud. When I wham her leg she moves the way I want her to. She was my only friend until Annie arrived.

In the first month after Annie's arrival I pouted and stormed when she tried to make me eat from a plate; within two months I no longer stayed in the big house with my mother. I no longer needed to be violent with Martha Washington.

No. I spelled *w-a-t-e-r* under the backyard pump, and Annie took me to live in the tiny house, the cabin next door, just Annie and me. It seemed, during those days and nights alone, the darkness was mushroomy, basil-scented in my child-mouth. When we left that house after several weeks to again live with my family, Annie and I were wrapped in a secret girl pact. I would be hers; she would be mine.

She would be my raft out of darkness.

So I felt Annie's face. "Is it your eyes? You've gotten a letter from your eye doctor?"

"How could I be your constant companion if I couldn't see perfectly? Between us we need at least two good eyes."

What Annie said was ironic, because growing up, the world for her had always been a blue-black place, its people and objects in a haze. When she was very small a burning started in her eyes. When she rubbed them and cried out, her mother bathed them in geranium water because they couldn't afford a doctor. By age seven Annie was legally blind, groping her way from place to place.

She saw the world as matted, moving swirls of colors and gray. From the age of ten to fourteen she lived in the disreputable Tewksbury poorhouse. When a man from the welfare department came to inspect the poorhouse, Annie threw herself at him, saying, "I want to go to school." He arranged for her to go to Perkins, where she learned to read and write completely at the age of fourteen; she graduated when she was twenty. During those years she had five operations at the charity hospital, and by her late teens she saw well enough to pass for sighted. Annie craved normality, and if she lost her sight again she'd lose everything, including me.

"I can see perfectly," Annie said. She nudged me to get up from my chair.

I exhaled.

"I can even see a liar a mile away."

I squirmed in my chair.

"Come on. I'll prove it to you." She led me through the hall.

"Where are we going?"

"Your study. I've been looking through some letters."

"You were spying on me?"

"Not spying. Investigating. And it's Peter I'm after."

"Shouldn't we respect his privacy?"

"Respect this." Annie plunked me into a mohair chair by my desk and rattled a letter in front of me. "It's addressed to Peter. Get ready, Helen."

"Ready for what?"

"To bid him good-bye."

"Don't . . ." Whatever the letter said, I didn't want to know. But Annie spelled rapidly into my hand:

Miss Dorothy Eagan, 17 Eagleview Point, Albany, New York

Peter Mine,
I crave your scent on my hands. I crave your letters, asking what I'm wearing. I'll tell you. I am wearing only desire for you.

I need to see you. I'm coming to Boston next week. Can you
meet me at the two o'clock train? Please wear your blue suit. You
always look so handsome in blue.

> Yours deeply,
> Dorothy

Annie and I sat together, her hand firm but nervous in mine.

"So he really loves someone else," Annie spelled.

Fire, a roiling thing in me.

"Your time with him is almost over."

"It's not." Deception comes to everyone sometimes. If I could
deceive Annie and my own mother, there must be a reason why
Peter would deceive me about another woman.

"What's the date on the letter?"

"Helen, I'm sorry. He's a charlatan. All men are. You have to face
facts."

"Tell me the date. It may have been written before he met me."

"What?"

"He can't be involved with her. He's—"

"You should have believed me when I told you what John re-
ported about him."

"Oh, Annie. You know John's a liar."

"True." Annie pulled back, and I felt her hands cool as she held
mine, her whole self assessing me. "He was, is, a liar. But this letter,
Helen, is incontrovertible proof."

"It proves nothing."

Annie smoothed my hair.

"Helen," Annie spelled softly. "He's an opportunist. I asked him
to clean out some of your old correspondence files last week; he
pulled out a stack of letters from Mark Twain and said, 'Did they
correspond a lot?' I told him Twain had loved you like a daughter
until the day he died. Helen, remember having tea with him in
New York? He even left whiskey for you in your room when we

visited him at his Connecticut house, saying everyone needed a friend in the night."

"Yes." Something was wrong. But I didn't want Annie, or even myself, to know what it was. I nudged the bedroom floorboard with my shoe.

"So the look in Peter's eyes when he heard how close you were to Twain, well, I could just *see* him imagining himself flitting around with all the other people you know. Mark my words. He wants so much to be famous he'll stick to you like glue." She snapped her fingers so hard I felt the *snap* deep in my hand.

"You don't know that."

"Helen. If you could have seen him, you'd agree."

I felt a bit of fear. Could I really know Peter without seeing? A blind man once said he didn't want sight. He wanted longer arms. Arms so long that if he wanted to understand the moon, he would simply reach up and touch it: he would rather *feel* the moon than see it. So no, I didn't need to see Peter: the hot skin of his neck, his mouth on mine, said all I needed to know.

"People aren't always what they seem," I said.

"Want to bet?" Annie spelled back, her hand still holding Dorothy Eagan's letter. I steadied myself in my chair.

"At least you'll be rid of him," Annie said a few minutes later. I sat so still in the chair. The air near her bed seemed dense. "Read me the date on the letter," I said. "A date will tell me if it is recent or not." Annie did not move.

Another thing no one tells you about being blind is the utter dependency, the way I have to cajole, plead, persuade those around me to do the simplest things, like read me the date because I can't do it myself. If Annie refuses, how can I know if Peter's been deceiving me? It's hard to believe how many of my desires I've had to bury, because they didn't fit the whim of someone else. But it's like

I've caught a fever. I want to run away with Peter, and my hands shake uncontrollably.

"The date," I repeated.

"It's too light to see."

"Your vision is not the best," I tried to joke.

Annie coughed. "So true."

"It could be an old letter."

"And I could be President Wilson," Annie said.

My deepest regret? How easily I would have excused him for anything. I've said it before and I'll say it again: there are so many, many ways to be blind.

Chapter Twenty-three

America's First Lady of Courage. That's how I am known, for my relentless fight for the deaf and blind. It's true that I've crisscrossed the country tirelessly, that I've raised more money than anyone else, that I demand the same rights as anyone in the hearing and sighted world. But I can't claim to be the First Lady of Courage. It took all the courage I had to walk away from Annie and find my way down the hall, alone.

So I don't remember the vibration of Peter's footsteps, but he followed me into my study. I sat at my desk, my hands tracing the letter Annie showed me. Panic filled me, but I was determined to show Peter that I was strong. I won't let anyone take my dignity, especially him. I hid the letter behind my back.

"What do you have there?" He laughed, pulling my hand toward him.

"Nothing." I kept my hand in a fist.

"Good. Fight me. I love a good tussle." He leaned me against the wall by the bookshelves.

"Stop it." I pushed him away.

"Yes, tell me to stop." He put his mouth to my neck. "Say, 'Peter, stop,' and I'll say—"

"You'll say you're sorry."

"Sorry?" He lifted his head. "The only thing I'm sorry about is this damned corset of yours," he laughed, trying to loosen the waist of my skirt.

"You have plenty to be sorry for. Deceiving me."

"What are you talking about?"

"Read it to me." I handed him the letter. "I want to hear it from you."

"Oh." Peter paused. His hands shook.

"Yes?"

"Oh." Peter laughed. "Did Annie show this to you?"

"Of course she did. She, at least, wants to protect me."

"She wants to keep you in a gilded cage, is what she wants."

"Who is she? This Miss Dorothy Eagan?"

"She's not important now."

"But she must have been. Tell me."

"The truth? She's nothing like you. I met her at a charity ball, her father knew mine."

"And you loved her?"

"No, Helen. I thought I did."

"But you made love to her?"

"Helen, please let's not talk about the past."

I didn't speak for a long time. "Leave me alone. I need time to think," I said. Smoke from Peter's cigarette filled the air as he left the room. I can tell you that I sat at my desk and pulled open the drawer. I took out my cloth journal written when I was seven years old. In it I had recorded:

Tuscumbia, Alabama

Annie's gone away.
She left me with Mother.
My doll won't stop crying.
I hit her with a stick.

How painful it is for me to lose someone. But I never told Annie I missed her. Too painful it was, to let in desire. So Peter had loved someone before he met me. So what? I tried to push the doubts away.

"Helen." Peter came in and took my hand. "That's over. This is now. And we have a date with destiny."

"A date with what?"

"The day we go to Boston City Hall, dummy. To get a marriage license."

"Don't call me dummy." I almost laughed. "I'm a bit sensitive about that."

"Helen." He pulled me close. "For a woman who can't speak, you sure have an awful lot to say."

I'm ashamed that I didn't ask the questions that rose in my mind then. I regret that I did not say, "Did you want to marry *her*?" Why didn't I ask? Not because I was afraid that other women would fall for Peter because he was so handsome, funny, and smart. No, I was afraid that if he could leave one woman so suddenly, why couldn't he leave me?

Peter stood beside me, his whole body shaking a bit, radiating a kind of queer heat. I rubbed his shirt cuff, the fabric so worn. "Peter, I'm not saying you don't care for me . . ."

"Care for you? You're a miracle to me."

"A miracle, yes."

"Someone who showed me a life I had never thought of before."

"Yes."

"Someone who showed me I could live in a way I didn't think possible."

"Yes."

"Helen. I should have told you. But—"

"You don't have to explain."

He kissed me and took away my breath.

"Helen, pack your bags tonight. The rally in Boston is in three days. We have to be ready." He traced along my neck with his thumb. "Annie and your mother will be expecting me to pick you up after breakfast. We'll drive to the train station and take the eight forty-five to Boston."

"What about the marriage license?"

"Right after the rally, my pet. Try to get some rest tonight."

"I won't be able to."

"Well, you'd better, because you'll need your beauty sleep." He slid his thumb into the opening of my blouse.

I know Annie is not a saint. Nor is Peter. Nor am I. I need them. Without Annie or Peter I don't have a home to call my own. But I know this: with Peter engulfing me I feel so strong I can suddenly see the sky.

Chapter Twenty-four

I once wrote that my blindness never made me sad. But I was not telling the whole truth. After Peter left that night I felt sadness pitch and fall through me. If Annie hadn't shown me that letter, Peter wouldn't have told me about Dorothy. What else was he hiding? I was so dependent on others, so vulnerable, that I was more aware of my blindness than ever.

Still, I craved Peter. I didn't care who I hurt, or what I refused to see. I only wanted him, so I didn't say a word when he found me in the backyard the next day.

"Where's Annie? Your mother?" Peter turned around as if inspecting the yard. "Lurking in the shrubs to spy on us?"

"They're in Boston. John's baby is due any day now, and Annie will be damned—her words, not mine—if he and Myla bring that baby back to the apartment Annie and John used to share. She won't allow them to use what's hers, so Annie's there right now dragging out her maple bureau, taking away her kitchen chairs. She's even pulling the telephone out of the wall."

"She's a force of nature." Peter laughed. "She'll probably scour the linoleum off the floor."

"With her bare hands."

"Hell hath no wrath." Peter took my hand. "By the way, I wrote to Dorothy. It's off now."

"For good?"

"Forever."

I inhaled the chill air and pulled my jacket around me.

Peter tapped out a cigarette. "One more thing," he said. "This apartment of John's. Do you and Annie still pay the rent?"

I didn't answer.

"Helen? You can't pay for your own house."

"Annie won't let John have her books, pots, and pans. She's even taking the pillows off the couches."

"That'll show him."

"Peter."

"Yup. Annie's really taking a stand. Her husband has a child, and she still—"

"Loves him."

"She's too loyal."

"People are, sometimes."

Peter's deception was still on my mind. My image of him as a courageous, honest man had started to fray. But I was determined to seal off that knowledge. Of all people, I knew how one must hide parts of oneself to succeed in the world.

Peter's coat gave off the woody scent of the neighbor's fire, where they burned their fall leaves. He fiddled with the buttons on my jacket. I wanted him to kiss me, to slip his hand inside my jacket, but I held back.

"Hey," Peter said. "Those two gals are out of town and we're alone."

"No. Ian, the boy who mows the lawn, he's out in the garden shed, fixing the mower. Mother and Annie would never leave me here alone."

"Then let's make a run for it."

"A run for what?"

"That meadow behind the house. No one will see us there." He tugged at my sleeve. "Hurry, Helen. And once you're warmed up you'll need to loosen those tight clothes."

"Yes, sir." I let him lead me under a thicket of trees.

"Come on, lazybones." Peter led me into the meadow. Pine needles crunched under my shoes, and the cool scent of mint rose from the garden beyond the pines. Under a tree, Peter slowly pulled at the silk bow of my blouse.

"Too bad this knot is so tight. I'm afraid I'll have to use my teeth."

"What a shame."

"I might have to tear it."

"I'm sorry to hear that." I raised my neck to him. "Let me help."

"Ah, good girl," he said. "I love a woman who takes the lead."

"Do you?"

"Yes. But I also like a woman who submits. Like this." He clasped my wrists behind my back, and I couldn't move my hands.

He held them high above my head, and I remembered when I was a small child and had just learned language—hundreds of new words a day—and constantly "talked" to myself by spelling words into my own hands. Annie, upset that I'd seem blind to others, told me to stop. For her lesson I would pay a heavy price.

"Hey." Peter dropped my hands. "What's this?"

I felt the ground with the toe of my shoe. "Croquet hoop."

"All these years you've been out in this meadow playing what? Croquet?"

"You bet. On good days I dominate the field."

"My athlete." He turned. "I love a woman with energy." I felt him reach down and tug something out of the grass. A metallic scent, mixed with old wood. "This old mallet." He pressed the wood against my arm. "It has the initials HK on it."

"It's mine. I know how to use the mallet."

"Something tells me you're excellent at it."

"I know how to play, all right."

Far off a lawnmower's vibrations *chut-chutted*.

"But you always play it straight. Helen Keller never keeps secrets." He made me lean over, guiding the mallet in my hands.

"I hide things all the time. You wouldn't believe the secrets I keep." As he shook the mallet beside me, I tried to cover my nervousness.

"Well, Helen." He traced the mallet up the back of my calf. "Is there anything you're not telling me?"

"Besides the obvious? Like I can't get dressed in the morning: someone needs to choose my clothes, and help me."

"Sign me up for that," Peter laughed.

"Oh, and I have no idea how to fix this crumbling house—"

"I'll be too busy dressing and undressing you to worry about that."

"I think that about wraps it up—oh—except that Mother will kick and scream once we're married, and Annie will insist on living with us."

"Annie, live with us?"

"She'll want to."

Peter pressed the mallet closer to my back. "The list grows."

"Yes."

"I don't have any real worries," he said. "Except that . . . I may not be up to the task."

"I'm quite a task."

"Are you ever."

I know people's jobs by their scent. I can tell where a person has been when he passes me in a room. As a stranger walks by, if his clothes give off an ink scent, I know he's come from a print shop. The flint smell of iron means factory worker, a flour scent trails the baker; ivy, iris, and mulch rise from the hands of a gardener. And the man who's worried? His hands give off the tinny scent of fear.

"I can still take care of you."

"I'll take care of you right back."

"How do you propose to do that?"

"With my Andrew Carnegie money. I told you—didn't I?—he sends me an annual pension—not a lot, about five thousand dollars a year—so I can use part of it to hire another secretary, and you can write, do your work."

"Wait, what? You take money from Andrew Carnegie? Helen, you're a Socialist. He's a robber baron. Have you thought about that?"

"As a matter of fact I have."

"Well, you can't take money from him. His money comes from exploiting the poor. Steelworkers were shot by Pinkerton guards while on strike at one of his plants." Peter rapped the croquet mallet on the ground and I felt a thunk.

"So you can't take money from him, and you sure can't offer it to me, either."

"Watch me," I said.

I am made of contradictions. But I won't apologize. I seem independent, an ardent Socialist, yet my Radcliffe education, my house, my daily needs are paid for in part by a fund contributed to by America's great capitalists: Carnegie, and Spaulding the Sugar King.

Andrew Carnegie for years had offered me an annual pension as support. In 1910 Annie and I were short of money; the roof on the Wrentham house was loose in spots; the gutters were full; leaves covered the yard. We couldn't afford household help for the chores. Then my friend Sarah Fuller visited: upon seeing the state of my home she wrote to her friend Andrew Carnegie, pleading that I should not live in such disarray because of who I was and all I gave to the world. Carnegie offered to give me a pension for life.

I turned him down. I wanted to make it on my own. And I was a Socialist. Taking money from the richest man in America wouldn't do.

But Carnegie replied that he hoped someday I would accept his offer, and a few years later he invited Annie and me to his New York City apartment. In the library the leathery scent of his books and the heavy rug beneath us muffled all vibrations as, over tea, he repeated his offer.

"Helen," he said, as Annie translated into my palm, "even a Socialist needs the proper shelter." But I still refused.

"I'm a modern woman. I can make my own wage, and my own way." I accepted his tea, his meals, but not a cent of his money.

"If you don't take the money I'll take you over one knee and spank you," Carnegie said.

I just laughed.

But not long after, Annie and I were in freezing Bath, Maine, on a lecture tour. When I awoke on the hotel's third floor and felt my way to Annie's bed, she was burning with fever; within hours she was unconscious. Her hair was soaked with sweat under my fingers. I couldn't find my way to the desk clerk, I couldn't use the phone, I couldn't cry out to get a doctor. The room grew tighter around me, until it was without air.

A few days later Annie had recovered enough to get help for herself. We returned to Boston, but Annie was still sick and weak. I wrote to Andrew Carnegie.

His check arrived every month after that. I'll never turn it down again.

"Helen? Who's hiding things now?" Peter tapped my shoulder. He smoothed my hair, and then tugged it, hard.

"Ouch." I pulled back. "That hurts."

"So does hearing my future wife wants to support me."

"Annie depends on me. I can't just think of myself, of you and me."

"Helen," he said. "This is the craziest thing I've ever heard. You're a deaf-blind woman who bears the weight of supporting yourself and Annie, and now you want to help me?"

He traced my face with his fingers. "Look at me. Twenty-nine years old and two nickels in the bank, overeducated and underemployed. A real loafer, I seem."

"But you have hopes and dreams."

"Don't we all. The best one is to marry you."

That was the moment I felt real intimacy between us. He put down the mallet, and when he kissed me, it was salty, tart, as if we both knew the burden of crossing, and recrossing, into different worlds.

Woods, trees, air, brine.

He *was* mine.

Chapter Twenty-five

The scent of pine needles, damp wood, and acorns filled the air as Peter led me to the cabana high above the pond later that afternoon. "Right this way, mademoiselle." He pried open the door and led me across the sloping floor. The warm day made the cabana musty, and heat seeped through the closed windows. Peter took my hands; they felt tense but I felt utterly calm. I had wanted him for months. The last time we came to the pond I lured him in but I wasn't ready; this time I wouldn't let him go.

"If being an activist doesn't work out, you may have a future as an actress."

"You mean the way I got your attention the last time we were at the pond?"

"Yup."

I reached up and pulled down from a wooden peg the sleek, black satin bathing suit I had worn that day. "Remember this?"

"*Do* I." He laughed back. "The very suit you lowered that day at the pond."

"You mean the straps."

"Good enough for me. I have eyes, and you're a gorgeous woman. Do you think I haven't imagined the rest?"

"One can only hope."

"I believe that is the moment I began to fall in love with you."

"Flatterer."

"I prefer intellectual. First I was taken by your mind."

"Love me for something else."

He lowered me to the bench in the corner and yanked off my jacket, pulling me to him.

"Wait." I got up, felt my way to the cabana door, and closed it tight.

Suddenly I was desperate for him. He was behind me, his hands on my waist, his thighs taut against the backs of my legs. He pulled off my blouse, his hands warm on my corset. The afternoon heat rose to the windows and seeped in. Then he took my hands and raised them above my head.

With one hand on my hip and the other on my corset, he began to move me back and forth. He slid his hand down my hip to my thigh and raised my skirt. I felt his belt buckle press into my back.

"You're my captive."

"For how long?"

"An hour at least." With great leisure he stroked my bare thigh. "Or longer."

Tick, rick, tick. I felt him unbuckle his belt. And while my skirt was still between us he pressed hard into my hips.

He yanked up my skirt so that I felt the hem on the backs of my thighs. Still, the coarse fabric stayed between us. But I felt in waves. With my hands holding the doorjamb I felt him pummel me. "Do you like that?" he spelled to me.

"Yes."

"How about this?" With one knee, he pressed open my thighs.

"Turn around," he said.

Now my back was against the door.

He reached inside my corset, his breath like bitterroot leaves. "Do you want me to take your corset off?"

"Please."

He lowered himself and pulled open the corset laces. Then I felt his tongue on my breast. He reached up and held my bare shoulders, and I arched my back. Nothing had prepared me for this. "I can't . . ."

"Quiet." He pressed his hand over my mouth. "We're not done here."

He grabbed my hands and held my wrists together. I squirmed, but he had my wrists over my head.

He found my palm. "Give in," he spelled.

"Never."

"Give."

"Give what?"

"Everything."

I stood on the balls of my feet, my head to one side, my corset open. Then he took off my skirt. I inhaled.

He was up against me. I raised my hips to him.

"Take."

Peter pushed his life into me, he pushed into me with his thin hips, pushed in again, again.

The sky opened. The world came in.

I can't really remember what happened next. I know great flocks of Canada geese honked outside the cabana as I woke and felt Peter beside me. Their cries seemed to unsettle the sky, bring a chill, so I pulled my jacket over my bare skin. "Take that off," Peter said, stroking me. "I want to see you."

He trailed his fingers over my mouth. I read his lips. "Russia," he said. "Helen, I'm planning a trip there. There's a revolution brewing. It will change the world."

"You're like Emma Goldman," I said.

"I'm not an anarchist."

"I know. Do you know what she said about me?"

"Do tell." He moved his palm over my belly.

"She said, 'All my life I've searched for one great American woman. And Helen Keller is the one.'"

"Are you ever," Peter murmured. "I'll take you with me. To Russia."

"Every girl's dream honeymoon." At that moment I didn't care about the future. I slid closer to his warm body. He tugged me up until I was over him.

"Again?" he said. If I could go back to that time, it would be then. When all my worries floated out into the woods, far, far away.

Before nightfall Peter guided me out of the cabana. I walked so easily over the bumpy wooded path back to the farmhouse. When Peter tried to open the back door, it got stuck.

"Push," I said, standing on the grass behind him.

"What do you think I'm doing?" The door opened. He pulled me into the back hallway. "What the hell?"

"What is it?"

"This." He guided my hand to a long piece of metal. Rounded, smooth, it curved down to a cloth canopy.

"Is it a . . ."

"Stroller. A baby stroller. Lifted from John's apartment by a furious Annie." Peter held my wrist. "Here, shake." I felt the *rat-a-tat-tat* vibrations of a toy rattle. "My God, she's even taken the kid's toys."

I stood still. "Peter, what if someday, you and I—"

"Don't get any ideas, darling."

That night I had trouble falling asleep. Annie was pacing in the hallway. When I finally did drift off, I dreamed of a small child lying between Peter and me. Sun, earth, moon. We three.

Chapter Twenty-six

❦

October's wind blew brisk the next morning. Mother and I, out for an early morning walk, passed the lopsided oak tree by the side of my house and turned into the hallway before breakfast, our faces chilled. Beyond the hallway was the music room, where a piano, a violin, and a gramophone sat covered with dust. "Annie took every last thing out of that apartment that she could carry," Mother said. "She even had this piano shipped here, express. What could she possibly want with it?"

"It doesn't matter." I couldn't stop thinking about Peter.

"Does she still play it?"

"Play what?"

"The piano, Helen." Mother shook my wrist.

"Oh, she will, you know, for concerts and such." We faced each other, and the wind rattled the windows. I hooked my arm through Mother's. I couldn't wait to get on the train with Peter, and I almost missed when Mother said, "Helen, remember when you were young, you used to try to play the piano?"

"Yes. Once I wrote that I often felt like a music box with all the play shut up inside me."

"And not anymore?" Mother said.

I just smiled.

"Helen, did you wash your hair this morning? It's still wet. You shouldn't bathe in this chill. It's bad for you. You could catch a cold."

"I've never felt better in my life."

"That's what Annie thought, too. But look at her now. You should be more careful."

"I'm beginning to think I should be less careful."

"Beginning to think?" I felt Mother laugh. "You weren't so careful years ago when you sent that letter about—oh, I won't say it."

"What letter?"

"Oh, never mind."

"Oh, *that* letter: the one where I talked about venereal disease. Yes, Mother, I did send that letter, to *Ladies' Home Journal*, in fact."

"What did they want with a letter on such a thing?"

"Mother, that letter saved thousands of babies from blindness. Doctors knew from the 1860s that venereal disease in mothers caused newborn children to go blind at birth—"

"I know, Helen. But no one would write about it. It *is* a delicate subject."

"That's why I wrote it: of all people they'd listen to me."

"Helen, why must you always be the one spearheading things?"

The tenseness in Mother's jaw told me it was a strain for her to be in Boston. She had to put up with my outspokenness and Annie's temper tantrums and her illness. "Look at this." Mother pulled a letter from her dress pocket. She spelled for me the invitation from the Mark Twain Foundation. "It's the sixth anniversary of Twain's death. You and Annie are invited to speak at a dinner honoring his legacy."

I said nothing.

"Helen, this is *exactly* the type of thing you should be doing."

"Of course, I'll go. But I can't leave this week. I'm going to Boston tomorrow with Peter—"

"You'll do no such thing."

"Mother, I know you don't want to think about it, but I do need—"

"What? Money? From a rally? Even I know that doesn't pay much."

"It's not the money, Mother."

"Are you doing it to get away from Annie and her grief?"

And then I lied again. "Peter and I are meeting with my publisher. They may want me to do a new book."

"I didn't know you were writing a new book." Mother put her arms around me.

"You won't believe how many new things I'm doing."

Mother stepped back. "Why don't you tell me? I have all day."

"Peter will be here any minute now. I've got to get ready. We need to go over my speech."

"Helen, I'm writing your sister, Mildred. You and Annie simply can't manage here, and soon Mr. Fagan will be . . . leaving your employ. If it turns out that Annie does in fact have tuberculosis, I'm taking you to Mildred's house in Montgomery immediately."

"Perfect. I can't wait to leave," I said.

I need to remember happiness, because of what happened next. Rain pelted the kitchen windows, and dampness permeated the house when Annie's scent of camphor and medicine told me she'd walked into the hall. "Helen, my room. Now," she said. Surprised by her staccato fingerspelling in my hand, I left Mother by the fireplace in the kitchen and followed Annie. The rug was thin under my feet, the chair by her bed stiff. As I ran my palm over Annie's face, her mouth tightened, and the narrowness of her lips made sympathy enter my heart.

"I want you to be the first to know, Helen."

"Know? About Peter and that woman? But I do know."

"Will you for one minute stop talking about Peter?"

"I can explain."

"Helen, I don't want to hear his name again until hell freezes over."

"That long?"

"The doctor was here. Yesterday, while you were out . . . ."

"Walking."

"Yes, Helen. While you were out walking, the doctor came. The results are unequivocal." She brought a handkerchief to her mouth and coughed, coughed.

"This damned disease. They should call it the Red Death, not the White." The scent of blood rose to my nostrils from her handkerchief.

"Three days, they've given me," Annie said, her fingers unsteady. "They say I have to be there in three days."

"Be where?"

"A damned sanatorium, in upstate New York. Here's their cure: I go to this rest home with a bunch of other sufferers and we wrap ourselves up in woolen coats; they cart us out onto a cold porch and we breathe fresh, frigid air all day. Not for me. I'm not going there. Last week I saw a sign in the window of the Wrentham Travel Agency for sunny Puerto Rico. That's where I'll go to recuperate. At the very least I'll be warm. Helen, get out of the way." She pushed past me, and a moment later I felt the closet door open, then the thump of her suitcase on the bed. "Let's fill this up with my best clothes. If I'm going to die I'll be tanned and well dressed."

"Annie, stop it."

"Tuberculosis, the gift that keeps on taking. It's taking me from you, and leaving you with that damned Fagan. Thank the lord your mother is here."

Too nervous—panicked, really—to help Annie, I walked up and down her room, ambivalent. Peter loved me, promised to care for me. But I smelled the rose perfume from the gray chiffon dress Annie packed in her suitcase and I remembered her wearing it at our last dinner. I realized with a terrible ache that she would soon be gone. I put one hand over my mouth to keep the grief out.

I stopped pacing and sat beside Annie again. She had a pile of blouses on the bed, and I handed them to her to put in her suitcase. "I have tuberculosis, and John's having a child with another—well, I can't call her a lady—that *person*," Annie said.

"Annie, you know you're the only woman in my world. Do you remember when I was eight? You were teaching me words and geography. You gave me an orange surrounded by raisins to show me the place of the sun and the planets."

"Are you trying to cheer me up?"

"You wanted me to know about the sun's heat. So you took me on a long walk—we walked all morning to see that furnace."

"I took you over half of creation, Helen. That was my job."

"The closer we got to that enormous furnace—it burned, what? Two tons of coal an hour? The closer we got . . ."

"The more you recoiled from it. You stopped, three blocks away, and your dress was drenched with sweat from its heat. It was a blue pinafore, the fall of 1899."

We both paused.

"I know the real reason you took me to see that furnace. It wasn't to feel heat like the sun's."

"No, no, it wasn't."

"It was Mother and Father fighting that day in the house, wasn't it?"

"They were fighting. They were—"

"I felt the china shatter. I picked up the broken shards."

"Your father said you were a drain on the family. That your mother was not herself anymore." Annie paused. "He wanted back the young woman he'd married."

I sat right against Annie. Our legs brushed; her shoe touched mine.

"He didn't want a child who saddened her."

"No."

"He didn't want sickness."

"Not all the time."

Annie put her head down on the suitcase, and I stroked her hair. Once, twice, three times I stroked that rough hair, and then she took my hand in hers and held it, like old times. Finally she said, "The strange thing was, I found your father's eyeglasses two weeks later, high atop the bookcase out back. Did you have anything to do with that, Helen?"

"I hid them there."

"What on earth for? They were covered with coal dust. Your mother had to use kerosene to get them clean."

"She'd been crying, and I knew it was because of me. So I hid his glasses. If he couldn't find her next time, he couldn't throw things."

"You didn't need to be exposed to that."

"You wanted to keep me from suffering."

"Yes."

"So you took me to see that furnace, to get me out of the house."

"I'll never forget that monstrous heat. That day you said, 'Did the sun fall?'"

"That's what I imagined."

"That's what I feel like now. My husband has left me, had a baby. I have damned tuberculosis and am going away. I don't know if I'm coming back."

"If you go, who will take care of me in the future?"

She patted the suitcase, and I felt the *ssnnaap* as she fastened it shut.

"I'm contagious," she said. "Starting now, it's best to keep your distance."

I felt dizzy.

"If there is a future," Annie said, "it's something I can't see."

Chapter Twenty-seven

Ssssssuuuuuup ssssssuuuuup. Lying in bed that night I felt the *thump-ca-thump* of a car coming up the driveway; I drowsed again and was awakened by the ping of rock against my bedroom window. Peter, agile but afraid of heights, had climbed the rickety rose trellis on the side of the house. When I slid open the window he climbed in. The rose thorns had torn at his sleeves.

"I heard about Annie. John called to rant and rave about her taking his things."

"You talked to John?"

"He's really steamed. Said she had no right." But then Peter must have felt my hand stiffen, because he stopped. "Helen, they had the baby two days ago. Now the house is all torn up and he . . ."

I stood still.

"I should stop, shouldn't I?"

I said nothing.

"No, I shouldn't have started. Helen, I'm sorry. It turns out Annie called John this afternoon—"

"She told him about the TB before she told me?"

"You were . . . tied up."

"Oh." A wash of pleasure ran through me.

"She said she was sick, he had to come home, to take care of you like he used to."

"She did? What did he say?"

"He said he has a baby now, and can't leave. But Helen, you've got me."

"I've got you. But Mother threatened to take me to Alabama if Annie was sick."

"She's probably booking you passage on the SS *Savannah* as we speak. But if she does take you south, don't worry. I'll take you off the boat in Georgia. I've got a minister friend in Florida who will marry us. I'll take you there and we'll wed." I felt a click as a light in the hallway went on, signaling someone afoot. He spelled even faster, "But your mother's not taking you anywhere. Our license is ready in two weeks, anyone at Boston City Hall can marry us. You, me, two weeks from now. Are you in?"

"I'm ready." As he started to climb down the trellis, footsteps neared in the hallway. I leaned over and kissed him and he pulled away.

Stay with me. Stay.

The next morning I plummeted out of a dream of Annie, myself, and John Albert Macy living in the Wrentham house like a family. Then I remembered it was the day to go to Boston and hastily got dressed. The sudden thump of Peter's car bumping up the gravel drive at six a.m. made me find my way quickly down the hall, and as I reached the first floor and the front door closed behind me, I knew I had won.

No one could stop me now.

I leaned against the window the first half-hour of the long train ride to Boston, even when Peter tried to tug me out of my seat by the window to come with him to the sleeper car at the far end of the train. "You need rest," he said. But it wasn't rest I was after: I needed balm for my bruised heart. I had the urge to race through getting my marriage license in Boston, skip the rally on Boston Common, and get back to Annie.

"Why so blue? Come on," Peter said, pulling me away from the window. "Annie's a fighter. She'll be back in Boston in a month, she'll shake this thing." Peter suddenly stood up. "I'm still learning this secretary trade. I got us the tickets to Boston but I forgot to bring food. Coffee? Rolls? The club car's open."

I reached for my bag and pulled out my wallet.

"No, Helen. We're going to get our marriage license. For God's sake, I can pay for a couple of sweet rolls."

"You're my sweet roll."

"Sweet I'm not."

"Right. You're actually quite tart."

"You're the tart," he laughed, and I felt him nuzzle my bare neck. A flood of memories came to me from the cherry tobacco scent of him opening me, opening.

I leaned back in my seat, remembering how Peter had pushed my cream-colored skirt to the floor. Peter's hand drifted to the inside of my thigh.

"We're in public." I pushed his hand, reluctantly, away.

"We'll have a good trip back." I felt his warm hand on my back. "I've booked us a sleeper. So let's get some food and eat. You're going to need your strength."

The train windows vibrated, and cold air scented of granite, water, and steel swooshed into the car, telling me we passed over a bridge, a river swirling far below. I tried to act calm when Peter slid back into the seat next to me; the metal tray he held out was cool to my fingers. "I've brought breakfast. Just toast and coffee. Now open up." He handed me a cup of coffee.

"Swallow, missy. Open up and swallow."

The coffee's warmth flooded through me, and when I took a bite of toast I tasted the bittersweet tang of marmalade.

"That's my girl. Eats like a horse, even under stress."

"Peter."

"Well, it's true, isn't it? Didn't you tell me you've never been sick a day in your life?"

"Yes, except the day I went blind and deaf." I brushed my hair behind my ears.

"Sorry. It's just that, well, you're so damned robust."

"Annie's always been the susceptible one."

"Helen, you're not going to like this, but John doesn't even think Annie *has* tuberculosis. He says he knows Annie, and he's seen her with these coughs before. Doctors misdiagnose things all the time. Helen, I know you're worried—who wouldn't be? But keep your eye on the ball, here. It's possible she's just sick—run down—and that a few months in the tropics will . . ." He paused.

"Will what?"

"Well, let's just say that a little time in the sun might help her get ready for whatever comes next."

I thought at that moment that no matter how healthy Annie might be when she returned to Wrentham she'd still have to come home to the reality of John's mistress and their newborn baby, but the fact that I'd married Peter behind her back would be the biggest betrayal of all.

The train raced down the tracks, then the Pullman's whistle shirred the air three times, loudly, shaking us. "South Station," Peter said, squeezing my hand.

When we clambered off the train, the metal steps clacking beneath my low-heeled shoes, the air was filled with the scent of leather briefcases from commuters rushing past, of pretzels and ham sandwiches from open lunch stalls, and then the sudden rush of chill air as someone, far off, opened the great doors to the streets of Boston.

"Where are we going? What do you see?"

All around us, Peter said, war posters gleamed from the station's walls: "Patriots! Use cornmeal! It Saves Wheat!" urged a green and red one; "Buy a Bond of the Liberty Loan and Help Win the War!" shouted another.

"Look at that messy pack of kids. Italians, I'll bet," Peter said. He described the vast crowds of immigrants, most of them clutching straw baskets filled with matches, their voices a kind of strange music in the vast hall.

"Oh, perfect," Peter said.

"What?"

"Here comes one of the mothers, barreling toward us. She's left her six kids sprawled on a bench, and she's got her baby rocking in a sling in her arms. Jesus, she's almost here. Let's get a move on."

Within seconds I smelled the sharp scent of talcum powder and felt the woman's hand sticky from a pear she had been feeding the child.

Peter tried to pull me away, but I resisted. "Yes, she's Helen Keller." Then to me he said, "You won't believe this: she wants you to touch the baby for good luck. Is she crazy?"

"People do it all the time," I said. "Once a lady in Wrentham came to King's Pond just to swim where I'd been. She said she wanted to be in the 'angel water.' "

"You're kidding."

"No. They think I'm a miracle. That's what people want, some of that. So if she wants me to hold the baby, please, yes."

People believed something magic would be theirs if they touched me. Yet Peter knew, as few did, the price of that miracle: I always needed a constant companion, someone with me, day, night, day— to dress me, lead me through strange rooms, protect me from harm, even at a cost to themselves. It's why Annie once said, "I sacrificed my life so Helen could have one."

I wanted to be like that mother, my own hands sticky with pear juice. So when she gave me the child I pulled its warm body close in my arms, and when it bit me, hard, I welcomed the sting. "Is she beautiful?" I asked Peter, my arms cool after he handed the baby back.

"Most babies look the same, squashed faces, kind of like pups. Even John's daughter—"

"You saw her?" I stood still.

"John couldn't get to the hospital without me. Two nights ago— he called me when Myla was in labor; I gave them a ride. You didn't think he'd have cab fare, did you?"

"Was he . . ."

"Drunk? Couldn't tell."

"That should have been Annie's girl."

"Judging by the circles under John's eyes, and the thinness of his wallet, Annie's better off. It'll be no picnic raising that kid."

"Peter."

"It was right up the street, in fact. Charity ward at Boston Hospital. You wouldn't believe the scene. If you want to know the truth, Helen, John tried to call Annie that night. Right after Myla gave birth. He went to a pay phone—I know because I had to lend him a nickel."

"But Annie never heard from him."

"I know. The minute after he dialed her number he hung up. He had to go back to Myla and the baby."

"Of course. Babies need attention."

"As far as I can tell they don't leave time for much else." He lifted my bag, smoothed my hair, and turned me toward the exit. "Come on, lady, we've got a speech to give in a half hour and a marriage license to track down after that. I can barely keep track of you, and you can barely afford me. Thank God we don't have another mouth to feed."

"How right you are," I lied.

The space around us seemed suddenly too large. Peter led me toward the exit; crossing the station, he eagerly grasped my hand.

He hurried me past the children crowding the doors, his whole body pressed forward to get outside, fast.

"So, Helen, if you ever have a . . . scare. . . you'll talk with me, right? If you're in trouble?"

"You mean pregnant?"

"Yes."

"Peter, do you think there's anyone more important to me than you?"

"What matters is that we're married."

"Now you're talking," I said.

"We'll live in Wrentham, cut our expenses, let Annie recuperate."

"That's a picture I like."

I lied so easily, to keep him with me.

Peter turned the revolving door, stepped in with me, and in the crush of people we were swept out to the sidewalk with the city roaring around us. Peter drew in his breath: away we walked, into the sunshine of the day.

Chapter Twenty-eight

❦

We had outwitted Mother. Annie was too sick to push Peter away. But the events that would start to unfold in Boston would prove that the future was out of our hands. We were too delirious with happiness. Peter hailed a cab outside South Station, and as we sped through the Boston streets I rolled down the backseat window to inhale the city's dense air. The thrum of hundreds of people, the odor of trolley cars and warm brick buildings made me giddy. As we swung closer to downtown I suddenly sat up straight: the car's engine vibrated at a red light.

"Catholic," I said. "A wedding."

"What are you babbling about?" Peter edged closer to me on the warm backseat.

"Church. It's a Catholic church across the street, right?"

"Yep."

"And there's a wedding party. They've just come out onto the steps."

"Right again."

"The door's wide open and the bride's holding lilies."

"You're a . . ."

"Genius," I said. "Did you think I can't tell what's going on outside? It's the incense." I told him that's how I recognize a Catholic church, by the aroma of incense and palm, its open door giving off a different scent from the Episcopalians, whose churches smell of cool marble, leather books, and mothballs.

"St. Peter of Columbine." Peter read the sign outside the church. "They're flowing out after a midday mass. Too happy to be Episcopalians. This is perfect," he laughed. "The divine Miss Keller can tell what kind of buildings we pass. What next? You'll drive the cab?"

"Why not? We just passed the Trinity Church—the Episcopalian church—three blocks back. It's across from the Boston Public Library. Annie and I gave a talk there last spring. We're on Boylston Street, and soon we'll come to Boston Public Gardens; the Boston Common is just beyond it." I felt the cab lurch forward, and then turn left. I leaned into Peter as we moved closer to the Common.

"All right, smarty. Thanks for the guided tour." Peter handed me a Braille copy of my speech. "We've got ten blocks to go, so let's get a little work in. Let's run through it one more time." He inhaled the fall air.

"I don't want to talk about speeches. I want to talk about weddings. Yours and mine. I'll wear white."

"There might be a problem with that." Peter laid his hand on my thigh.

"Are you saying I'm not pure?"

"I'm saying you're the purest thing I've ever seen."

At times what I say or do is turned against me. In 1891, when I was eleven, I sent Michael Anagnos—the head of the Perkins School for the Blind—a gift that would change me forever. I'd written a story called "The Frost King." Anagnos couldn't wait to publish it to national acclaim: "Look at blind and deaf Helen Keller! She can write; she can create; she is not what blind and deaf people are thought to be!" He claimed my story was astonishing.

But soon enough he and the Perkins School charged me with plagiarism: the story was too close to one published years ago. Had Annie read me the story when I was a child? Had I inadvertently thought the story was mine? Had I, in my dark and silent world, made the words my own, because words were all I had?

At Perkins, Annie and I were led into a classroom to face a panel of eight officers of the school. Annie was asked to leave; I faced my interrogators alone. The blood throbbed at my temples and I could hardly answer during the hours of questioning: Was I a liar? Had I stolen the story? Did I know those words weren't mine? Even worse: Had Annie put me up to this, for fame and renown?

I wished I could have disappeared into the sky.

I wished Annie hadn't burned with disappointment.

I wished not for what people thought I wanted—sight, sound. I wished only to speak for myself and to not be a burden cursed with pleasing those who carried me. And if I made a mistake, would Annie, and others, leave me? If I was isolated, how would I live?

God forbid I should utter a mistaken word.

That night, after I'd been sent home from Perkins, I lay in my bed, weeping. I've said in my books that I wept as I hoped few children had wept. I felt so cold, I imagined I should die before morning. I can say now, as I've said before, that if this sorrow had come to me when I was older, it would have broken my spirit beyond repair.

Later I learned that the board had voted and were tied; Anagnos cast the vote in my favor, to exonerate me. But I never wrote a story again. I watched my words carefully: one mistake and my reputation would be shattered. I was an acorn, a snowflake, a leaf a man could hold in his hand, easily broken.

"We're almost there, Helen," Peter spelled to me. From the cab's open window I smelled the pond water from the swan-boat area in the Boston Common. I inhaled the scent of Peter's tobacco. His warmth comforted me. Soon we would marry; Peter would protect me. I would help him write and publish. No one would get in our way.

I turned toward him and spelled into his hand. "I can't wait to be alone with you."

"Not long, my pet. We've got a sleeper car for the train back."

"But I'm not tired."

"Me neither." Peter brushed my leg with his hand, and I moved closer to his scent of musk, tweed, and smoke. But the cabdriver must have turned around to stare. Peter shifted away.

"It's going to be a knockout, that speech of yours. It'll be all over the press."

"Perfect. No one will suspect we're about to sneak off. They'll be too busy talking about Helen Keller, the rebel girl. Taking on President Wilson in her speech, no less."

"He deserves to be taken on. We have no right to be heading toward war . . ." His palm warmed under my fingertips. "And you're just the girl to do it."

"I'm not a girl."

"Sorry. You're a beautiful woman. And you'll knock it out of the park today. I'm betting on you," Peter said.

"I'm not a gambler." I dropped his hand.

"Well, I am, Miss Keller." He took my hand back. "And you're a sure thing."

I wasn't always a sure thing. After the plagiarism scandal at Perkins I had felt hollowed out, bereft. Annie brought me back to Tuscumbia. But even there, a cloud of suspicion hung over me. All that broiling summer Annie spelled into my hand, but I wouldn't respond. A rage twisted inside me. A feeling of a hand slipped over my mouth. No one—not Annie, not Mother or Father—could reach me.

But I was not entirely alone.

Listless, I sat on the front porch. Daily, the servants plodded across the floorboards and gave me water, or porridge hot and sweet. Humiliation still burned in me. But as their footsteps faded across the porch, I sat up. I suddenly knew: we—the servants and myself—I'm ashamed to say it, were in some way the same.

Even though the South had lost the Civil War, families like ours were still on top. Our servants were descended from slaves. They were powerless, trying to find their way after the war, forced to build gaiety out of sorrow. But so was I. Like them, I was invisible, vulnerable, easily shamed: a self-hatred burned at our core.

Later that fall Annie wrote to Michael Anagnos at the Perkins School that I was "restored to myself." But that wasn't true. I wasn't restored to myself. I was different. From then on I knew that my life would be dedicated not only to the blind in later years, but also to anyone who was vulnerable, unable to speak.

My lot would be to side with the marginalized.

I was no longer frozen in my grief. I had a voice, and I intended to use it.

Even so, as the cab lurched up the steep hill of Beacon Street toward the rally, I became unsure, even panicked. What Peter couldn't know, not in the caustic way I had to learn, was that my success as an advocate for others had its price: loneliness. I'd been isolated from the deaf-blind community: they called me a plaster saint, because my successes were held up to them as impossible feats that only I could achieve. One deaf-blind man, very successful, found a statue of me at his place of work and promptly hid it.

I will never fully belong to any world. Not any. But I refused to be isolated. I was defiant, ready to break into a new life. Still, when Peter put the Braille copy of my speech in his pocket, I was more determined than ever not to be left alone. "Did I ever tell you that I once said any man who married me would be marrying a statue?"

"I love art," Peter spelled into my open hand.

The cab stopped, and Peter pulled out his wallet to pay. I felt his hand waver, then go still.

"Let me." I slipped my wallet into his hand. "Why don't you hold on to my wallet while we're here. It's so easy to lose."

"And you're so easy to see through." Peter handed back the wallet. "I'll take the cab fare, since this is official Helen Keller business, but carrying around a wallet embossed H.K. just doesn't suit me."

"It's just that . . ."

"Helen, you have more money, and you're more famous. It's something I can't forget."

Peter said the Massachusetts Statehouse loomed on our left, with its dignified brick facade and shining gold-leaf dome, and a statue standing on the side lawn.

"Ah, Miss Anne Hutchinson, a woman after my own heart. An early Boston colonist, hmm, in the 1700s, no—" Peter paused. "Okay, the plaque says she was around from 1591 to 1643." He put his arm around my waist.

"I know my history."

"You didn't go to that fancy school for nothing. But just for once, Helen, let me be the fountain of wisdom." Peter said Anne Hutchinson actually believed she had the right to express her own views; she told those Puritan boys there were other ways to think. "That riled them up: she was expelled from Massachusetts for preaching her own beliefs. She was a smart aleck."

"Like me?"

"Absolutely. People were drawn to her. She raised their hackles. In the 1600s she said women's souls were as important as men's—"

"She was right about that," I said.

"Even had prayer meetings just for women at her house—a regular rabble-rouser, like you, Miss Keller."

"And what did she get for it?"

"The usual. Banishment from proper society—sent to what's now

Rhode Island to live her life in exile—and an early death." Peter tightened his hand on my waist.

"Lovely."

"Don't forget, they made a statue of her, to remind everyone of her virtues."

"Statues are for smashing." I opened the door.

Chapter Twenty-nine

❦

The vibrations of a marching band shuddered up my calves as Peter and I stepped out of the cab. In the chill wind of Boston Common Peter took my arm and guided me along the sidewalk, where I felt the streams of people pushing past.

"What's going on?"

"It's unbelievable. There's a whole marching band, fully suited up, blaring their horns and beating their drums right down the middle of Beacon Street, and, wait, behind them a regiment—looks like an army regiment. There must be six, ten, no, twelve columns of kids—boys, really—all suited up in uniforms. Volunteers, ready for the slaughter." Peter pulled me back from the crowd.

"But isn't it the day of our rally?"

"You got it, sister. How handy that they're out marching, to remind the faithful of the importance of war."

"Don't call me 'sister.' " I pulled his hand under my coat.

"Right. Mrs. Fagan, I should have said."

I walked by Peter's side into Boston Common.

"Banners everywhere," Peter said. "Extolling the war. And the boys—they look fifteen, eighteen, like babes, really—gawky, chewing gum, tramping past—are they in training? Wait, yes, Boston Reserves Unit 18. They're part of this clamor for young guys to get ready in case we go to war. Preparedness, that's Wilson's whole idea: let's get a hundred and fifty thousand young men into the army and ready to die."

As they tramped past in their heavy army boots, I inhaled the oily scent of their guns. The European war was coming closer.

"It's unbelievable," Peter's hand spelled rapidly. "Wilson's campaigning for reelection with the slogan 'He Kept Us Out of War.' But he signed the National Defense Act last June, remember? Now he's building up the national guard to four times its size, says he'll make our navy as powerful as any in the world, and has these high school kids out in droves as recruits for the army. Tell me, Helen, exactly how is he keeping us out of war?"

"Our whole country is blind," I said.

"You said it. Don't they read the newspapers? Over one million soldiers killed in the battle of the Somme since July—one battle, Helen, and one million dead. And it's still going on."

"Are people clapping?"

"Oh, only about two hundred prowar people—they're crowding the sidewalks, cheering these poor kids on. The traffic on Beacon Street's stopped to let them cross."

"What else?" I shook Peter.

He said that across Park Street throngs of protesters held signs, chanting against the war. "And the sidewalks are crammed with the usual reporters, gawking at the whole scene. There's O'Rourke, and Danson . . ."

"The ones who came to my house?"

"The very same. O'Rourke's a real troublemaker. Let's steer clear."

Peter led me across the street; I was set to talk in five minutes, but someone pulled my sleeve.

"Great," Peter said. "The boys from the *Globe* have caught up with us. They want to ask you some questions before you go onstage. Danson is first. Watch out for him—he's a joker."

"Fire away."

"All right. He asks if you can tell the color of his coat?"

"It's blue."

"Wrong. He says it's black."

"Well if he knew, then why did he ask me?"

I felt laughter in waves. But then the air turned heavier.

"O'Rourke's asking your take on the war."

"Tell him President Wilson is as blind as I am."

Then Peter leaned forward, his hands tense. "O'Rourke's a real crank. He says you have no right to speak here, no right to speak out against the war."

"What he means is how can I, blind and deaf Helen Keller, have any thoughts worth hearing about something I can't see. That's his point, isn't it?"

"Yup."

"Let me finish his sentence then—I've heard it only about a hundred times before. He's saying, 'Has Miss Helen Keller experienced war? Has she seen the battlefields, heard the soldiers' cries?' He wants me to stay away from topics of national interest and stick to the sole topic allowed me: blindness. Am I right?"

"Right as always, my pet."

America's leading newspaper editors said over and over that because I was deaf and blind I could have no real knowledge of politics and the world. When I wrote about anything besides blindness or deafness they said, "Why, Miss Keller, thank you for your lovely article on the state of our economy. But we don't want to hear your opinions on labor, jobs, or peace. Better minds than yours are working on those subjects. But please, won't you enlighten us on what it's like to live in the dark?"

Do they think that just because I can't see or hear I don't have a brain? I am trained to think, and unlike most editors I know, I can do so in five languages. I read papers daily in German, English, Italian, and French. I've read both Marx and Engels in German Braille. I dare any of them to surpass that.

I felt O'Rourke's footsteps on the sidewalk.

"Peter," I said, "ask Mr. O'Rourke if he has read *Le Monde* lately? I certainly have. Would he like me to update him on firsthand reports from the front?"

"He says he doesn't speak French."

"Oh, then maybe the report from yesterday's *Der Spiegel*?"

"No, not German either."

"A shame. Tell him it's easier for me to learn about the world because I can read all night in the dark."

O'Rourke's footsteps were behind us when suddenly Peter moved away and I stood alone, unanchored, with the crowds of people bumping and jostling past me. When he returned he took my arm. "The coast is clear. That O'Rourke kept buzzing around. I told him to get lost."

"You're my hero."

"But do you know what O'Rourke said next?"

"No."

"He said that I'm the one who's lost."

"He's just jealous."

"Of what?"

"He's chasing you for a story while you're heading onto the stage with me."

"Right. I'm next to the beautiful Helen Keller while he's filing stories people stuff in windows all winter to keep out the chill."

The cheers of the crowd were so strong, I felt them in the air as we approached the stage area. "Jesus, Helen, they're stamping their feet. The crowd is all riled up, and I've got to get through this mess. Let's take a minute." We stepped off the path and moved behind a grove of trees. "Helen, my dear, if I get you through this I believe I deserve a raise."

"A raise? How about this." I stood on tiptoe and kissed him.

"Well, that's one kind of raise. But I meant the cash kind. Do you realize what I need to do before we leave here today?"

"I have the feeling I'm about to find out . . ."

I felt him tick his fingers together. "I'll strong-arm my way through your adoring crowds, then call out your words from the stage. When it's all over I'll get you out of here safely."

"Your work never ends."

He plunged through the crowd, me by his side, and we began to climb the stairs to the stage. "Watch your step. I'd hate to see you get hurt."

But neither of us would come out of this unscathed. I had violated my word to Annie, lied to Mother, and Peter had become something of a joke among some of the reporters. But I was at his mercy. If he had regrets, I couldn't bear to hear them. So I turned and smiled at him. "Lead on," I said, and he lifted me, in one fell swoop, over the last step and onto the wooden stage.

As I spelled my words to Peter he called them out to the crowd. "Rumors have begun to spread about this war," I said. A wave of applause rippling, moving the air. "Rumors that this war is just, that it is necessary, or called for, for us to intervene in the lives of other people when they have the right, the need, to stand on their own two feet."

"Helen," Peter spelled rapidly. "You're departing from our speech. The one we wrote together in Wrentham." But I went on pressing my words into his palm.

"These countries were our friends, and we respected their independence," I said. I stood still while Peter repeated the words, then I went on: "Then the imperialists came in, demanding they bow down. It is their *right* to determine their own futures, their *right* to make decisions on their own." I felt Peter's arms as he began to rouse the crowd. "It is our absolute *need* to let them determine their own futures, whether we like their futures or not."

"You tell them, Helen."

The audience burst into rousing applause.

On stage I am the center of the universe. Wherever I am—Boston Common, Carnegie Hall, or under the burning sun of Colorado's Rockies where dust swirls and wind whips my face—on stage I am in control. Yes, I still need a guiding hand's help to cross a strange room, to comb my hair, to put on the right clothes, to leave the stage gracefully. Yes, I need Peter or Annie to translate my words, to make them ring out to the crowd, but it is the one place where I am surer of myself than any other. It's the place where I have a voice, and with any luck it would soon be Peter's most important place, too. Beside me.

Applause flowed over us and Peter held my hand tight. The thrum of floorboards told me the crowd was inching closer. "Let's get a move on, missy. We'd better make a run for it, or they'll keep us here all day."

"Yes, boss." A jolt of happiness running through me.

"Hold on." I felt him wrap his arms around me, leading me down the back steps to avoid the crowd. But they surged forward so forcibly that even with Peter protecting me, when we pushed our way through them behind the stage, they tore at my dress. Peter tried to push people back, but the crowd was too much for one man. I felt the press of people around me, and I felt myself about to fall. Finally, two strong hands on my shoulders and I was pushed free of the crowd.

"You're my hero," I exhaled.

"They're your heroes," Peter said.

"Who?"

"The policemen lined up outside. They got the crowd under control; they're keeping this rowdy bunch of Keller worshipers at bay. Not me. I could use a cup of coffee," Peter said. "There's a café right across the street." He hustled me into the café, where we sat across from each other.

"Peter. Let's get married, today, here."

"What? You want to take your sacred vows in a coffee shop?" He laughed.

"No. At Boston City Hall. We'll be there for our license and—"

"The license takes two weeks. It can't move any faster than that. As soon as it comes to your house in the mail, believe me, Helen, we'll marry."

But I had the distinct sense that if it didn't happen now, something would prevent it. "It has to be today," I repeated. "Can't you . . ." I fumbled in my purse, found my leather wallet. "Here."

"Why, Miss Keller, are you trying to buy me?"

I pulled out a twenty-dollar bill. I always kept one tucked into my wallet for emergencies.

"Or are you asking me to bribe a public official?"

"I'm asking you to . . . make things happen."

"I'm shocked at the things you know."

"No, you're not." I slid my hand into his pocket. "Peter, today, if you can."

"A Socialist I am, a lawbreaker I'm not. Sorry, Helen. We'll wait two weeks, then we'll tie the knot."

Was Peter stalling? No. I was the one who needed to move fast. Because Peter couldn't foresee what life would really be like with me. Caring for me every day might begin to seem like a burden. How I wished, for one moment, to be a regular person, less of a responsibility, "normal."

And at that point Peter did not really know the toll I would take on him. The longer we delayed, the more likely he would realize. I could not take that chance.

I wanted him to marry me before he found out.

Peter led me through the coffee shop door.

Chapter Thirty

Breathless, Peter and I climb Boston City Hall's granite steps, our coats whipped by the wind. As we cross the slippery hallway tiles the fact that soon I will have a license to marry makes me so dizzy that I grip Peter's hand. When he pushes open the door to the city clerk's office I smell cigar smoke, must from old filing cabinets, and the tang of typewriter ink.

"Right this way, lawbreaker." Peter leads me to the counter. "I'll have this filled out in a jiffy." I hold on to the cool edge of the counter while Peter fills out our marriage license. When it comes time for me to sign it he pushes the paper across the counter. There is a pause as he hands the application back to the clerk, then says, "Oh, great. Another Keller fan."

"What? Someone's followed us here from the rally?"

"No, it's this McGlennan, the clerk. He says he saw you raising money for the blind in downtown Boston—hold on, when? Oh, back in 1905. He still remembers it because when you spoke, the women in the audience cried, and the men had to look away."

"As long as they looked in their wallets, that's all right with me."

"You're a stellar fundraiser, promoting goodwill around the world."

"I'm an international beggar."

"I'll make you beg."

"Seriously, Peter, if this McGlennan knows who I am, he needs to promise to keep our marriage license a secret."

"I've already asked him. He can't—or won't—keep it quiet." Peter's hand felt tense in mine.

"What do you mean? He'll sell it to the highest bidder?"

"A marriage license is public information. According to McGlennan, if anyone asks for it, he's obligated to show them the application. But if no one asks, well then we're two free birds." Peter looped his arm through mine. "It's okay, no one saw us come in here—I looked. We're fine. We'll return in two weeks for the license. Now let's get back to Wrentham before anyone sees us."

We slipped out into the warm Boston sunshine. "Wait here," Peter said. "I'm going to get a cab." One minute passed, then two. I put my hand on a cool marble pillar of the building to steady myself—under my feet the sidewalk trembled from the subway beneath the street. When his footsteps thudded back across the pavement minutes later, a familiar scent made me take Peter's arm.

"He's back." I held my coat closed against the wind.

"Who?"

"O'Rourke."

"How do you know?"

"He's a drinker. I can smell whiskey a mile away."

"If you're quick on your feet we can get in the cab. Too late. He's coming toward us."

Peter turned from me to talk to O'Rourke.

"What does he want?" I took Peter's hand.

"He's yammering away about what we're doing here. Were we at City Hall? Why were we in McGlennan's office a few minutes back? 'Miss Keller,' he wants to know, 'are you planning on marrying?'"

"If Mother finds out . . ."

"You forget, Helen. Reporters are trained to tell stories. I just told him we've never been to City Hall."

"You denied it?"

"One hundred percent. I said we have no intention of marrying.

I am your humble servant, that's all. That's why I'm accompanying you on this trip to Boston."

"You're not humble."

"True, but he doesn't need to know that. Now let's get going before he snoops around even more."

We sat together awkwardly in the cab all the way to the train station. "If he files a story, it would run . . ."

"Tomorrow. Otherwise, we're safe. You're important, Miss Keller, and yes, the world is hungry for news about you, but there's this little thing called a war going on, and let's see." I felt Peter check his watch. "Today's the third. President Wilson is scheduled to give a press conference tonight, and whatever he says, I guarantee you, will be all over tomorrow's papers, upstaging any story that says 'Helen Keller to Wed.'"

"You're sure?"

"Yup. I'm sure there will be no newspaper story about you."

"No, you're sure about today's date?"

"Positive."

A wave of happiness ran through me, but not for the reason Peter thought.

From the time I was fourteen, cramps sent me to bed the first week of every month because of "female troubles." If I had a speech scheduled during those times, I canceled it. If I had classes, Annie let me stay home and rest in bed. So in the two days after Peter and I were alone in the cabin by the pond, I should have felt that familiar cramping, but nothing had happened. I began to think that I might be pregnant. I could have everything: Peter, marriage, a child.

Nothing felt as wonderful as that moment. Annie had told me stories about women who had children after giving themselves to a man only once. I still remember how she paced the hall of our house when she told me this, berating herself because after over ten years of marriage to John she never got pregnant. Mother said women like me should never have families, that God had given me a special role to play in life. But since I'd met Peter, I didn't want to be a saint anymore. Maybe, just maybe, a miracle had happened.

A thrill, a feeling of new grass, hot stars, moved through me.

After we boarded the train home he led me down the swaying corridor to our sleeper car. I held on to the seat backs as we walked, but the train swayed so much that I stopped. "Peter, I have to . . . sit down for a minute." I felt so close to him when he led me to a seat, and tucked a blanket over me because of the window's chill. In that warm, closed space with Peter I felt the outside world recede. But as the train rattled farther from the station, he leaned toward me.

"Out with it, lady," he said.

"Out with what?"

"Don't kid a kidder. What are you keeping from me?"

"Nothing."

"Then why are you turning your head to the left, the way you do when you're avoiding something?"

"Well, I am a leftist," I laughed.

"Okay, lefty. Fess up. What's the big secret?"

I wanted to say, "Maybe I'm pregnant," but I knew I shouldn't say anything. I ran my hand through Peter's hair. If I were pregnant I'd need Mother, or Annie, with me once I married, to help raise a child. And the closer that would make me to my mother and Annie the farther away it would take me from Peter.

So I kept it from him. Instead I said, "Mother's done it. She told me last night she's taking me to Alabama next week."

"Just you? Without me?"

"Right. She booked passage on the SS *Savannah*. She said she's had enough of you and doesn't know what to do with me now that Annie's going away."

"Mothers," Peter said.

"Children." I shifted in my seat. "She wants to protect me."

"Protect you? She wants to keep you the size of a flea. And she's made a religion of it."

"Peter, please—"

"Okay." He cut me off before I could say anything. "She's not to be criticized. That bread pudding of hers at dinner last week was fit for a king—but listen, Helen. She wants nothing more than to keep you exactly as you are—outspoken, yes, but not free to be a woman. If she's scheming to sweep you away, then lucky us. We'll move up the date of our escape. We'll marry sooner."

"But the license takes two weeks."

"Not if you've got this." Peter put the honorarium envelope from the rally in my hands.

"It's empty."

"No, it's full—of freedom, my dear."

"I don't get it."

"The honorarium. I spent it for a good cause."

"You gave it to the antiwar people?"

"No. I followed your advice."

"What advice?"

"I've known McGlennan for a while. I've run into him at press conferences at City Hall, mayor's breakfasts, pub crawls. He's always hungry for a little extra cash. He took the twenty, and while he couldn't guarantee some bozo wouldn't get ahold of our marriage license, he did say he could rush the application through . . ."

"I thought you weren't a lawbreaker?"

"I'm not. I'm a lawbender, when I need to be."

"I'll keep that in mind the next time I need a lock picked."

"I don't do break-ins."

"But you've broken me in."

"I have, haven't I." He leaned his knee into mine. "Helen, have I told you . . ." I held my breath. In all our time together, he had never uttered the word *love*. I put my finger to his lips, held it there, as if I could draw the word out.

But this time Peter was the silent one.

So I moved closer. I put my mouth to his ear and slowly moved my lips across his skin. Then, carefully, I spelled *I l-o-v-e y-o-u* into his hand.

He put his mouth to my neck, and with his fingertips in my palm wrote, "Yes, I love you, too." I could hardly hide my pleasure. I instinctively wanted to cry.

Whatever Annie, or even Mother, said, I knew Peter was not an opportunist. He was vulnerable, like me. Because he was a hostage to my fame. Once we were married, people would stare at him, I knew. Whisper about our relationship. Constantly wonder if Peter had taken advantage of me. But they can stare all they like. He knew that and still had reached out to me, across my void, and filled me with pure joy.

Moments passed. Then Peter touched me again. "I'll tell you more when we get to the sleeper car."

I couldn't wait.

"Helen, in the meantime, check your mailbox in the next few days. The license will be here in two, three days at most."

"We'll leave before Mother can . . ."

"Get you under her wing."

"I can't just leave her."

"You can. Do you want her to take you down to Montgomery for the holidays? Let me guess." He leaned back and ran his hand through my hair. "First there's the annual pre-Thanksgiving afternoon where you gals get fussed over by the local women's club, who come in carting tea and little biscuits the size of a child's fist . . ."

"How did you know?" I laughed. "Then Mildred's card party will visit, and on Thanksgiving we'll get up early to see the men before they tramp outside to hunt, coming back close to supper, when the turkey's dried out and we've been alone by the fire for five hours."

"Okay. Is an early wedding to me looking better?"

"Come with me." I took his hand.

"Charmed, I'm sure."

I stood up, a surge of desire moving through me. He'd bribed McGlennan; he loved me; we could leave in a few days, marry, run away. I wanted to get to the sleeper car, fast.

Peter closed the compartment door so it made a solid *thunk*. He turned me around and eagerly pulled my hips toward him. With my hands pressed on the door, I felt his thighs against the backs of my legs. I arched my back as he lifted my skirt. As I raised my hands further up the door, Peter turned me around and put his mouth on my neck.

I began to unbutton my blouse.

"I can see I'm going to have to teach you some manners, miss." Then he led me toward the bed and pounced beside me like a cat. He had my hands above my head. "Gentlemen first." He peeled off my blouse.

I lay back.

"Wait, I've got a treat." I felt Peter move away.

The train was speeding down the tracks.

"Merry early Christmas." He leaped back onto the bed.

"Christmas isn't for six weeks."

"Well excuse me, Miss Pious. But still, I've brought you something."

"What is it?"

"This." Peter helped my hands trace the bottle of oil, then stretched out next to me on the bed. He took off my blouse, then poured the oil on my skin; it pooled there slightly between my breasts and he massaged me, then he pulled my knees apart. My skirt fell to the floor and I felt the heavy, warm press of his hips, as his whole self came in.

Time passed. We tossed together like a world without end, until we both slept; the train swayed over a bridge. I felt Peter tense. "We've missed our stop, my dear. We're goners," he said.

"Oh my."

"We're so far past Wrentham I'll bet you can almost smell the swampy banks of Cape Cod. When we get to the end of the line we'll turn around and go back home."

"Mother's going to kill me."

"You'll die of happiness first."

Again, I raised my hips to him.

Chapter Thirty-one

The night air turned chilly around us when we finally stumbled off the train in Wrentham two hours late. Peter led me to his car, and as we bumped over East Main Street the floorboards felt cold beneath my feet. I knew by the fragrance of the pines, willows, and water that we were nearing my house when I felt the car lurch suddenly to the right.

"What are you doing?"

"Fixing the mirror. You need to freshen up."

"You're joking?"

"Helen, my dear, you're a mess. A gorgeous mess. Your hair's all tangled and your blouse looks like it's not buttoned right."

"No. You're kidding about my using the mirror, right?"

At times Peter seemed to forget about my disability. Hopeful, pre-occupied, he didn't fuss over me. He didn't think, as Annie and Mother did, *What does Helen need next?*—and that freed me. But I worried that he was deceiving himself. His vision of us was too easy. We'd secretly marry in Boston. I imagined fall's chill air, the scent of turning leaves. But how would he get me there? Where would we go after that? How would the two of us make a real life? I rubbed my hands together in my lap, trying to push the thought away.

"Oh. Sorry about that remark." Peter slowed the car, and as we sat together by the side of the road he softly brushed back my hair, and then unbuttoned and rebuttoned my blouse. "Will this be part of my regular job description?" He rubbed my smudged lipstick off with his thumb.

"Absolutely. But don't expect any extra pay."

"If this is work," he leaned toward me, "it's work I really, really like." He slid his hand inside my blouse.

"Drive the car." I slapped his hand away. "Mother's expecting us. We're already hours late."

"Your wish is my command." Peter steered the big car back onto the road.

I've never seen my face. As we bumped up the driveway, I remembered a woman who visited me in my Wrentham house once during a party. She wrote that she saw me standing in my living room, a mirror behind me, and speculated that I was incomplete, unwhole, because I'd never seen myself reflected in a mirror's gaze.

Without a mirror to guide me, she wrote, I twitched and turned, alert to every vibration. I was strange, even startling, with my muscular neck, a pretty beaded ribbon, like a flapper's, round my forehead, but with a lurching, moving body that pieced together the world around me in the strangest of ways.

What she didn't realize is that Mother—and Annie—were my mirrors. They reflected my self back to me: it was through them, their reactions, their words in my palm, that I made myself whole. How could I go into my new life with Peter without that?

"I want to tell Mother," I said.

"And I want to be King of England, but that's not going to happen, either." Peter stopped the car. "Of course you wish you could talk to her, you don't want to betray her, okay. I know. But Helen, it's just two more days. As soon as we're married we'll write her a letter, invite her to . . ."

"To what?"

"To acknowledge that her dear, saintlike daughter has started a new chapter."

"Peter, I can't betray her."

"Helen. You already have."

As Peter led me out of the car, and then up the front steps, I yearned to go to Mother and say I am in love, I crave this man, he has taken off my mask, set me free. "I'm not clearheaded like you. She's my mother. I need her to approve."

"Listen, Helen." We stopped by the front door. "Not a word. There's no need to tell your mother why we're late, or where we've been. You've got a family made of iron, they're so strong, and if you breathe one word about our afternoon she'll see through your mask and whisk you away from me."

"But I . . ." My hand was on the front door.

"Take a deep breath, Miss Keller. Remember that book you wrote, at twenty-two?"

"*The Story of My Life*?"

"Yep. Well, that was the prelude. You're thirty-seven now and about to elope with me in two days."

"I'm ready."

But there was a smaller, more pressing problem. We stood there, Peter touching my coat collar. "The house is ablaze with lights," he said. "That can only mean that Mama Keller is on the prowl, waiting for her innocent Helen."

"And we're so late."

"Not late enough, in my opinion."

"Peter, stop. If Mother asks why we're late, it's because we were meeting with my publisher. I told her I would be doing that today."

"She may not buy it, being that it's Saturday, but stick to your story."

"How do you know so much about lying?"

"Don't call it lying. I prefer the term 'multiple truths.'" He pushed me inside, and when he left me I walked into the house, the memory of his hands warm on my skin.

The living room air smelled damp, full of fall's chill, heavy with the rains of the last few days. Mother took my hand. "Careful. My trunk's by the ottoman." She guided me around it, my left foot grazing the leather corner. "Yours is by the sofa." She led me past the coffee table to a chair by the fireplace. Heat rose toward me from the fire, and the scent of maple came to me as I sat down. It was a relief, an escape from my worries, to sit by the hearth with Mother. She would attend to every detail of my needs. But she was suffocating, too.

"Why all the packing?" I asked.

Mother passed me a cup of tea and spelled, "You seem to have forgotten that we're taking the boat to Alabama soon. Did you think your clothes would pack themselves?"

My heart thumped wildly. I wiped beads of perspiration from my brow.

"By the way, what kept you and Mr. Fagan?"

"I saw my publisher."

"He must have been very keen on your new book." Her fingers tightened.

"Yes."

"He's a hard-working man, to be in the office so late on Saturdays."

"You have no idea how hard he works."

"He wasn't there." Mother's fingers tapped mine. "Your so-called publisher."

"How do you know?"

"Did you think I wouldn't call the office when you were out so late?"

I swallowed hard. "You called?"

"Correct. No one answered."

I said nothing.

"Why on earth did you lie to me?"

I pushed around the biscuits Mother had put on my plate, tapped my fingers restlessly on the table.

"You know I dislike clichés, Helen."

"Yes, Mother."

"But there's one that seems quite apt right now."

"Is it about playing with fire?" I tapped my teaspoon against my cup.

"Yes, and how easily one can get burned," Mother said.

I tapped the teaspoon against my cup.

My mother still saw me as a vulnerable child. Yes, at age five, two years before Annie came, I stood by the living room fireplace in Alabama, searching with my hands for the fire's warmth. Cold, I was so cold, and inched closer to the flames. Then heat, exploding, terrible, searing heat on my arms, my chest, and then Vinny the maid's strong arms around me, pulling me back. My dress had caught some embers, and Vinny wrapped me in a blanket to smother the flames. For nights afterward I dreamed of smoke, my whole body peeling away.

"I'm . . . sorry, Mother."

"This isn't about being sorry, Helen. It's about being irresponsible, about getting hurt. It's about putting yourself—and me, even Annie, in danger. Do you think we aren't looking out for you? Helen? Are you listening to me? Do you remember our last visit to Montgomery?"

"If I don't, I know you'll remind me."

"Annie gone, you were alone in Mildred's guest room. At thirty-two years old you slept soundly even when the heating duct under your bed caught fire."

"Mother, I was fine."

"You were lucky. There was no one there to warn you of the danger, and when you finally woke you were covered with ash."

"I didn't smell the fire."

"You didn't, that's right." Mother pulled away.

I took my hand from Mother's. With her shoulder leaning against mine, we sat together in front of the fireplace. She was determined that I admit my vulnerability, but I was having none of it. Finally she said, "No matter what, we're leaving for Alabama in two days." I just smiled, and for the next hour Mother and I immersed ourselves in packing our suitcases.

She was determined to take me to Montgomery, and I was equally sure that before two or three days had passed Peter would sweep me off to Boston City Hall. Just before I went to bed Mother said, "Annie wants to see you. You'd better get up early. Helen, I know you don't want her to go, but you must face her. She needs you. After all these years she thinks . . ."

"Thinks what?"

"That without John, without you . . . she's no one."

I couldn't tell Mother that Annie's desire to always be with me depended on my life shrinking. I wanted to run.

When I walked down the hallway the next morning, the fragrance of coffee from the kitchen filled the air, but the closer I came to Annie's room, the more I inhaled scents of camphor and cough drops, cloyingly sweet. Outside her door my feet felt heavy. I couldn't do it, knowing that in two days she'd be gone, and I might never see her again. But as I walked into her room and the door thumped shut behind me, I remembered that I was now Helen-and-Peter. I might be having a child, I was a loved woman, I knew the roll and pitch of a man's body, the feel of his racing breath while he held me.

Annie pulled me toward her bed. "Helen, remember this?" She patted her down pillow. We'd stood high above Niagara Falls, all its tons of water churning, pounding below us, and as we stood there Alexander Graham Bell had put a pillow in my arms so I could feel the vibrations of the crashing water even more strongly.

But here in Annie's room there was a different kind of vibration: the slow, slight shattering of air from her cough told me she soon would be gone. So I was startled when she said, "Well, it's official. There's a new mother in the room."

"What?"

"A new mother. John's had a baby, I'm married to John, so even though he'll never let me see the child—not that I want to—I'm a stepmother."

"Annie," I said.

"Do you know what she does?"

Who? The baby?"

"No. Myla. The mother. She's a sculptress."

"I know. Peter told me."

"Peter? You've been talking to Peter about this?"

"He was there, Annie. John asked him . . . the night of the birth."

Annie stood still. "Did John . . . ask for me?"

"I'm sure he did," I said. "And I'm sure he will again, once things have calmed down." I felt Annie rubbing her eyes. She and I both knew the truth: John would probably never ask for her again. He had stopped loving Annie long ago, and was furious with her for not agreeing to a divorce. I curled her hand in mine and touched her nails bitten to the quick. Suddenly I felt sorry for her, Annie who never knew the possibility of having her own child.

"I don't like myself," Annie said.

"Please, don't."

"Do you remember what John said about me? That I never fully acquiesced to the marriage? That I was too busy with you to ever be a real wife?"

"Annie, don't do this."

"He said you were Helen Keller Inc., and I was your chief cook and bottle washer. John was your errand boy, and we revolved around you instead of each other . . ."

"You loved John, and you loved me."

"I did terrible things. I took his damned furniture. Even the baby carriage."

I imagined her heart beating at her throat.

"Listen, Annie. You gave John everything. You even gave him money from our bank account when he needed 'rest' and went to Europe for four months—four *months*, Annie . . ."

"Right." Annie lay back. "While you and I tramped across the country, belting out your story from every sorry stage from here to Timbuktu. Did he think I *liked* doing that? While he was downing Chianti and sleeping till noon in Rome?"

"I understand your rage."

"Do you want to know the worst thing?"

"Not really."

"Good. Because I'm going to tell you anyway." Annie sat up. Bad news energized her, made her more alive. "Now I realize the truth: Myla was with him on that trip. John, my John, that ingrate I devoted my life to, was having a love affair behind my back."

I bit my lip.

"I was busy with you—you needed me, damn it—and he was off in Rome seducing Miss Myla . . ."

"Annie, you're upset. This will only make it worse."

"Make it worse? It helps to know what a bastard he was. Why else would he deceive me?"

"He wasn't all bad. He was—"

"He was a professional deceiver. Look at these." She pulled out a box, its cardboard rough under my hands. "All these postcards." The scent of musty paper filled the room. She put one of the cards in my hand. "This one, it says, 'Annie, Rome is the perfect place for me. Feeling better already. Ciao, John.' "

Inside, Annie had a spring coil, a bit of metal, sharp-edged, that kept people at bay. At that moment I was afraid she would find out about Peter and me: it was only a matter of time until she knew of our affair. But I had the terrible feeling that if she did find out, she'd never, ever let me go.

"Annie"—I rubbed my fingers over the worn postcards—"he left you because he needed you, and you were so devoted to me."

Annie didn't see John as a lover. Not when they first met. No, John came to us when I was a sophomore in college. I had a contract to write *The Story of My Life*, but I couldn't organize my words. Sheets of the manuscript were piled high on my desk, and as my deadline approached, Annie decided I needed help. She found John Macy, a young, snappy Harvard instructor of English. During the day he organized my manuscript, in the evenings he took Annie out into the warm Cambridge night and brought her back so energized she paced the halls till all hours. Ten years younger than she, he was a rabble-rouser, a poet, and a persistent lover: he asked her to marry him four times before she said yes. The three of us laughed when, the week their engagement was announced, a Boston newspaper carried the headline "Helen Keller, ALMOST Wed."

When they married, we three lived in Wrentham, where John helped me pin up the big red Bolshevik flag in my bedroom. He made my life a red flag—bold, outspoken, alive.

I knew the rumors: that John had married Annie because he secretly loved me. Yes, his hand flooded mine with warmth when he spelled Shakespeare to me the days Annie's eyes hurt her too much to read. Yes, we dazzled each other: nights sitting up late, reading John's Socialist newspaper *The Call*, where Margaret Sanger listed her demands for birth control to be made legal. I believed him when he said anything was possible for women. We plotted a move to Schenectady, New York, where he'd be the Socialist mayor and I'd be in charge of helping the poor, and we'd drive to Lowell as strikers flooded the streets, thirty thousand strong. Life coursed through me in those years.

The truth is, I thought of him as my brother. Annie was his lover, his wife.

Yet it was because of Annie's dedication to me that she never fully gave herself to him.

"Don't blame yourself, Helen. Who's here now? You and me. It seems I made the right choice. At least, when I come back—*if* I come back—I'll have a purpose. Helen, we'll go on tour again. The audiences will listen. Because at least we'll still have *your* story to tell."

We were stitched together, the room a small pocket, with little air.

All night I sat beside Annie, wiping the sweat from her forehead, holding a cup of water to her lips when she coughed. With my hands on hers I remembered when I was seven and Annie was my teacher. She was twenty-one and slept beside me in my small bed, and between us every night I placed my doll, Nancy. One morning I woke up and there was only an empty space where my doll should have been. I patted my way across the bed and my hands came upon Annie. She was rocking Nancy, combing her hair. When I reached for the doll, Annie pulled it away.

She played with my dolls many nights, for years.

So I did the only thing I could this night. As she slept, I held Annie in my arms like a child.

Chapter Thirty-two

⟢⟡⟣

It was out of my control, what happened next. Over lunch Mother handed me a letter, but she didn't tell me what it said. "This is no way for you to ring in the New Year," she spelled. I felt the clink of her fork against her plate. It was all I could do to sit still, delicately slicing roast beef, dabbing my mouth with a napkin. It was twenty-four hours away from my wedding day. I could hardly eat, so I was glad for the distraction of the letter.

"What is it, Mother? Read it, please."

"No. You're not going." I felt a wave of air as she pulled the letter away. "You'll be in Alabama with me, anyway. This goes right in the trash." She scraped her chair as she moved away from the table, but I followed her to the kitchen.

"Annie would never, ever, keep something from me. If the letter has my name on it, it's mine. You must read it to me. It's not up to you to decide what I can and cannot see," I spelled into her hand.

No betrayal is greater to me. When another person decides what I should know I bristle with anger. No one is going to tell me how I should perceive the world. I felt Annie's footsteps approaching. "What's going on here?" Annie rapped me on the wrist.

"Mother won't let me read my own mail. I told her she has no choice."

"Helen, don't talk to your mother that way." Then Annie spelled to Mother and me, "Kate, please give me the letter. After all these years I can handle Helen."

I waited while she read. Then Annie said, "Congratulations, Helen. You're invited to speak at Carnegie Hall on New Year's Day. I'm sure all of Manhattan will be there. These antiwar people can't think of anyone better to rouse the crowds against Wilson's war than you, my dear. Too bad you can't go."

"What do you mean?"

"Well, how will you get there, Helen? I'll be coughing up blood in Puerto Rico and you'll be eating mincemeat pie at Mildred's in Alabama. I doubt your mother is going to haul you up to New York, and you can't go alone. Face it, Helen, our days as rabble-rousers and independent women are over."

"That's what you think."

I stood up.

The vibrations of Peter knocking on the front door made me turn from Mother and Annie. Knowing it was he, they both left the room. Alone, I couldn't wait to tell Peter. The money we'd get from the talk in New York might help me keep the farmhouse, if only for a few months; I was sure he'd be thrilled to accompany me to speak out against the United States entering the war with Germany. Yes, he would be my translator on the great stage of Carnegie Hall, my voice, my life.

When he rapidly crossed the dining room to me, I gave him the letter. He read it, and pushed it away.

"That's nothing. Look at this." He pulled out an envelope and put it in my hands.

"Is this . . ."

"The marriage license, yes. It came this morning. Let's get Annie's trunks moved to the front hall and then we'll plan our escape. Helen, dear, let's leave this afternoon. We can be in Boston by two, and be wed by three."

"This afternoon? Peter, Annie's still here. You know I can't . . ."

"Can't what?"

"Leave before she's gone."

"Helen, the longer we stay here, the more likely it is that your mother and Annie will find out, and then we'll never leave at all."

"I'm here until Annie goes. And that's the end of that."

"Yes, boss." Peter withdrew his hand from mine.

I had been special too long. Yes, I was dependent in painful, even excruciating ways, but because of my dependency too many people gave me what I wanted, acquiesced to me, so I got used to having my way. Now I wish I had slipped out the front door with him, and sped to Boston.

I wish I had fled that very instant.

Peter's footsteps faded as he crossed the dining room. I followed him down the hallway, patted my way past Annie's trunks by the front door, and turned to the pantry, where Peter's scent of cigarettes and pine rose from the walls. I crossed the linoleum floor to him.

"What are you doing?"

"Now that Annie's shipping out, my job description has expanded."

"You got a raise?"

"No. I got her most-hated job, taking out the trash." The slight clank of the trash bin's metal lid told me he'd opened it. "Hold your nose, Miss Smell-Sensitive." I felt a thump as Peter deposited the bin by the back door. "Wait a minute." He paused while tying it up. "What's this?"

"What?"

Peter pulled a book from the trash and put it in my hands. "*Most Cherished Baby Names*. Annie must have filched it from John's apartment the night she stole their baby stuff."

"When she got home she must have thrown it in the trash."

Peter paused. "You know what else she brought back from John's? A false sense of what it means to have a child: it's not all cooing and nights around a warm fire."

"You're an expert on fatherhood?"

"I've seen John. The man's rail thin, smoking nonstop, and happy, yes, I'll give him that, but do you think he'll write anything good for the *Herald* now that he's got that kid crying for food day and night? Give Myla two months, a year at most. She'll have John hawking carpets at Filene's department store, his bald spot shining under the lights."

"That's not true."

"Just you watch. By the time the kid's first birthday rolls around John's name will have faded from the newspaper world faster than you can say *papa*."

"So all fathers suffer the same fate? They lose their dreams?"

"Luckily I'll never find out. It's just you and me. Here's to Margaret Sanger and birth control." He pressed me against the back door, his hands suddenly tangled in my hair, his hips pressed into mine.

"Peter, we're in my house. Mother and Annie are right upstairs."

"It's high time you said good-bye to them and, oh, to this house, too."

"This house?"

"Looks like you're going to get a pretty penny for this shack of yours." Peter traced my palm with his fingers. "Annie's found a buyer. With the money we'll get a smaller place. Not a cracker box, Helen, but two bedrooms."

"Two?"

"Yes. Ours." He traced my face and pressed me hard against the door. I held my breath. "And a shared study. We both have work to do."

I took a deep breath. I knew I'd have to share my secret sooner rather than later. I couldn't put it off. I'd tell him when we got to his house; I'd tell him that evening, regardless of what he might say. But as we moved down the back steps Peter still held the book in his hands. The slight movement of air told me he was flipping through the pages, and then he stopped. "Helen," he said, "is it true that your name means 'light'?"

"Read more closely. It means 'brilliant light.'"

"What your mother must have thought when you went blind."

"Why, Mr. Fagan, are you developing a soft spot for my mother?"

"I wouldn't go that far."

I waited, the driveway cold beneath my shoes.

"Peter, what does your name mean?"

"The rock."

"You're steady."

"Yup. And I roll over whatever is in my way."

Nine months, maybe less. I may hold a baby in my arms. I'll spread, grow larger, fast. I'll need new clothes, I'll need to tell Peter that I have no idea how to be a mother, how to care for a daughter or a son. Poor child. All her—or his—life, the center of attention, simply because of me. People will say the child is the next miracle. And Peter and I? Even more delirious with—what? This lightning strike of joy.

Peter opened the trash can, and I felt a whoosh of air as he dropped the book into it. He guided me into a kitchen chair, rattling the table when he sat in the rickety one next to mine, and then pulled my foot into his lap, untied my shoe, and massaged my heel.

"What are you doing?" I pulled my foot away, but he grabbed my arch and held it.

"Checking to see if you have cold feet."

"Very funny. And what about you? No nerves?"

"Why should I worry? Okay, you won't go with me today, but Annie leaves tonight; I've booked train reservations for us both tomorrow morning; a quick ceremony at Boston City Hall and boom—you're Mrs. Peter Fagan. Once we've tied the knot, I'm your legal mate, and no one, not even your dear, lovely mother, will be able to separate us."

"You think of everything. Almost."

"What do you mean, 'almost'?"

"Shall we send out wedding invitations?"

"It's a bit late for that."

"Annie postponed her wedding to John so many times he threatened to write 'Subject to change without notice' at the bottom of their invitations."

"Too bad she went through with it."

"Too bad he left."

"She didn't see what was coming." We moved Annie's trunk to the front hall and sat down. A great sadness filled me, and I don't know why I said this, but I did. "No matter how it turned out, she doesn't have any regrets."

"Helen, that's not true. Annie's never gotten over John leaving."

"Fine. But you said yesterday to always stick to your story, and that's mine. She loved her husband, she tried, and it—"

"Crashed and burned." Peter stacked the small suitcase atop the trunk.

"She had no regrets," I said.

When Peter turned to the hall telephone to order Annie's cab, I stood alone on the rug, my fingers moving as if repeating my words. But when Peter hung up, recrossed the hall, and took my hands, he held them so tight, I couldn't say a thing.

Chapter Thirty-three

Books are the eyes of the blind, I wrote in one of my publications. But nothing I ever read gave me instructions, a manual, on how a woman like me breaks away from her family to start a new life. I had only my desperation to get away, my craving for Peter, my foolish belief that I could have everything normal women had.

Peter released my hands. "Annie's asleep, your mother's napping, too. Helen, I want to be alone with you one more time before we marry. Come to my place this afternoon. We'll have an hour alone, maybe two. We'll be back for dinner . . ."

"No." I backed away. "I'm too nervous."

"Come on. We can practice our lines in the car. I'll say, 'I, Peter Fagan, do take thee, Helen Adams Keller . . .'"

"I know my lines. Let's practice something else." I leaned over and kissed him.

"Ah, a girl after my own heart." He led me across the kitchen, out the back door, and down the steps. I couldn't wait for him to open the car door and start the engine; I couldn't wait to be alone with him, as if it were the first time.

At Peter's house something inside me tipped and spun. The cool scent of fresh water filled the air when we walked in the front door. "Oh, perfect." Peter dropped my hand. "Just what I need. Instead of seducing you, it looks like I'll be repairing a broken water pipe instead." Peter plopped me into a chair by the front window. "Water's spurting from the damned pipe, all over the floor." In moments I felt a *chut-chut-chut* as Peter dragged a wooden ladder across the floor. "Damned cheap house. Flimsy construction. There's a leak in the back hallway, and no one to fix it. This place was probably a slave shack before Annie rented it for me."

"We citizens of Massachusetts never owned slaves."

"You sure did. Whole packs of them in the 1600s and 1700s."

"Well, *I* personally never owned slaves."

"Come on, Miss Born-in-Alabama. The Keller family churned out Southern cotton for centuries. They must have had the help of slaves. Or do I have my history wrong?"

He didn't wait for an answer. He just propped the ladder against the wall and climbed the teetery rungs. I held the ladder in place with all my strength.

I don't see black, white, or even gray, but I've known from a young age that nothing is simple, or clear-cut. Everything has its price. "Did the Keller family own slaves?" Annie asked my father when I was eight. Every night in the Tuscumbia dining room Annie threw herself into a pitched battle with my father about the Civil War. "Yankee horse thief," my father ranted at Annie, refusing to answer. "Coming down here and criticizing our way of life. Why don't you go back where you came from?" He shook his fist at her.

"Fine," Annie said. "I can't wait to be back where people are treated with dignity."

"Dignity?" my father said, as Annie quickly spelled his words into my palm. "You're telling me the North treats its people better than the South does? Listen to me, *Miss* Sullivan. It is Miss, isn't it?"

"You know it is," Annie snapped back.

"Well, Miss Sullivan, we *may* have owned slaves, but we didn't send our white girls, our white women, out to *work*." He said this last word as if it hurt.

I sat by Annie, quivering.

"You think work is a dirty word?" Annie said. "Look around at all your finery. Maybe you didn't work for this, but back in your father's generation some slaves on the Keller plantation certainly did. Why don't you acknowledge that all you have came from the backs of slave labor? *Slaves* made your life of leisure possible. Yes, Captain Keller, I work. *I* don't depend on the labor of others to support me."

My father waited a long time to answer. Then he said, "Why, Miss Sullivan, we lost our money after the Civil War. But the little that's left, yes, some of it came from the old slave-owning days of the South. And that's what makes your paycheck so fat."

Annie said nothing.

"So tell me, Miss Sullivan. Do you still think you're so almighty free?"

I remember Annie shaking with rage in the dining room. Part of her salary, or at least the home she lived in with me, came from a past of which she wanted no part. But since that day, I've understood that nothing is black or white.

I was still holding the ladder. "Peter, we have only an hour together here. Why don't you come down? Call a plumber, that's what Annie and I do when there's a leak."

"Numbers. I want numbers," Peter climbed down and took my hand. "How many times in the past year, when you and Annie didn't have two nickels to rub together, did you call some poor soul to fix something in that rattletrap house?"

"I don't know. Five, maybe ten times."

"And how many times did they get paid?"

"Peter."

"Don't 'Peter' me." He pushed the ladder away and held my hands. "You know as well as I do that Annie either charmed them into doing the job for free or tossed their bills in the trash when they left. Am I right?"

"Peter, you know the answer. But I'm glad she did. Have you seen the bill for Annie's trip to Puerto Rico? She refused to go to that sanatorium in New York. She's rented a cottage outside San Juan, where she says she can rest. So she'll need to pay for the ship, a car, a room, and food for three to six months."

"One thing about being blind, no one ever tells you the cost."

"On the contrary. I know the cost of everything." Maybe that's why the idea of having a child frightened me less than it did Peter. I had my principles, but blind and deaf, totally dependent on others for my life, my sustenance, I knew that nothing came without a price. And I was willing to pay it. If I had to take more money from Carnegie to support myself and this child, well, I would swallow hard and do it.

Peter led me toward his bedroom. "Helen, you're one of the lucky few who make money, and even luckier still because you're about to marry a great guy like me." He shut the door to his room and pulled me to him. "But, Helen, tell me. Just how many deaf-blind women have kids?"

"What?"

"You heard me. How many women just like you—deaf, blind, unable to get around on her own, dependent on a surly teacher—"

"Peter—"

"Or a handsome man to take her around all day and night—how many of those women have kids?"

"Do I look like a walking encyclopedia of the blind?"

"No. You look like a woman who's been dropping hints right and left about children. The day Annie ransacked John's apartment and brought home that baby stroller, I remember you said, 'Peter, what if someday you and I . . .' You didn't finish the sentence, but

I'm a word man, remember? I filled in the blank. 'Had a baby' is what you meant. So what's really going on, missy? Anything I'm missing?" He leaned against the door.

"Peter. The only thing you're missing is the chance to unlace my dress."

"Like this?" He slid his fingers inside my dress.

"Yes."

"And this?" He pulled my dress up over my head, and kneeled down. I arched my back, and he pulled me closer. The warmth of his mouth on the inside of my thighs made me gasp, then I felt his warm breath at the very center of me.

He wrote on my thighs, "This is how fingerspelling was invented."

"For monks to talk during holy hour," I spelled on his neck, his curly hair in my hands. "They didn't want to break their vow of silence."

He slid his mouth closer, and I arched my whole body back and eased him into me. "How would you feel about having a baby with me?" I spelled impetuously into his hand. But he didn't listen, he pressed his hips to mine and the world fell away again.

Later he rolled to the farthest edge of the bed. I stiffened as I lay beside him, afraid of what he'd say. "Helen, I heard you."

"So, what if I were pregnant . . . someday?" I said.

"That would be an unwanted complication." He gave off the scent of a metallic fence, part seaweed, pulling him out to sea. "We can't afford—"

"Can't afford what? The farmhouse is on the market. And Andrew Carnegie sends my pension every month. I told him to keep sending it."

"You did that? Even when you knew I was against it? Well then I'll let you in on some news *you* won't like, either. Did you know that the *New York Times* returned my article about shell shock? They hire prominent journalists, not stringers like me."

"Peter, you know I publish there; I could have gotten you in."

"Don't you get it, Helen? I'm not going to ask you. Not ever. If we have a child we will have nowhere to live, and little money at all."

I moved closer to him, breathing heavily.

"I thought you wanted a child," I said.

"Yes, but not *now*." Something jittery, wrong in his palm. "I'm still draft age, I could be drafted—President Wilson will be calling up troops to fight this war."

"You want a baby," I repeated. "Just not now, or not with me."

My own voice seeped out. Loose like rolling pebbles. I was talking to him, unsure if my speaking voice was pitching up, or down, raw as I was.

He said nothing. I fished in the air for him, my hands touching pockets of emptiness.

All the air left the room. At that moment I understood Annie's self-hatred, sharp as a knife. *I was an unexpected complication.* He did not want a baby, or did not want one with me. Deep inside my body, I felt a tell-tale, familiar cramping.

"I'm not saying never." Peter took my hand. "Just not now."

I pulled my hand away and made a fist.

Peter did not reach for me.

The whole long minute we sat in silence.

"We have a lot to do before tomorrow." He stood up and left the room. I felt the *ssssup, ssssup* of his bare feet on the pine floor.

I got up, slipped on my dress. Peter was in the kitchen making coffee. I sat on the edge of the bed and put on my shoes. The silence around me was deeper than any silence in my thirty-seven years.

Chapter Thirty-four

⊰⊱⊰⊱

As if nothing was wrong, I followed the scent of Peter's cherry tobacco into the kitchen and sat at the table in the corner. Outside a truck rumbled up the road, and the heat of the overhead lamp warmed me, but the heaviness of Peter's footsteps as he rapped across the floor by the stove told me he ached to leave.

So I ran my fingernail over the table's soft wood, and then I rubbed my eyes. Rubbed as if to erase an old, piercing pain, like I was going blind for a second time. But I could not stop what was happening. All I knew was that Peter had teased me into life; I was alive and vulnerable. I could not go back. So I approached Peter, but as I got close enough to feel his warmth the telephone rang. Within seconds Peter hung up. "Just what we need. Your mother is hopping mad. I'm to get you home, now."

"Is it Annie? She's worse?" I pulled my coat around me.

"Something tells me Annie's just fine—ready to head off to Puerto Rico to heal on your dime. No, the contempt in your mother's voice means only one thing: when I drop you off at the front door Mrs. Kate Keller will stand tall outside my car and order me to drive off, never to see you, my dearest, again."

Peter backed his car down the driveway, the wheels making the floorboards shake beneath my feet. I knew I had to soothe him, make easy the rough spots between us. I reached across the front seat, put my hand on his, and said, "About the . . . pregnancy. I'm probably just excited, overstating things, as usual. It's only been two, three days since . . ."

"Since what?"

I said nothing.

"Oh. Your . . ."

I nodded.

"Helen, are you kidding? I'm no doctor, but it's only been two or three days? That's nothing. You're not pregnant. You're probably just . . ."

"Don't say it."

"Overexcited."

"You really mean hysterical. That's what the press calls me when I get all worked up."

"Well, I am a member of the press."

"Indeed."

"And you do get excited."

"Right."

"So this is probably nothing at all." He laid his warm hand on mine. "Come on, Helen. Someday, maybe, we'll have kids, but let a man know he can support a family first."

"Why, Mr. Fagan, you're so old fashioned." I held the door handle as he rounded a corner.

"I'm a man, Helen."

"I've noticed." Maybe he was right, I was just tense. Maybe some distant day we'd have a child.

Driving through Wrentham's streets, I relaxed beside Peter. The tires vibrated on the road as if to say one more day, one more day. Suddenly Peter swerved to a stop. "What's going on? Are we home?" The scent of willows told me we were close to my house, so I reached for the door.

"Not yet, Helen," Peter said.

I don't know how long we sat there together. The scent of

chimney smoke inched into the car. Finally Peter said, "Helen, your mother is a frugal woman, right?"

"Frugal? She invented the word. Why?"

"Because I'm staring up the driveway toward your house, and the whole first floor is lit up. The second floor, too. The damned house is shining like a Christmas tree, and she's standing in the doorway."

"That can't be good."

"Nope. She's got the door flung wide open on a chilly night like tonight . . ."

"Does she see us?"

"Not yet."

"If there's bad news," I said, "I don't want to know it."

"You and me both."

Peter idled the car by the curb. "I'm not letting this Keller clan stop our plans. If anything happens tonight, if we get separated— say, your mother boots me out and takes you to Alabama—don't fret. I'll follow you down to Montgomery. Remember I told you about my minister friend in Florida? I'll whisk you to him and marry you before your mother even knows you've crossed the Alabama state line."

The car shuddered beneath my feet. For the first time I felt real fear slice through me. Peter stroked my hair. "Helen, I'm willing to chase you all the way to Montgomery if I have to, but please tell me that you don't have a passel of gun-toting relatives down there."

"Mr. Fagan. I come from an old southern family."

"My point exactly. Southern families own stacks of rifles."

"Well, Warren collects Smith and Wessons. He keeps them in a showcase on the living room wall."

"Warren? Who's Warren?"

"Mildred's husband. Peter, if you're marrying me you really should learn the names of my family members."

"Okay. Mildred: your loyal younger sister. You adored her—"

"Actually, I was so furious at her birth, so jealous, I tipped over her cradle when Mother was out of the room. Luckily Mother came running back and saved Mildred from falling five feet to the floor."

"So Mildred still nurses a grudge."

"No, she's a soft soul. Kind as the day is long. It's Warren . . ."

"The husband."

"He's the one who holds a grudge. If a Keller woman offends the family honor—"

"Let me guess. He gets his gun and brandishes it until the threat to the Keller honor is gone."

"How did you know?"

"A wild guess. But I hope I never have to find out."

As Peter led me up the driveway and toward the house, all I knew was that I was in love, I might be having a child, and I was suddenly filled with the desire to be comforted, soothed, by my mother. More than ever before I wanted to tell her the truth. "I'm getting married, Mother," I wanted to say. *I need you to know.* So I pulled away from Peter just a bit; as I approached the steps he slowed me down.

"Easy does it. That lady looks spitting mad."

"My mother never spits."

"Well, she reads. She's got today's *New York Times* . . ."

Peter stopped.

"Do you think?"

We both stood on the driveway, acorns beneath our shoes, and I knew. A thudding started in my chest. "Peter." I turned toward him. At the steps, I had a hard time moving my feet.

Peter said, "Whatever happens I'm not going anywhere. We can't let them hold us back."

Then Mother's footsteps tapped relentlessly on the front porch. I was in front of her. She took my hand from Peter's. I was breathless as she rapidly spelled the newspaper headlines.

The New York Times November 18, 1916

HELEN KELLER
ENGAGED TO MARRY

Special to the New York Times

BOSTON, NOV 18——Miss Helen Keller, the most famous blind and deaf woman in the world, is engaged to marry her private secretary, Mr. Peter Fagan. Confirmation of the engagement comes from Mr. Edward McGlennan, the City Registrar of Boston, Massachusetts, who recently issued the couple a marriage license application at Boston City Hall. A copy of the application shows the signatures of Mr. Fagan and Miss Keller, hers in the square hand used by the blind.

Mr. Fagan denies both the engagement and any visit to Boston City Hall. However, friends of the couple report that Mr. Fagan has talked with them about his plans to take Miss Keller away from her family for a marriage in Florida.

"I've booked tickets for us to Montgomery tomorrow at eight a.m.," Mother said. "Now step away from that man. You are never to see him again."

My voice, when I use it, slides up and down—first too high, then pitching perilously low, a gargling, choking sound, some tell me. But the moment Mother read me the article I felt for the first time as if I could hear my voice, and as I stood by the door clenching my fists, for the only time in my life I let my voice hurtle wide open, shouting no, no, NO!

————

We stood by the front door as Mother went on, Peter spelling her words into my hand.

"I advise that you leave quietly—now. You'll spare us the humiliation of a scene. That's the very least you can do, after acting like a traitor under our roof."

"I'm not a—"

"We fed you. Paid you. Trusted you with Helen . . ."

"Two out of three isn't bad . . ."

"I beg your pardon?"

"You fed and paid me, that's true. But trusted me? No."

"And we were so very right, apparently. Now stop spelling to Helen. She's not your property."

"She's to be my wife."

"She'll never be anyone's wife."

"What have you got against—"

"How dare you interrupt me? Did *you* raise a handicapped child, Mr. Fagan? Did *you* fight with your husband for her very life? Did *you* lie awake night after night with no breath in your throat, trying to see a future for her?"

"We *have* a future, Mrs. Keller."

"You think it's a game, taking Helen for little walks, bike riding—did you think I didn't know where you'd been? Even taking her—my daughter—to your house and compromising her reputation? I know Helen wouldn't do anything to bring shame to her family, but you . . . you're impertinent. When Annie wakes up I'll tell her and she'll have your head . . ."

"I'm a scoundrel—say it. But a scoundrel who loves your daughter, and she deserves to be loved."

"Deserves? Who are you to say what she deserves?" Mother turned to me. "You did this. Now you must undo it. You must choose. Your family or Mr. Fagan. You can't have both."

"Mother, please."

"There is no choice," Peter said. "Everyone knows now. There's nothing to hide. Helen wants a life—a family—with me."

"A family? Helen has a family."

"Apparently she thinks otherwise."

"Helen, tell Mr. Fagan your choice."

"Mother, Peter, he's . . ."

"He's what, Helen? He's not what I think?" I felt her rattling the paper. "He let you sneak around, he led you into an arrangement that you kept from Annie—and from me. What kind of a man would do that?"

"I did it, not Peter. I wanted to be loved."

"Choose, Helen." Mother said again. Anger like steam rose from her skin.

Sun came in from the living room window, warming my arms, but my heart was breaking into slivers. I knew it was over then. Peter would go; I would be alone with Mother, who had been lonely in the deep recesses of her being for most of her life.

"Well, Helen . . . ," Mother insisted.

I squeezed her hand tightly.

"Now, Mr. Fagan," Mother said. "The door is open. Please leave."

"No." I tried pulling away, but Mother held my hand tight.

"Don't tell me," Peter said. "That old line about blood being thicker than water. Helen won't choose you, Kate."

"It's *Mrs.* Keller to you. My lawyer is arranging a press conference where I announce that Helen was never engaged to you—and she never will be." Mother dropped my hand and I felt cold air rush in through the open front door, swirling my skirt.

I moved toward Peter. "I didn't . . . choose her."

"I know. And I've chosen you. Damn her and her lawyers. I'll spin some tale for the press about how this was all a lie, what do I care? I did it when the *Times* reporter phoned me yesterday about our engagement, and I'll do it again at the press conference. But when I rap on your door in Alabama one week from today I want you to move so fast to the front porch and my waiting car that this mother of yours—this whole family—can never stop us again."

The door banged shut.

Chapter Thirty-five

"Stay right here in this living room." Mother swung the front door shut. Outside the vibrations of Peter's footsteps faded, and I was seized with a desire to run out the door after him. As the car thumped away, a pain, tin-sharp, moved through me. I struggled to push past Mother.

"I need to be with Peter." I tried to open the door, but Mother locked it with a *sshhhk* and took my arm.

"Helen, that man—I refuse to use his name—is not to be trusted. He's a liar, and an opportunist. How can you trust a man like that? He has been banished from this house for good. You won't see him again."

The afternoon dissolved around us. I wanted to believe that Peter was trustworthy. But why didn't I recognize then how easily he could lie? He'd lied to the *New York Times* reporter, saying that we weren't engaged, and then lied to me by omission because he didn't tell me what he'd done. Yet, I see why he kept it secret. He understood that our future was at stake. He wanted to protect me, to cover for me, and for that I am grateful. There are so many ways to show love.

Mother shook me by the hand. "Now for the last time: What were you doing with that scoundrel? *Tell* me."

"Mother, please. *Let me go to him.*"

"No. You'll stay right here with me."

I stood by the front door, searching for the lock, but Mother coolly held my hands. "Yes, life was good to us both for a few brief months," Mother used to say. She loved to talk about the nineteen months before I lost my hearing and sight, when she was a normal mother, and I a normal child. Ever since my "tragedy" she saw those months as the best time of her life—and mine. Yes, she also had Mildred, and Phillips Brooks. Even two stepchildren. But had father touched her, hungrily, like Peter touched me? His mouth like a furnace, his body all hers, like Peter's was mine?

I was her love, and also her sorrow.

I straightened, head high. If I wanted Peter back, I'd have to fight for him. What frightened me was my anger. If I could have burned, I would have.

Mother led me farther into the house. "You're going to have to speak with Annie," she said. "If you're not going to tell me what was going on, then at the very least you must tell her."

"Mother. She leaves for Puerto Rico soon. She's already upset; this will make it worse."

"Your concern is touching, Helen. But before Annie departs she must hear about your affair. Perhaps you should have thought of the repercussions of your actions earlier." Mother urged me down the hall toward Annie's bedroom, and I followed, ready to fight. She pushed me across the bedroom's threshold and soon I stood right by Annie's bed. "Tell her," Mother said. "Now, or I will."

"With pleasure." I reached across the wrinkled bedspread and put my hands on Annie's face. Her cheekbones were so prominent beneath my fingers that I pulled back, startled.

"Annie, you're . . ."

"What? Wasting away?" Annie struggled to sit up.

I sat down, suddenly weary. "You've got to fight. You can't just—"

"Helen, the battle is over."

"No—"

"It is. This useless, stupid battle—was a complete waste of time."

"It wasn't, and it isn't over."

"You've been too busy with Mr. Fagan to keep up with the news."

"What?"

"Helen, haven't you read the lead story on the front page of the *Boston Globe*?"

"No, I . . ."

"Then listen up, lady. With all your incessant protesting against the war you'll be glad to hear this:

The Boston Globe

THE BATTLE OF THE SOMME ENDS

PARIS, FRANCE, NOV 1916 — The Battle of the Somme, the scene of heavy fighting since July 1, 1916, is finished. British troops suffered nearly 60,000 casualties on the first day. Tens of thousands of soldiers suffered shell shock, and casualties on both sides total over one million.

"The world has gone mad," Annie said. "A million killed—for what? Why don't they think of the toll these battles take on families? The mothers who've lost sons, the wives who will never see their husbands again. That's the *real* tragedy."

For once I didn't care about others, their misfortunes. I even forgot that I might be pregnant. Sitting by Annie, the air in the room heavy, I was just relieved that she didn't know about my affair with Peter. Then, under my fingers Annie's face felt dry, and she suddenly spasmed into a cough so harsh it made the air shudder.

Mother adjusted Annie's pillows, I smoothed her damp curls, yet Annie coughed so that I almost panicked; it seemed as if her lungs had filled with water, and she struggled to breathe. All that afternoon she tossed in her bed, the sheets crossed over her body until she flung them off. Her distress gave me a reason to forget myself, and I pulled my body onto the bed and lay beside her, the way I did as a child.

After what seemed like hours, she relaxed, and there was a long interval of tense stillness. Annie didn't cough, Mother didn't say a word, and I was loath to have the moment end. Once Annie sipped some water Mother said, "Annie, it's not the world that's gone mad. It's Helen."

Annie turned toward me. "Helen, do you have something to say?"

"No." I stood up, defiant by the bed.

"Helen, if you won't tell Annie, I will." Mother rattled the newspaper, preparing to read the engagement article, as I stood helpless.

From the time I was seven Annie taught me to describe the world just as hearing and sighted people do. So in Vermont I wrote letters about the blue mountains visible outside our hotel window; in California I told audiences I loved the sound of the Pacific Ocean cascading on Pelican Beach; on the banks of the Mississippi River I wrote in my journal that the muddy waters leaped before my eyes to crash thousands of feet below in a resounding roar.

But critics hounded me: Who did I think I was? They complained after my words were published in books and articles. How could a deaf-blind girl use language to describe anything, especially the natural world? I responded in my autobiography that the deaf-blind exist alone on an island. We are surrounded by deep silence, impenetrable. We must learn the language of the hearing and sighted world to survive.

Yet that day I could find no words to explain to Annie my deception.

Annie's hands felt weak in mine. "Helen, in exactly sixty minutes I leave this house. I don't know when—or if—I'll be back. So whatever you have to say, just spit it out. What have you done?"

"Nothing."

"Not according to the *New York Times*." Mother handed Annie the paper.

A long while passed.

"Perfect," Annie said. "'Helen Keller Engaged to Marry'—people will eat this up. Kate, the press loves to make up stories about Helen. Their lies sell copy, you know that."

"Annie, Helen has lied to us—to *you*."

"Helen hasn't done a thing. Some reporter saw her and Peter in Boston, jumped to a conclusion, and wham—whipped up this lie. Helen's not capable of this kind of deceit, especially with as unimportant a man as Peter Fagan."

Maybe Annie believed what she was saying, or maybe she was too weak, too exhausted, to keep me from harm's way. I had only to escape Mother, and I was free.

Mother left the room, her perfume wafting in the air. "She's calling the lawyer," Annie said. "You're going to have to face the press." I held her hand, wishing I could tell her the truth. "I want to go away, Helen. You've tired me out. I've never said it before, but it's true. I need to be away."

An hour later a cab rolled up the driveway. "Wake up, Helen," Annie said. She picked up her suitcase and I followed her down the hall. At the front door she said, "Without me you're going to be bored to death in Montgomery. And if you think you made a mistake already with this Fagan mess, something tells me you'll do even worse with just Mildred and your mother as your constant companions." With a thump of the car door she was gone.

I stood alone in the driveway. With one hand I tapped on a maple tree's cold bark, a deep loneliness filled the branches, even the sky.

Chapter Thirty-six

The scent of honeysuckle and steel told me my train had entered the Montgomery station. Mother, seated by my side, had not spoken a word to me since we had left Boston five days ago. She pulled down our luggage, and I felt the sweltering heat of the station. Finally, she spoke. "Helen, your sister has no idea what you've done, and I have no intention of telling her. The last thing we need is for all of Montgomery to know about the scandal you've created—"

"Mother, it was in the *New York Times*."

"Helen, you've been in the North too long. Do you think Mildred—or anyone in Montgomery—reads the *New York Times*? As long as you keep quiet, they won't know about it. You will simply conduct yourself as any visitor would: If Mildred asks you to deliver Thanksgiving biscuits to the poor, you'll do it. If her card party wants you to join, you will. Do you understand me? Not one word. You've caused enough problems already."

The train shuddered to a stop. I stood, smoothing my dress, and held on to the seat back to follow Mother onto the platform. But she paused just before we stepped off the train.

"I did mention it to Warren."

"Warren? Why?"

"Because someone has to protect you."

"From what?"

"From yourself."

With that, the doors bumped open, and as we walked out I smelled a familiar scent of wool and rubber. "What is it?" I asked Mother as hundreds of footsteps fled past.

"Nothing." Mother hurried me through the crowds. Only on the way to Mildred's did she say the station had teamed with hundreds of soldiers, readying for war.

Steamy heat rose from Mildred's house on Seventh Avenue, and the scent of corn bread wafted out of the kitchen in preparation for Thanksgiving. When I walked in the front door Mildred put her new baby, Katherine, in my arms. I had to sit down at the table, so weak did I feel when I inhaled the new-baby smell of talcum powder. I ran my fingers over her tiny ears, and practically blurted out to Mildred, "I may be having a child." Instead I silently rocked Katherine, aching for Peter to come bounding up the front porch steps.

"Let's leave Katherine in her bassinet." Mildred took the baby from my arms. "You look so pale, Helen. I've never quite seen you like this. Mother's resting upstairs—let's sit by the fire in the living room. The trip must have exhausted you." She led me into the front parlor, where leather-bound books lined the walls. As I moved toward the couch, my hands skimmed the glass case where Warren's gun collection was on display.

"Is Warren . . . home?"

"Oh, no. He's out celebrating the city's finally passing that new statute."

"Why, Mildred, have you gotten all political since the last time I was here?"

"I pay attention to politics when politics affect me. The Yankee factories are paying agents to come down here and recruit the Negroes. Every day they camp out, telling the Negroes to move up North because they'll have better lives far away from their homes. Can you imagine?"

"Absolutely."

"You're always sympathizing with the wrong side, Helen. The Negroes are fleeing Montgomery in droves, so the city passed a statute making it illegal for anyone to recruit them to work in any other town or city."

"I'll bet they're going anyway."

"Without looking back. I'm without a cook, can't get a nanny, I've been up nights with Katherine so long I'm falling asleep talking to you. Soon I'll be doing our laundry, too. Every last one of them will have fled. Now Katherine's up. That's enough on that topic. Let's leave that to the men. Would you hold her, Helen?"

I rocked Katherine, but the room felt empty. Without Peter, life felt achingly constricted. "Explain it to me again," I said. "The Negroes are free. They can't go and make their own lives?"

"Absolutely not. We've been like family to them."

As Mildred talked, my mind wandered. I knew it wasn't the same. I've said before that I have rights, white skin, a chance to travel if accompanied . . . I'm free, and educated, and have never suffered like the Negroes, but I couldn't help thinking how I, too, was demonized for trying to flee.

"Now, about my card party tomorrow . . ." Mildred shook my shoulder. "I don't have bridge cards in Braille, but you could still sit with us. We can . . ." I began to feel a familiar ache in my abdomen, so I turned away from Mildred. At first it seemed like nothing, but soon I stood up and started to pat my way down the hall to the washroom. Mildred followed and turned me to her.

"Sister Helen, you look . . . Let me get you to your room." She led me up the carpeted stairs.

Within minutes I lay on the guest-room bed, the familiar small cloths I'd used since age fourteen unpacked by Mildred and placed on my nightstand. The cramps intensified and a heaviness came over me, the acrid smell of blood telling me I was not pregnant. I had been so eager to have a child, and to know I was not made me turn toward the wall. But relief flooded me, too. Peter might want a child someday—he said so—and when the time came he might be ready.

I stayed in the room as long as I could, pressing a wet washcloth to my forehead as Mildred thumped at the door.

"Helen. You've been weeping." She handed me a hanky.

"I . . ."

"You've never been separated from Miss Annie for long." Mildred always called my teacher "Miss." "She always kept you so busy, connected to everything," Mildred said in her clumsy fingerspelling. "I've found a nice Jewish girl, she lives in Montgomery, and wants to meet you. She wants to learn fingerspelling. She could be a . . . paid companion of sorts for you now that—"

"Now that what?" I pulled away.

"Miss Annie's . . . away. Mother's older and needs her rest, and I'm so occupied with the babies. You need someone just for yourself." Mildred put Katherine in my arms.

Katherine sucked my thumb.

Mildred sensed my loneliness. When Katherine started to cry again she said, "It's not for the faint of heart, a husband, a family."

"You said it."

After Mildred put the baby down for a nap she brought me a cup of peppermint tea. "This might cheer you." She slid a letter into my hands. I ran my fingers over the envelope: the Braille dashes and dots meant it was either from Peter or Annie. I tore it open.

San Juan,
Puerto Rico
November 1916

Helen Dear:
Your mother has told me that you are in love with Peter. Could this be true? She wants me to recover, fast, and return to keep

you safe. I want to protect you. But understand: I cannot leave Puerto Rico now. I cannot face the cold of our Wrentham house, the uncertainty about money, the secret that John has had a baby with another woman.

I am trying to get better. Even one short week in Puerto Rico has improved me immensely. I'm sure a large part of my recovery is that this place is an island of joy. When I arrived here I had only a dull ache where my heart should have been. But here I wake to the sound of birds, the scent of fresh pineapple in the warm air. In the heat of the day I eat fruit that has grown to be as large as a tree. As large as the mulberry in front of your house in Tuscumbia—the one we were in when that storm came. Do you remember, Helen? How you shook in that mulberry tree, afraid of lightning, until I came and took your hand?

When I came to Tuscumbia, I wanted someone to love. And you loved me, Helen. Now I am too tired to fight; you must have someone *else* to love. It may sound strange to you that I believe that you should hold on to Peter. Don't lose the man you love, as I did.

I have tuberculosis. The White Death. It is unthinkable that I should not live, but if I do not, remember that you were like a daughter to me. I have given you my life. Never have I had the chance to see what talents I might have had on my own. You must see this. Face it: If I die, who will care for you?

Peter will.

Helen, fight for what you have.

Fight for *your* island of joy.

Love,

Annie

That night I dreamed of Peter leading me into a sleeping berth on a train, his hands on my ribs, then on my hips, as he rolled over me on an unmade bed.

Chapter Thirty-seven

⊰❁❁⊱

On the day of my elopement, the vibrations of Montgomery were strong around me. Inside the house, Risa, the girl Mildred had hired to entertain me, sat at the sewing machine in the living room. As I walked in Mildred's backyard, with one hand on the fence, I stumbled over small rocks and children's toys. Mother and Mildred were shopping in Montgomery and I was alone, when a familiar scent of muskrat and warm rain swam over the humid air.

Peter walked toward me from the piney woods. As he got closer I burst forward to take him in my arms.

"Peter, it's not until tonight, what are you doing here now?"

"Don't fret, missy. I couldn't just hang around Montgomery all day. I was here, and I wanted to see you." He took my hands.

"But—"

"But nothing. I rang the bell, your new . . . assistant—though if I may say so she doesn't look nearly as exciting as me—pointed me out here."

"You told Risa about us? How did you—"

"Relax, missy. I told her I'm working for the *Montgomery Monitor* and wanted to interview you."

"You're a master of disguises."

"To get to you, yes." He pulled me close.

"Ow," I said, lifting my foot. "Red ants. They're biting me, like fire."

"How I love rescuing a damsel in distress." With one brisk movement we fled the yard and walked down the wooden path behind Mildred's house to a small clearing where the ants wouldn't be.

Then I felt Peter turn toward the flagpole in the side yard. "Hey, rebel girl. What's with the Confederate flag?"

"It's my brother-in-law's."

"And just where is he now? Sniffing around the property, hoping to find me?"

"No. He's out hunting for the Thanksgiving turkey."

"He's quite the patriot."

"Indeed. He lowers the flag before he goes to bed."

"So when the flag goes down tonight I'll know he's safe in bed. That's when I'll creep up the steps . . ."

"And whisk me away."

"So good of your brother-in-law to help."

"He lives to serve." I laughed.

But there was something distant about Peter. "What is it?" I asked.

"Oh, just two or three things. One: this place looks like a fortress. Two: I'm being hounded by the press, the Keller family, and their damned dogs. And three: Macy wrote that if I marry you I'm . . ."

"You're what?"

"I'm like a person boarding the *Titanic*—ready to go down."

"John's hardly a reliable source about life."

"True. But he has experience with . . ."

"What? Me and Annie?"

"Well, theirs was a . . . tempestuous marriage."

"Tempestuous? John had the best days of his life with us until whiskey soaked him through. He brought his troubles on himself, and don't you forget it."

"Yes, ma'am."

"Besides, I'll make your life better, not worse. Has one week apart caused you to forget? Then let me remind you." I pulled him to me and opened his shirt.

"Ah, that's what I love. My fighting Helen. I love it when you get mad." He drew me to him.

Then a snap in the woods signaled someone was coming.

"Tonight." He pushed me toward the house, but I didn't want to go. I crossed the yard with small steps, as if to slow down time.

I didn't show up for lunch or dinner that day. It was past seven when Mother pushed open the door to my room, shook me by the shoulder as I read by my desk. "Helen, your house in Wrentham has sold. I've engaged a rental agent and she's found a new house for you and Annie to rent. It's in Forest Hills, outside Manhattan. When Annie returns, the mover will come to the Wrentham farmhouse and pack up the heavy things. What do you want them to take?"

I said nothing.

"I assume you'll want your most precious things."

"Yes, indeed." I already had my most precious thing. My suitcase was packed and locked under my bed; it would be only three hours until I grabbed it, walked briskly to the front porch, and took Peter's hand.

"Helen," Mother said, "make a list."

She put a piece of paper on my desk and left the room.

November 25, 1916

Dear Mother,

I've married Peter Fagan. Believe me, I've never been happier in my life.

I know you'll come to understand.

Your loving daughter,
Helen

I folded the letter and left it in the middle of the desk.

———

Warren's truck rattled up the driveway at dusk, and as the scent of night settled around me, I felt the staircase vibrate as he climbed wearily to bed. When Mildred and Mother finally crept upstairs at nine thirty, I felt their bedroom doors close firmly behind them, so I got my suitcase, tiptoed out of my room, and left the house. I waited on Mildred's front porch, my luggage packed in one tidy bag. Peter slipped hurriedly out of the woods and I felt his footsteps as he ran up the porch steps.

"Let's go, Helen." He took my suitcase and then my arm. "Now."

A breeze shook the honeysuckle vines.

Just then the front door swung open, a rustle announcing that someone was coming out of the house. Peter held firmly to my hand, but Warren pushed past me and grabbed hold of him. Clutching the railing, I smelled the cold metal of a gun, and Warren's yell split the air.

Peter pulled me toward him. "Leave us alone," he said. "Helen's coming with me." He tried to lead me past Warren, but the strong scent of metal told me Warren had raised his Smith and Wesson and was pointing it right at Peter.

"No one tells us what to do with Helen." The vibrations of Warren's voice moved through the porch floorboards into my legs and I panicked. A cold, icy fear sluiced through me. Peter pushed me back, away from Warren. Alone by the railing I couldn't breathe. Instead I inhaled fear—iron, bitter, metallic—rising from Peter's jacket as he struggled with Warren.

The floorboards thudded as the two shoved each other, and I waited, helpless, for the air to split open: for my nostrils to fill with sulfur and gunpowder—and though Warren didn't fire his gun, I knew. Even as Peter's footsteps punched the porch floor, even as he was brash, a daredevil, even as his love for me was unwavering, his skin gave off the scent of a frightened animal caught in a trap. Because he faced the impenetrable fortress of my family.

He would never win, he couldn't. No one could.

Let me go, I wanted to say.

I tried to run off the porch, but Warren blocked me at the railing as Peter's scent drifted away into the woods.

I still held the railing, suddenly lightheaded, as Mother came out of the house and took my hand. I pushed her away. "I *won't* go inside—*no*." Mother left me alone on the porch, and complete darkness closed over me.

I remembered the time when I was six and sensed that Mother wished I would die. It's not that she didn't love me. She did. It was the overwhelming pull of me. *Helen can't hear. Helen can't see.* Helen can't make her way from table to door, never mind make her way in the dangerous world.

That was when I began to crave being perfect. *Mama, I'll be good. A saint. Don't leave me. Don't leave me. I promise to be good.* This, the deaf-blind woman's promise. I will reflect your desires all the days of my life. In return, you will never leave me.

But now I craved freedom. That night in my room I kept my suitcase packed. I knew Peter would be back, so all night I tossed in my white iron bed in Mildred's house, gesturing with my fingers as if calling to him.

Chapter Thirty-eight

⊰≻⊰≺⊱

I wish I could have changed what I wanted, but my desire to leave only intensified. The next morning, scents of biscuits and eggs rose from the kitchen, but when Mildred knocked on my door I refused to come down to breakfast. I was lost in thought: Peter's hands in my hair, the feeling of him by my side, the excitement of our wedding day—tomorrow, when I would be separated from my family, but united with the man I loved. An hour later, when Mildred tapped on my door for help with chores, I finally dressed and went downstairs.

On my way to the kitchen the aroma of tobacco told me Warren was nearby.

"Helen, you owe me a 'good morning.'"

I tried to walk past, but he took my hands and held them tight.

"You tried to run off with that Yankee."

"I'll do it again."

"You had no right to . . ."

"To what? Have a life, a family, like you, Mildred, and Mother do?"

"Your mother is racked with a migraine; my wife—your sister—refuses to accept that you would do this, but if you ever try . . ."

"What? You'll use your gun again?"

"No. I won't use *that* gun. Next time I'll use one I actually fire."

I stormed into the kitchen and slid closed the lock. When Warren rapped on the door, I refused to open it.

——

I had reached my limit. Mildred did not mention anything about last night. Instead, she turned from the counter where she was chopping apples for a Thanksgiving pie and said Mother had gone to her room with a headache. "Make her some tea, Helen." She handed me the teakettle and placed it under the faucet. The cold water rushed over my hands as I awkwardly filled it, so Mildred took the kettle from me. "There's Bailey," she said. "Helen, go open the door and let him in." I opened the back door and turned, expectantly. With a rush of warm air Warren's hunting dog made his way into the kitchen and thumped his tail against my leg, bits of branches sharp in his fur.

"I've never seen such a mess," Mildred said.

"Me either."

"I'm talking about . . ."

"I know what you're talking about, Mildred. Warren takes Bailey out with him nights, and that's how he got like this. Give me the brush. I'll clean Bailey up."

Mildred put a steel brush in my hand, and with great vigor I moved it through the tangles.

"Mildred, will he . . ."

"Be out tonight? I didn't ask. And he didn't say."

I had to warn Peter that it might not be safe to come tonight. But if I wrote him a letter, how would I get it to him? Mildred would see me at the mailbox; I couldn't walk through the woods to downtown Montgomery; I couldn't even get to the sidewalk without guidance. The air around me darkened.

"Helen, stop. You're hurting Bailey."

"Don't be ridiculous. I've never hurt a living thing."

There was a long pause.

"Perhaps not on purpose. Remember Martha Washington?"

"Who?"

"The little Negro girl, the daughter of Mother's cook. She was seven, you were five. You used to play with her. One day something enraged you—God knows what—so you grabbed Mother's scissors and cut off all of Martha's curls."

"So?"

"You were always . . . determined to get your own way." Mildred took the brush from my hands.

I had to contact Peter. Was there a chance that Mildred would speak up for me?

"Mildred, I . . ." I wanted to tell her that I was sorry.

"He's my husband, Helen." Through the floor I felt the vibrations of Warren chopping wood in the yard. "He paced our bedroom all night. He feels *responsible* for you."

"Could you . . . talk to him?"

There was a long pause as Mildred moved to the table. "Do you remember what happened after you cut off Martha Washington's hair?"

"No."

"She was punished for causing trouble. I was there. Her mother took her and whipped her good for 'disrupting Miss Helen,' but worst of all for disturbing the household—Mother was beside herself. I can't be a go-between for you with Warren or Mother. Can you understand, Helen?" Mildred's hand stopped spelling in mine.

The stomp of Warren's boots on the back steps made us pull apart.

Why couldn't I have what was my right? I wanted to protest. I was unable to leave, unable to reach out to Peter, but I needed him to comfort me. For him I would make any sacrifice.

"He's a good man, Helen," Mildred said.

"I know."

"He just wants what's right for you, for all of us."

"Yes."

"But Risa."

"Risa?"

"The girl who writes Braille, like you and . . . Peter do. She'll be here at two this afternoon. To . . . *do*. . . for you."

The day lightened.

Within minutes I sat in the warmth of my room, typing a letter to Peter on my Braille writer. Please, meet me tonight. Warren may be out, so be careful. I tucked the letter into Risa's pocket when she arrived, and for the rest of the afternoon Mother, Mildred, and I sat on scratchy living-room chairs to play an agonizingly slow game of whist. When the living room floorboards shook just a bit, I knew Risa had opened the front door.

"Let's go upstairs," she said when she reached me at the card table. "I have something for you."

I pushed my chair back

"You'll stay right here, Helen. I want my eyes on you." Mother put her hand on mine.

My fingers trembled just slightly in Mother's palm when I told her I had to work with Risa. I had letters I had to answer.

"You may certainly attend to your duties," Mother said.

When Risa and I left the room, I felt confident that Mother was satisfied that if I stayed busy, my future with Peter would also be kept at bay. Then Risa leaned toward me with a note from Peter.

Dear Renegade,
Well, they're hankering for a fight, aren't they? All right, then. Fight we will.
   Be outside at two a.m. No one will be awake then, Mrs. Fagan. And if Warren does go out searching the woods, he and that mangy old dog will limp up the front steps into the house by two a.m., tired of tramping through the woods.
   I'm betting on it.

My life flashed before my eyes last night, and once was definitely enough.

> Yours,
> Peter

At two a.m. Mother was asleep in her room, and while I couldn't be sure, I hoped that Warren was asleep beside Mildred in their room across the hall from mine. I relaxed my whole body and paused before walking downstairs. I was sorry to leave Mother and Mildred, but my way ahead was clear-cut.

Suitcase in hand, I closed the front door behind me. Stars must have shone down, lighting up my face as I stepped out onto the porch. My hands shook as I set down my suitcase and stood poised for the vibrations of Peter crossing the yard.

That long first hour of waiting, the warm Alabama wind sweeps past, and I clench my teeth, telling myself his car must have stalled. By the second hour I shift in the rocking chair, turning left, then right. Where is he? As five o'clock comes, I ache for his mouth on mine. Now the early-morning sun warms my arms. My heart pounds; blood, rushing to my throat, thrums in my ears.

I strain over the porch railing, my whole body a vibroscope. I imagine Peter writing his note, scoffing, like he always does, at the threat of my family. But then I remember the last line: "I saw my life flash before my eyes, and once was enough." Has he finally felt the weight of the dark I live in? My eyes blink. Who would have the strength to come into my world forever?

All through the dawn I push away the truth of what is happening. But when I feel daylight's heat on my arms I know. The crack of a twig, of trucks rumbling up Seventh Avenue, the faint flutter of birds move over my skin like dark rain.

I have lost Peter. I cannot stay still for fear of breaking apart, but I cannot move either. I have nowhere to go. And I can't return to my room, not yet. The sun has fully risen. My breath comes in short clips.

How I ache to get away. Peter is not going to walk up the steps, and the Montgomery daybreak seems a selfish thing, bristly, in its chill.

Now there is a slight *sssnaap* at the front door behind me. When I turn, a hand falls on mine.

"Helen, Warren sent me to bring you back into the house." Mildred tries to help me up.

I sit in the chair like a pillar.

Chapter Thirty-nine

Say God is blind and deaf, his hands rubbing the bark of earth's trees, searching for someone to hold him close, rock him in his sightless, mute world, warm him in a mother's arms.

Say God feels fear. A cold, moving thing.

The morning Mildred led me back into the house I paced my room in devastation, refusing to speak to Mother, Mildred, or Warren. My mind raced. Had Peter been run off? Or had he simply gotten frightened? Had he stood at the edge of the woods, suddenly aware of the weight he would shoulder by marrying me—the unrelenting care he would have to provide for the rest of his life? Did he start to cross the lawn and then, seeing the house in its towering darkness, feel the hostility of my family toward him, and realize for certain that they would never truly let me go? I knew he loved me. If he had come, his face would have been contorted in sorrow as he withdrew and stepped back across the yard, watching me and knowing even *he* could not take me out of my isolation.

Maybe he was afraid of the same things I was: loneliness and oblivion. And he simply couldn't enter into them with me.

But if Peter could not really come near me, who then?

I am a floating bit of ash.

In my small room I move to the desk by the window and back, restless, trapped in my craven desire, my need to see him. When I fall into a sudden, uneasy sleep the dream comes. The one where I have the deathlike feeling I first felt a few weeks ago when Annie said she had tuberculosis and was going far away.

In my dream I soothe Annie with my hands, trying to erase the White Death. *Not true*, I say in the dream. *Do not leave me.*

And God rocks high above the blind universe, sorrow on his tongue.

When I wake up I feel vibrations in the hallway. Warren, Mildred, and Mother all pace in the hall, but I don't allow anyone in my room.

I lie awake all afternoon, the sheet over me like a shroud.

That night a sudden freeze descended on Montgomery's avenues and fields, covering everything with frost. When I woke up not in my honeymoon cottage but in Mildred's guest room, I was freezing cold. Mildred came in and tried to warm me by putting quilts on the bed.

"Get some coal for the fire," I said.

"We have no coal."

"Please, Mildred."

"You have to go back to Wrentham. Mother wants to take you tomorrow." Her hands shook.

"No. I want to stay here. He may still come."

"No," Mildred said.

"Was Warren . . . out last night?"

"He hunted the woods until dawn, Helen. But he found nothing. Nothing at all."

"Nothing?"

"No." Mildred waited a long time. "Not a living thing. And Warren can track prey as well as anyone can."

A chalky darkness filled me. Heavy, that dark, as if I could take it into my mouth.

It occurred to me then. Perhaps Peter had not made it to the edge of the yard last night. Had Warren run him off with a gun? Had that stopped Peter, finally, from coming for me? Perhaps at daybreak he sat on the edge of his bed, listing the reasons to be with me. *A woman like Helen needs to be loved.* And at the top of this list, finally, he put the reason to stay away: *to save his own life.* A life not entwined with mine. A life where he could rise, or fall, on his own. He knew I would be devastated, there would be no deeper hurt. Nevertheless, he had to let go. I imagined him standing up, pulling at his frayed shirt cuffs, locking his suitcase, and closing the door behind him.

"Helen, a letter came for you today." Mildred hesitantly took her hand from mine.

"Is it from—"

"I can't tell you, Helen. I'm under strict orders not to show you anything."

"What?" I sat up. A rage moved through me. Peter had not come, but he had loved me, treated me like an equal, and I had become louder, more combative by knowing him. And I liked that. I pulled the covers off and stood by Mildred, my anger mounting.

"Mother said—"

"Read it, now," I demanded. I might still win. Mildred read:

Washington, D.C.

My Dear Helen,

Congratulations, darling girl, on your upcoming marriage. I am delighted to read that you finally heeded the advice I gave you so many years ago. May you and Mr. Fagan, if my *New York Times* is right in the spelling of your fiancé's name, have all the pleasures of this blessed institution.

As Mark Twain once said, you truly are the eighth wonder of the world. May your beloved always treat you so.

Sincerely yours,

Alexander Graham Bell

I am a human being, with a human being's frailties and inconsistencies, I once wrote in a book. As I held the letter in my hands, Mark Twain's words reverberated within me. When I was younger, unaware that a man would ever love me, Annie and I had visited Mark Twain in his white Connecticut mansion. We walked into his cigar-scented living room that cold December night and sat by the fireplace as he read aloud to Annie and me.

Later, he led us up the thick-carpeted stairs to our bedrooms. I turned to go into the first one, on the left, but he quickly shut the door. "No, not that one." Annie spelled into my hand that it was the former bedroom of his beloved daughter, who had died young. At nineteen, she had fallen deathly ill in that very room while Twain was away in Europe; he was rushing back to her, his ship halfway across the Atlantic, but she died before he arrived.

The next day we stood with Mark Twain outside in the snow, waiting for our car to return home. I knew that his fame was worldwide, his humor unending, but as Annie and I said good-bye, his voice under my fingertips felt rough as stones. When we drove off, Annie turned and saw Twain alone, white hair blazing. She said he looked back at his empty mansion as if yearning for a sound he no longer heard.

Now I know what Mark Twain wanted.

For the one you lost to call your name.

I traced over the note with my fingers. Mildred took it from me and packed it in my suitcase. All night I lay awake. We had no coal. The stars were dead, the universe stalled. I had no burning thing at my center.

Peter was gone.

Chapter Forty

⊰❈⊱

Days passed. Rain battered the house. Thanksgiving was ush-
ered in with all of us seated at Mildred's oval dining table,
Warren passing platters of food that no one ate; Mother on my left,
refusing to speak, Mildred on my right, urging me to eat something—"Even a bit of turkey. Just one bite, please, Helen." I pushed
the plate away, my own feelings dulled, emptiness filling the place
where Peter's love had been. As dinner went on, a curious darkness
roamed the dining room, slid over the damask tablecloth, hovered
over the heavy silver as we passed the food, then moved beneath
my skin, pushing up through my muscles, circulating in my blood.

Then came a knock on the front door. With a scrape of his chair
Warren stood, walked heavily to answer it, then returned to the
table.

"For you." He put a bouquet of gardenias in my hands.

"Let me." Mildred read the card, "To Helen Keller, whose
courage inspires us all. Best wishes on Thanksgiving from the
Montgomery Ladies Auxiliary."

Had I dared hope the flowers were from Peter?

By evening I ached to leave. Warren had not returned from
hunting, Mildred fed Katherine in the kitchen, and Mother sat by
the living-room fire with her back to me. I sat alone in my scratchy
chair across from her. I wanted to write to Annie, *Please, help me.*
But a dull ache in my heart told me it was futile. Peter was gone for
good. The price of my deaf-blindness weighed heavily on me. If

Annie didn't get well, and Peter was gone, what would become of me?

Mother broke her silence. "Your house is ready."

"What house?"

"The one in Forest Hills. The one I rented for you. I'll stay there with you as well."

I said nothing.

"The farmhouse is sold. Your lawyer signed the papers since you've been . . . ill."

"Please, Mother . . ." I took her hand. "I wasn't ill, I was—"

"This would be a good time to do as I ask. If anyone questions—and believe me, we'll do all we can to make sure very few people find out—but if anyone insists, Helen, we will say that you were very ill after the departure of Annie and simply made a very poor decision, which you now greatly regret."

I didn't reply.

"Helen, that's the very least you can do."

I couldn't speak. I wasn't sorry; I hadn't made a mistake; I wasn't ill. I'd never been healthier, happier in my life. I would have thrived with Peter if only, if only she had let me go. I leaned in toward her, my face warmed by the fire.

"I'm waiting," she said.

I took her hand in mine. Soft in my palm, Mother's fingers suddenly felt different. They felt drained of life, fragile. I realized how afraid she was. Annie was gone, I had betrayed her, and now she would have to care for me. She had suddenly become old.

I had become old.

"We leave tomorrow." Mother turned away. "Mildred will help you pack."

The chaos of my sister's house rose around us. Mother went to bed and I stood in the kitchen with Mildred. I couldn't face resuming my life without Peter, but I couldn't stay in Montgomery, either.

Katherine banged on her high chair tray, and acrid smoke from the waning fire told us we needed wood. When Mildred put baby Katherine in my arms, I felt dizzy with all I had lost, and afraid of how to go on without Peter.

"Come." Mildred took the baby from me and led me upstairs. As rain tapped on the roof, Mildred said, "Helen, I won't—I *can't*—mention what you've done. But you're a Keller. Do you know the way we get over things? We keep moving."

Down the hall in my room I thought of my loss of Peter, but also of Mother's great loss when I was young. The way she threw herself into work after I went deaf and blind. A kind of frenzied pace kept her going, until she could find her way after life had taken such a wrong turn.

Maybe Mother felt blinded then, as I am doubly blinded now.

Mildred lifted my suitcase out of the closet, opened it, and put my hands on it. The lock was cold to my touch. My heart cracked open.

"You leave tomorrow. Mother has rented a car to take you north."

"I'll pack," I said.

How does a deaf-blind woman pack up memories? I get up from my chair, and fold my coat, lingerie, and dresses into my bag. My Braille writer sits atop a crate. Mother has arranged for my books and furniture in Wrentham to be moved. They've already been loaded onto a truck to New York.

Slowly, I walk the bedroom where I'd hoped to leave behind my single life. Why did Peter betray me? Why did he not fight for me? Humiliation tastes bitter in my mouth. My dream of escape, vanished. Yes, I lied to Annie and my family, maybe I even lied to myself about Peter. Still, I don't regret our wild love.

Once I wrote, "I remember things through my fingertips." Anytime I want to remember Peter, I bring my fingertips together, and the sparks of his touch burn in me like blue flame.

————

Daybreak comes soon. Mother waits for me outside, and I am glad she does not see me cry. I leave Mildred's guest room. I close the door, hard. I cross the drive, get in the car, and inhale the scent of loss.

We drive down the streets of Montgomery, then past the pine forest at the edge of town. I open my window and inhale the heaviness of the South. The car rolls over roads, a brisk wind picks up, Mother turns a curve, and we drive north.

I never saw or was in contact with Peter Fagan again. Eighteen months after he left me, he married another woman; they had five children. I kept the letters he wrote me in a box on my library shelf in Forest Hills, New York, until all of them burned in a house fire.

Many years passed. One day I got a letter from Peter's grown daughter. Her father, she wrote, all of his life had kept a photo in his study, of me smiling outside a small cabin, a lake shining behind me.

"Why would Father have kept your photo all these years, Miss Keller?" his daughter asked. "Can you enlighten me?"

Afterword

⊰⊱

The love affair between Helen Keller and Peter Fagan was real. It occurred in the fall of 1916, when Anne Sullivan Macy was misdiagnosed with tuberculosis, and ended in December of that same year. Helen Keller never publicly spoke of her affair with Peter Fagan, and never married. She lived in Forest Hills, New York, with Anne Sullivan Macy, and together they became the major fundraisers for the newly formed American Foundation for the Blind (AFB). Helen channeled her prodigious energies into her work. With Annie and the AFB she helped to improve conditions for blind and deaf-blind people around the world. By the time she died, on June 1, 1968, she had met every sitting president since Grover Cleveland, was elected to the National Academy of Arts and Letters, and had won the Presidential Medal of Freedom, as well as innumerable other awards.

The actual letters from her love affair with Fagan were burned, leaving much to the imagination. Rich resources exist—books, newspaper articles, and photographs, along with letters in archives. My extensive research of these materials allowed the love affair to come to life in this work of historical fiction. Some places and dates have been changed to preserve the narrative flow. I was able to bring Helen Keller's voice alive through judicious use of her own words at certain points in the text.

I referred to many resources for information, first and foremost an excellent biography of Helen Keller, which details what is known about the Keller-Fagan love affair: *Helen Keller: A Life* by Dorothy Herrmann, and secondly a thorough and compelling biography of Helen Keller and Anne Sullivan, *Helen Keller and Teacher: The Story of Helen Keller and Anne Sullivan Macy* by Joseph P. Lash.

Equally important were letters and newspaper articles detailing the life of Helen Keller that are held in the Helen Keller Archives of the American Foundation for the Blind in New York City. The AFB kindly provided access to letters between Helen Keller and Annie Sullivan during Sullivan's convalescence in Puerto Rico; *New York Times* articles of 1916 to 1917, which chronicled Helen Keller's antiwar speeches and activism; and the letter written to Helen Keller by Peter Fagan's daughter. The AFB also gave me access to a recording of Helen Keller's voice, which helped me enormously in depicting her struggles with speech.

The Emma Goldman Archives at the University of California, Berkeley, also provided a key letter from Emma Goldman to Helen Keller regarding Keller's antiwar stance. The Wrentham Public Library in Wrentham, Massachusetts, provided a rare glimpse of Helen Keller's bathing suit—held in its archives—which became the basis for the imagined scene of Keller's swim in a Wrentham lake. The library also provided access to newspapers and private papers of Wrentham citizens from 1916 that helped fill in details about Keller's hometown during the time of her affair with Peter Fagan.

My understanding of Helen Keller's world was also deeply informed by a superb biography, *Anne Sullivan Macy: The Story Behind Helen Keller*, by Nella Braddy Henney, which greatly enhanced my understanding of Sullivan's early years with her family in Feeding Hills, Massachusetts; her years of poverty at the Tewksbury Almshouse; and her education at the Perkins School for the Blind. *Helen Keller, Selected Writings* and *The Radical Lives of Helen Keller*, edited by Kim E. Nielsen, and *Helen Keller: Sketch for a Portrait* by Van Wyck Brooks also enriched my view of Keller's complex life.

My knowledge of Helen Keller and her world was further expanded by the introduction to Helen Keller's *The Story of My Life: The Restored Classic, Complete and Unabridged Centennial Edition*, edited by Roger Shattuck. I also learned a vast amount from Helen Keller's own writings: the 1933 edition of *The Story of My Life*, which contains Anne Sullivan's early accounts of Helen's childhood; *The World I Live In*, in which Keller details her sensory relationship with the world; and *Midstream*, in which she writes briefly about her relationship with Peter Fagan.

I referred to *A History of the Great War: 1914–1918*, by C. R. M. F. Cruttwell; *Traumatic Pasts: History, Psychiatry, and Trauma in the Modern Age, 1870–1930*, edited by Michael S. Micale; and *A Battle of Nerves*, a PhD dissertation by Marc Roudebush for an understanding of the events of World War I and the impact of shell shock on soldiers.

I also learned from my correspondence with Kim Nielson, a disability scholar at the University of Wisconsin–Green Bay.

Acknowledgments

I have so many people and places to thank for help in bringing this book to life.

My friends Glo Richardson, Risa Miller, Martha Southgate, and Jessica Keener read the manuscript at different stages and kept me going with their enthusiastic support. Glo always believed in this project, and for that I deeply thank her. Carol Dine's poetic sensibility and line edits helped make the book shine. Rhonda Berkower was in my corner every step of the way.

Jim Schwartz provided encouragement and generously connected me with his agent.

Susan Sullivan, Hilary Nanda, and Jeremy Solomons contributed their love of literature and their collective wit every Tuesday and Thursday.

Suffolk University gave me a great place to flourish as a teacher and a writer.

Chris Castellani and all the folks at Grub Street Writers in Boston made writing and connecting with other writers a pleasure.

My superb agent, Stuart Bernstein, offered wisdom, ideas, and a path to publication that was a delight. My editor, Carole DeSanti, at Viking, contributed her keen editorial eye and full support.

Manon Hatvany and Marc Roudebush, the best friends anyone could have, made my life and the life of my family a pleasure.

My cousin Orna Feldman was my Boston family.

My sisters, Elizabeth Erskine, Catherine Tsairides, Carol Tudisco, and Maureen Bunney, and my mother, Mary Cardillicchio, gave their love. My brother, Nick Cardillicchio, was one of my real champions. His understanding of the importance of art was a gift.

My father, Nick Cardillicchio, was an inspiration to me. He died in 2008, and I miss him every day. During the writing of this book he always asked to see it. Now I can say, "Dad, here it is."

But my greatest thanks go to my beloved husband, David Rudner, and our dear son, Gabriel Sultan. Thank you, both, for your loving support. You are the center of my life.